AUTOGRAPH PAGE

To be used exclusively to recognize that special King or Queen for their support.

I0672507

This is a work of fiction. Any references or similarities to actual events, locales, real people, living or dead are intended to give the novel a sense of reality. Any similarity in other names, characters, places and incidents is entirely coincidental.

Envisions Publishing, LLC
P.O. Box 83008
Conyers, GA 30013

MVP (Murder Vengeance Power) RELOADED copyright © 2011 Jihad

ISBN: 978-0-9706102-6-3

First Printing October 2011
Printed in the United States of America

10 9 8 7 6 5 4

Submit Wholesale Orders to:
Envisions Publishing, LLC
P.O. Box 83008
Attn: Shipping Department
Conyers, GA 30013

APPRECIATION PAGE

There are so many wonderful Kings and Queens that helped make **MVP** RELOADED a reality, and I may miss a few but please family, chalk it up to my tired and exhausted mind.

First and foremost thank you GOD, without your inspiration and your spirit I would've given up long ago.

And I give a very special thanks to the Kings and Queens living behind America's prison walls.

MVP RELOADED IS FOR YOU, KING. **MVP RELOADED** IS FOR YOU QUEEN. By supporting my books, you help our young Brothers and sisters realize the kings and queens that they are.

Love and Life

Jihad

Murder

Vengeance

Power

RELOADED

"A revolutionary woman can't have no reactionary man. If he's not about liberation, if he's not about building a strong Black family, if he ain't about building a strong Black nation, then he ain't about nothing."

-Assata Shakur

THE BEGINNING OF THE END 2010

Karen Parker

"Ain't life just a bitch on her period," I said to the only other person on the late night Starbucks patio.

Irish Rose looked up from her kindle.

"Especially when your husband is screwing so many question marks." I continued as I put my vanilla mocha latte on the table and sat down in the green and black chair across from the fifty year old handsomely dressed graying, droopy eyed woman.

"Excuse me?" Irish Rose turned her plastic surgery augmented nose up. "Do I know you?"

"I don't know." I crossed my legs, showing Irish Rose, legs I'm sure she wished she had. "Do you know me?" I slid my iphone across the Starbucks black metal patio table in front of the middle aged appellate judges wife.

Seconds passed with no reaction. Understandably. At a considerable distance, the picture displayed on my phones two inch screen easily looked like someone smoking a huge brown cigar.

Irish Rose gritted her teeth before closing the cover on her e-reader. Her eyelids kissed the screen as she strangled the metal edges of my six hundred dollar computer phone. "What the.... Is that a dildo in his.... Is he... Is he smiling?"

I sat there cooler than the Atlanta moonlight summer breeze that was tickling and tantalyzing the thin, soft, almost invisible hair around both sets of my uncovered lips. "Press the arrow on the bottom, Mrs. Rose." I took a sip. "There are twenty-three pictures in all."

"Thirty-two years, two kids, four dogs, and a frigging cat." The judges wife slammed her fist on the table. "Mother-fucker," she growled.

"I'd have to concur." I nodded. "He is quite the mother-fucker and quite possibly a daddy fucker as well."

Irish Rose gave me a shut-the-hell-up look.

I shot her a Bitch please, look, right back.

"This is just... Just... Insane." Mrs. Rose remarked.

Mad. Mentally disordered. Thats what my therapist had said that I was. I had no idea what he had meant, until I went to dictionary.com and looked the word insane up. And sure enough, mad and mentally disordered were right there in black and white. And those three words were accurate in describing Judge Rose's wife's current state.

Einstein defined insanity as doing the same things over and over again expecting different results. I killed my father *one* time. I killed my brother *one* time. I killed my therapist *one* time. I killed one other judges wife *one* time. I'd never attempted or killed anyone more than *one* time. So, the definition of insanity definitely did not describe me.

Pissed the fuck off that Coltrane Jones was still sharing my air, *yeah*. Mad. *No*. And my mentality was very much ordered. I've spent two years, four months and sixteen days planning, putting my mentality in order. And if that afro-gray, bad-hair-day wrinkled genius Einstein was right, than his definition of the word really didn't apply to *yours truly*. I don't have the time nor the patience to be insane.

I turned my attention back to the nearly hyperventilating woman across from me. Twenty three times I counted. Twenty three times, Irish Roses chest had heaved up and down, before she put the phone on the table.

"I can not believe..." Her face was deep peach-pink as she violently shook her head, disturbing her perfect-in-place salt and peppered silver-gray and black shoulder length hair. She picked the phone back up. Her attention returning to the freaky photo gallery.

I knew it was coming. I was just surprised it had taken this long. I looked at my watch. Three minutes. The last judges wife was in tears in less than one. All of them said the same or some such similar nonsense. *I can not believe.* What the hell couldn't they believe. All men were the same. They lived to fuck or be fucked. And in Judge Royce Roses case, he enjoyed the best of both worlds.

For the first time in the seven minutes, we had sat across from each other, Mrs. Rose looked around the empty late night Starbucks patio. The same no ones and nothings that had occupied the tables next to and around us at 10:52 PM hadn't moved now that it was 11:01 PM. The only thing that had moved was my hand. I had no problem injecting the LSD into her arm, but her lackadaisical observance of nothing and no one gave me the ideal opportunity to plunge the needle into her Brandy laced coffee.

The judges wife, suddenly went into interrogation mode, standing up, gripping the edges of the round metal table. Eyes staring daggers into mine. "Why are you... How did you.... What do you...

It was time. She was definitely losing it, and the LSD wouldn't kick in for at least another fifteen minutes. I replied, "*Why. How. And what,* is not what you should be asking?"

"Who are you to tell me what *I* should be asking. I'm minding my business reading and enjoying my coffee when you invade my space and kidnap my conscious with these... these..." she pointed to the phone.

I finished her thoughts, "Pictures of your husband, the Honorable Judge Royce Rose getting his freak on with some woman wearing a white eighteenth century Judges get up, with a white haired wig, a cucumber, a dildo, and..."

She hand signaled. "Stop! Stop it! What do you want?"

With a dead man's calm, I said, "Revenge."

"Revenge? Revenge for what?"

"Infidelity." I held my left hand in front of my face as I admired the french manicure I'd received earlier that day. "Your husband is cheating on both of us."

Irish Roses expression went from one of horror, to hate, and then to a hyena like laughter in a matter of seconds. Eight seconds to be exact. "Where are the cameras," Irish Rose looked at the same nothingness she looked at five minutes ago. She sat back down. "Who put you up to this?"

"Mrs. Rose." I uncrossed my long tanned legs and leaned forward. My perky perfect 36 D cups hugged the tables metal edges. "This is no joke. I know where Royce is this very minute."

"I do too."

There was that high pitched irritating laugh again.

"Uhm- what did you say your name was?"

Ignoring her, I said, "Royce is not in closed chambers in Arlington, Virginia."

Her laughter did an instant cease fire.

"He is right here in Atlanta, not far from where we sit, and if you follow me, I will take you to him and the woman he is cheating on *us* with."

Again she jumped up from her seat and grabbed the tables edges. "First, Royce is not cheating on *us*. If my husband is having an affair, it surely wouldn't be with," Irish Rose turned her nose up as if I were last years sour milk, "with the likes of you."

I sat back in my chair, smiled, crossed my legs and said, "Lets talk about that a minute."

"I don't have to sit here and discuss anything with you."

"No, you don't. But you will, because you don't want the likes of me and my photos to get into the hands of the media."

Irish Rose smoothed her Auburn colored last years St. Johns dress out with her long fingers and sat back down.

"That's better. Now, look I don't care what you think or believe. Royce told you he was somewhere where he couldn't be disturbed, somewhere cell phones weren't allowed, so it's not like you can call him. But, like I said, you will follow me." I stood, put on my black leather driving gloves, picked up my phone and began walking toward the restaurant patio gate. "You will see for yourself."

I didn't look back until I was in the truck and turning right onto North Avenue.

Fifteen minutes later Irish Rose was having trouble staying between the lane lines. Three minutes later I began speeding down a steep winding hill. Seventeen seconds later I slammed on brakes. six seconds later, Irish Roses Lexus barely missed the tailgate of the stolen truck I'd borrowed earlier. "Damn!" I banged my hand on the steering wheel. Irish Rose must've been a racecar driver in another life. Instead of flipping over the guard rail and plummeting into the Chattahoochee River, the damn Lexus did a tailspin and crashed into a huge tree about twenty yards at the bottom of the hill. I shrugged my shoulders, "Oh well. Such is life."

I drove up as close as I could, put the black F-150 in park, got out, rubbed my gloved hands together and walked to the Lexus.

The convertible top was back, but the damn window was up. Irish Rose was a bloody mess. I couldn't tell if she was still breathing, and it wasn't important enough for me to check and run the risk of getting blood on my cute Marc Jacobs dress.

I called out. "Mrs. Rose, can you hear me?"

After getting no response, I opened the door and careful not to get her blood on me, I placed my gloved hands on each side of her forehead. I bent down and carefully whispered into Irish Roses bloody ear. "I just wanna thank you for being the dumb bitch that you are. If you would have looked closely at the woman in those pictures, you would've seen that she was shaped exactly like me. And the grey eyes should have given me away." I spoke to her lifeless body. "But rest assured, my dear. You're getting the best of this deal. Royce is not going to be a happy camper, trust me."

Okay, I know I said I had never killed or attempted to kill anyone more than once. What I meant was that I had never knowingly killed anyone more than once.

I closed my eyes and my hands began to form a necklace around Irish Roses bloody neck as I thought of the man that had ruined everything.

My brother Jonathon Parker had gone from being a Junior senator/presidential hopeful in the 2008 election, to a diseased shell of a man standing trial for the murder of our father. Ironically, I was the one that killed our father, and I had to kill Jonathon in order to avoid further scandal to the Parker name.

I squeezed.

Coltrane Jones, was going to die a thousand times, if I could help it. Not only could I help it, but I was going to kill Coltrane Jones and the ground he walked on, again, and again, and again.

"Snap!"

The undeniable sound of a human neck breaking brought me out of my future.

I didn't even remember removing my hands from her neck and to the sides of her head.

11

After wiping my gloved hand on Irish Roses salt and pepper, now ketchup colored hair, I walked back to the truck, one step closer to Coltrane Jones.

Murder was easy. Vengeance required strategic planning. Power was the intense pleasure derived from controlling the suffering of the hated. Being the MVP didn't give one the power of God. It made them God.

Chapter 0
Today: August 18, 2014

Cherry

"**God noooo.**" I sprang up with my arms reaching, fingers spread wide as if waiting for someone to pass me a ball. "Baby, I just had the craziest dream." I reached down. Felt around on Miles side of the bed, turned, looked down. Empty. The black twelve hundred count Egyptian satin sheets were drenched with sweat. My sweat. "Bay-bee?" I shouted breaking down both syllables as if baby were two words. "Miles," I called out louder this time.

The sun was wide-awake and shining through the bedroom blinds. I rolled to my right, opened the top drawer of the nightstand, put a hand on my .44 Desert Eagle, when I glanced up and saw that the alarm clocks red lights read 3:15 PM. I shook my head from side to side trying to shake off the cobwebs. I ain't never slept this damn long.

I got off the bed, gun in hand, ready to shoot anything, anyone and any sound that was unrecognizable. Who I really wanted to shoot was the two midgets wrestling inside my head. I squeezed my eyes together trying to stop the pain while

13

simultaneously trying to recall the events of last night. The nightmare that had woke me seemed so real.

I picked the phone up from the night stand, unplugged the charger and called Miles.

"I'm going higher.... Closer to my dreams."

I pressed END and walked around the California King I shared with my boo. I picked up his phone from the nightstand. A tear slid down my face as I thought back to last year, New Years in Maui, when Miles downloaded the ringtone from my now, favorite song.

****

"My Eve?" he'd said.

We were in Maui walking along the black sandy beach of Hana Bay. The full moon provided all the light needed to see the sparkle in his ocean deep tree bark brown eyes and his naturally swollen perfect brown lips.

He'd held my hands while facing me. We were as naked as the day we were born, having just finished serenading each others bodies with our God given tools of love, while a yesteryear ended and a new year began.

"My Eve," he'd said again. He took my face in both hands. "Cherry. You are my Genesis, my beginning. For forty years I've been just existing. With you I'm living. *My Eve*. The first woman. The beginning of creation. *My Eve*. My everything. I don't have a ring. We don't need symbols, to serve as a senator or representative to what we share. What we have is ours." He squeezed my hands. "No one elses." He brought my hands to his chest.

"You feel that?" He'd said.

Like the small child that I was, when I was in his arms, I nodded my head yes.

"That drum beat you feel is my heart singing the song *Closer to My Dreams,* by Goapele. And thats what you are. My dreams, my means, my Queen, my everything. And next year this time. In this very spot, I want to do this again. Naked, just like we are now. The only difference is, I want us to not only bare our souls to each other and to God, but also to his earthly representative, as we seal our love in matrimony as a new year is ushered in and another yesteryear ends. Cheryl Sharell," His lips barely grazed mine. "If God is love, I'm looking into Her eyes at this very moment, "I love you. Will you do me the honor."

I silenced him with a kiss. The love we made until the sun began to wake up was all the answer Miles Davis Jones needed.

Once we'd gotten back home, I moved in with my Adam. Back in Maui when Miles first described the beating to his heart with Goapele's song, *"Closer to My Dreams,"* I didn't know who the hell, Goapele, was, nor did I know the song. Didn't need to. Miles Davis Jones had the keys to my heart and the title to my soul. Miles hated ringtones with the passion of the Christ, but whenever I called his phone the lyrics and the music, "Closer to my Dreams," notified him and everyone else within hearing distance that I was calling.

****

Miles's phone was like American Express. He never left home without it. No need to panic. Take a breath girl, I told myself. There was a logical explanation. Had to be. I just needed to find it or him.

I searched both levels of the high rise condo we'd shared for nine wonderful months. Ten minutes later. Nothing. After returning to my starting point. I walked into the mirrored wrap around bedroom closet. Before I even felt the pockets of the black Roc A Wear slacks my boo had on yesterday, I saw the bulge. I stopped breathing. No way Miles left home without his wallet. After my hands verified what my eyes had, I breathed, not out of wanting but out of necessity. I felt his front pockets. Keys. Now, I couldn't stop, slow, or quiet my asthmatic breaths. I walked out of the closet, looked at the bed. Glimpses of the nightmare that had woke me, came back. My eyes dilated. I had to use the chrome stripper pole in front of our bed to keep from falling. What was wrong with me? I wasn't one to break weak. The way I was acting and feeling was beginning to piss me off. All the shit I'd been through. I closed my eyes trying to recall the nightmare I woke up to. The details were fuzzy. I walked back over to my nightstand. "Click, Click," I loaded a bullet into the chamber and took the safety off. "Now, I know my damn phone just ain't got up and walked a damn away," I walked around to Miles's stand, picked up his phone and dialed my number.

"Climbing the stairway to heaven, Here we go."

I let out the breath I had been unconsciously holding. If my phone had been a snake. There'd be a dead ass snake bleeding all over my six-hundred dollar black sheets. Just like the four bloody murdering-rapist sub-human snakes I left on and around that bed twenty years ago. My eyes watered as I travelled back in time.

****

With a surgeons scalpel, I had taken the lives of four men. The same four men that had forced my father to watch as they had repeatedly took turns. I was fifteen. Repeatedly, they'd used my body as a semen toilet.

If only I could've reached the scalpel before they had me secured to the bed. If only I could have reached the scalpel before they bashed my fathers head in on the marble floor of the kingpin drug dealers mansion.

****

16

I picked the phone up off the bed and looked at it the same way I had looked at that bloody scalpel after I had sliced the life out of those four men.

My body had healed quickly, but there had been no medicine for my soul. Six years, and three institutions for the criminally insane later, I was free to continue my killing spree. Men that raped and beat women didn't deserve to share my air. I had been the judge, jury, and executioner.

Thanks to the show *Americas Most Wanted*, telling my story and plastering my fugitive pictures all over the TV, women's rights advocate groups all over the world made it no secret that I was their hero. It was one of these groups that helped me flee to Cuba. There, US exiled freedom fighter Assata Shakur began saving my soul, by teaching me who I was and why I was. And not long after I'd discovered my real self, I was back off to war. And after I helped to topple the murdering and corrupt, Bishop TJ Money and his aspirations at becoming president, I received a medal of honor and a full pardon. And then, eighteen months ago I found God. I'd always been told about God. Even went to church from time to time. But all the shit that had happened to me and around me, no way there was a God, or if there was he wasn't my God, or so I had thought.

I had just finished jogging five miles around Stone Mountain. I was stretching, when God came up to me and smiled. "My name is Miles Davis Jones, Cheryl, Cherry Sharell, and I wanna let you know that I am a little crazy, but I assure you I am not insane and I am madly in love with you, and if you do not allow me to spend the rest of my life, loving and caring for you, than you will be responsible for yet another black mans demise." He'd said.

I remembered thinking that what he'd said was the nicest bullshit I'd ever heard. I ain't gon' lie, Miles was six foot of Dark liquor fine, standing in the grass in eighty plus degree weather at Stone Mountain Park, wearing a hot ass three piece suit carrying a dozen purple tulips, my favorite color and flower. And he said he was just a little crazy. Shit, I knew I was a lot crazy and besides I was in need of some new dick that I could work with, and by the size of the print developing in his brown and peach pinstripe slacks he might just be worth an audition, I'd thought. And he did have clean fingernails. His face and hands were moisturized. His teeth were Colgate white, and oh yeah, did I say he was fine. Not LL fine, more like Anthony Anderson, Gereld Levert fine.

I gave him a play. And please believe the man made me change my religion. I had never been loved. I mean really loved, like God meant for a woman to be loved. Miles Davis Jones, showed me everyday that I had known him, how a woman should be loved. That man fertilized my secret garden, played my piano like a black Beethoven. How could I not believe in God after knowing Miles. Only God, could create someone so perfect just for me. After all the hell I had been through and had caused, it was easy to see that Miles was my Stairway to Heaven, and that is why the Ojays hit Stairway to Heaven had become my ringtone when Miles called.

****

I called my girl.

"Girl, where you been?" Paradise asked. "You woulda thought I was Al-Qaeda the way I was blowing your phone up all day yesterday and this morning."

"Crack kills. You need to quit smoking; that shit," I joked. "P, we went to the shooting range and had lunch yesterday. Remember we were supposed to go to New Dimensions this morning."

"Cheryl!"

Ignoring her, I continued. "I know, girl. I'm sorry. I swear I set my alarm. I don't know what happened."

"Cheryl!" Again Paradise tried to interrupt.

"I'm just waking up and. . .

"It's Monday afternoon," Paradise interrupted.

"What?"

"We were supposed to attend Reverend One-Free's church service yesterday. Arthine Frazier's woman of the year award." Paradise paused.

I looked down at the phone. Fear rose up in my throat. Monday, August 18, 2014.

"Cheryl?"

What happened to Sunday? Okay. I closed my eyes and tried to think. I woke up yesterday morning and the first thing I did was. . . was. . . What did I do?

"You okay, girl?" Paradise asked.

"No. I'm not okay." Without much warning, the fear that had risen up in my throat exploded from my mouth and was all over the cherry hardwood bedroom floor.

"What's wrong? Cheryl?"

I couldn't stop. It seemed like my organs were coming up.

"Coltrane," Paradise called out to her husband, who was also Miles's brother and his best friend. "Have you spoken to Miles?"

"No, but I'd like to speak to you. Say things with my body that my mouth can't."

"Stop, boy," I heard her giggle. "Quit, you gon' hurt the baby. For real, Coltrane. I got Cherry on the phone."

"Hey future sister-in-law," I heard Coltrane say.

"Coltrane, this is serious. Miles is missing."

"Miles is what?"

Chapter 1

Karen Parker Rose

"Miles is what?" I mimicked Coltrane.

"You have my brothers house bugged?" Miles asked.

"No, I'm psychic," I said while watching Coltrane and his Parasite wife on my iphone screen.

"Why are you doing this Karen?"

Tired of watching and listening to Coltrane and his pet wife, I wedged my iphone between my twenty-thousand dollar 36 C cups, walked to the dining room table, picked up the silver metal tong like nut cracker and walked over to the wheelchair where Elmo and Bucky Barnes had Miles duct taped and twist tied to.

"Grammar school; my fourth grade teacher, Ms. Perry use to say that the only dumb question is a question not asked." I bent down kissed Miles's ear, before whispering, "That was some grade A kiddy bull dookey." I stood, put my hands on my nineteen-thousand dollar Beyonce hips, and shook my head. "Now Miles, that... Was a dumb ass question. And to show you how dumb, I'm going to put this nutcracker...."

He tried to struggle.

I put the nutcracker between his fingers. "No need to struggle. You look like a silver handicapped mummy with all that duct tape wrapped around your body. And trust, the Incredible Hulk couldn't move this chair. It's well secured, just like, " I ran a perfect finger nail down the side of his face, "your brother's fate. Now All you have to do is answer the question you just asked and I won't squeeze."

My eyes were diverted by my vibrating boobies. I removed my phone. "Damn." I looked at Miles. "Excuse me, my love." I smiled, before running thirteen steps into the kitchen. "What Royce?"

"Karen, where are you?"

"Oops. Hold on." I put the phone on mute, ran twelve steps back to Miles. "Shit, the duct tape." I turned and took three steps to the living room coffee table. Seconds later, I had four rounds of duct tape wrapped around Miles's head, covering his mouth. "Just the way I like my men," I said admiring my handiwork before running twelve steps back into the kitchen.

I took the phone off of mute. "You were saying."

"Why are you not here?"

"Because I am here." I threw my hands up. "What is it with the dumb ass questions today?"

"Where are you?"

"I'm where I'm at."

"Dammit, Karen. I told Ryan that we would be there when he made his plea on national TV in an hour."

"One hour, and seven minutes," I said looking at my watch.

"What?"

"He goes on in one hour and seven minutes. Don't worry, I'll be there in time."

"In time. Karen, we are supposed to ride with Ryan and Janet to the church. Why must you always be so difficult? This is an election year. Or don't you remember. Or do you just not care."

"Royce. I know what time it is and what type of year this is. And if I didn't care, not only would you not stand a chance at being appointed the next Supreme Court Justice, but the only bench you would be serving on would be a prison bench with your prison bitch."

"Don't go there Karen Parker Rose. Not now, not ever."

I removed the phone from my ear and looked at the screen before pressing the END button. That's why I would never understand this texting craze. When I was finished or was just tired of hearing the nonsense that came out of peoples mouths, I just pressed the END button.

For two years too long, I'd been married to asshole Joe, better known by society as the Honorable Judge Royce Donovan Rose. Judge Norman looked like an albino pit bull, but I would've taken him any day over Royce's old, boring, shriveled up pink behind.

Killing Judge Normans wife was a valuable and humbling lesson. Instead of digging for dirt on Ralph Norman, that I could use in the future, I had killed his wife first. That had to be the dumbest thing I'd ever done. I wasted six months and sixty-thousand dollars wiring his house and car, watching his every move from my iphone, listening, waiting on a skeleton to emerge from his closet. None ever did. I even tried to become a skeleton, but his holier than thou ass, steadily tried to save my soul. With my new face and body, I didn't think there was a straight man in the country that could resist my assets. Norman resisted. So, I was forced to go digging in another affluent judges backyard. And Royce's old ass had more skeletons in his closet than a cemetery. And he had a thing for young pussy. Extremely young pussy. Like the young pussy, I had on video. The same video I used to convince him to marry me, a year after I killed his boring, missionary position ex-wife.

Before sashaying back into the living room, I walked into the bedroom. The lighting. the cameras, the bed, everything was in place. I thought about waking the duct taped mummy, that was strapped to the bed, but decided against it. I fed him earlier, he'd be fine.

Moments later, I was standing next to Miles. He didn't look all that bad. The blood had coagulated well where I hit him in the head with the bat after the boys brought him in in the wee hours of the morning. My hands returned to their crimping position, fingers ready to squeeze the metal tong like nutcracker. "Okay, what's the answer."

"Uhm-mmm-mmmm-uh-uh-mmm."

"I can't understand you. Speak up Miles."

More mumbling.

"One more time Miles. Tell me why am I doing this?"

His eyes pleaded with me. His body language said he really didn't know. 'Scrunch.'

His eyes screamed. He convulsed. The veins in his neck bulged.

I couldn't resist. I had to hear his pain. I needed to hear his pain. I removed the duct tape.   "Ahhhhhhhhhhhh. Fuck. You crazy bitch. I ain't done nothing to you."

"Nothing but gave me an orgasm, but that was long ago. We were young. Kids. But, I was never as young as what you played me for." It took six steps to walk around the wheelchair. I did that three times before saying anything else. "Back then I didn't need to know that you were Coltranes brother. I would've never gave anyone anything to ever use against my brother. You tried. I came. You came, but it in the end it was my brother who got fucked."

"Coltrane lost everything, including nine years of his freedom.   Coltrane trusted your brother. Coltrane made Jonathon. And to rise to political power Jonathon set him up."

"That's the American way. Your people have been fucked everyday for over four hundred years. Been fucked so long, that you don't even feel the governments dick up in you anymore. So, you should do like you all do. Lay down or just bend over and accept reality." I knelt down in front of Miles, reached into the red tool box that had every tool that would free him. The tool box that was only one inch from his reach.

"What are you doing Karen?"

"Ah, there it is," I said, holding up the red handled wire cutters and the other iphone. I depressed a couple keys on the phone, and four small windows popped up. Windows that kept changing, showing different parts of Coltrane's house. "Let me turn the volume up so you can see and hear everything." I put the phone on top of the tool box and angled it so Miles could see the screen. I stood.

"Why are you doing this?"

"Didn't we just have this discussion?"

"What would you have done? My brother was innocent. He would've done life behind bars if I hadn't done what I did. Coltranes a good person. He didn't deserve...

"They write them every day in Memphis."

"What?"

I bent down behind him. My four thousand dollar Angelina Jolie lips tickling his left earlobe. "The Blues." I rose, put the wire cutters were my lips had been and said, "Sing me a song baby." Then, I cut part of his earlobe off.

His screams were so delightful. I closed my eyes and listened for eight seconds. "I so wish I could stay and play with your pain. Listen to the sweet sound that emerges from those chocolate lover lips of yours. But duty calls." I shrugged my shoulders before wrapping a couple rolls of tape around his mouth and head. "Gotta go love," I blew him a kiss. I looked out the peephole, turned and said, "Oh, watch the screen. Watch what happens when you fuck me and anything I love.

Chapter 2

Cherry

"On any and everything I love," I cried. "Please... Please... Please..." My long hair windmilled as I violently shook my head.

Coltrane grabbed me. Wrapped his arms around me. Held me.

"Let me go Trane! Let me go!"

His hug tightened. "Shhhh. Shhhh."

"No..... No...... No..... They took him. They took my world. Don't you understand. Miles is my... He's my.... I swear if they hurt him."

"Breathe Cheryl. Breathe." Coltrane spoke in a soothing tone. He sounded so much like his younger brother. "You have to get yourself together. Losing it won't help us figure out what's going on."

His words began to calm me. Trane was right. I couldn't lose it as I had after watching my father get beaten to death by my rapists all those years ago. I refused to go back to that place in my head where science, medicine, nor man could bring me

25

back from. That place were rational didn't exist. That place were there was no color, no moon, no sun, no light, no dark.

Still holding on, Coltrane ushered me onto the dark brown Corinthian leather couch in the den.

Paradise dabbed my eyes and face with tissue. "Drink this girl." She held a glass of water to my lips, before grabbing my free hand and sitting down.

Coltrane and Paradise waited. Patiently. Quietly. A minute... Two... Three... Four... I don't know how much time had passed before I began. "I was dreaming. At least I thought.... No, I know I was dreaming because I woke up in a panic. But, then again, it was so real. The details are fuzzy. I remember... I remember...."

Coltrane squeezed my hand. "Take your time Queen."

I closed my eyes, squeezed. "Two men. White, no, black men. Their faces." I shook my head. "I can't see them. Everything's blurry. A womans voice. Laughter." My eyes popped open. "Nooo!" I screamed, reached. "No... God no." I cried.

Paradise took me into her arms. Stroked my hair. Slowly. Calming. "Let it out girl. Let it all out. It's okay."

I pushed her back. "No, it's not okay. She, they pulled Miles out of bed and onto the hardwood floor and hit him in the head with a small baseball bat." I opened my eyes. "She's going to kill him."

"Who? "Who is she Cheryl? Who took Miles?" Coltrane asked. His voice louder. Higher pitched.

Paradise stood, turned and said, "Both of you. Calm down. Lets rationalize a minute." She paused. Her immediate stare was directed at Coltrane. A second later her eyes found mine. "Cherry, did you see any blood?"

"No." I don't think so. My knees had buckled when I felt Mile's wallet in his pants pocket. I had walked out of the closet and back into the bedroom. Again, my knees had buckled. I had grabbed onto the pole for support. I had looked down to the bedroom floor. "No! The floor was clean, " I said louder, with confidence. "No blood."

"Was there any evidence of breaking and entering? Like, was the front door busted open?"

I had ran out the front door so quickly. I was on the elevator. "No!" I said remembering that I had to get off the elevator and run back to the apartment. "I'd forgotten my keys," I began to speak out my thoughts, "I had opened the door, ran back inside, took my keys off of the ledge of the living room water fountain, ran back to the door. No! The door was fine. And I don't think they had a thirty-one or thirty-two story lift, because that's what they would've needed to get to the kitchen or master bedroom patio or any window."

"Baby," Coltrane exhaled, "You're right." He said, speaking to Paradise.

He turned to me. "Cheryl, maybe we are jumping to conclusions. After all, we're basing everything on a bad dream."

In a defeated tone I said, "Was the thirty-six plus hours I had slept a bad dream too? What about Miles's wallet. His phone. His keys."

Coltrane whipped out his flip phone.

"Who are you calling?" Paradise asked.

"911."

"Waste of time," I said.

"911, please hold," I heard the operator say.

Coltrane looked at his phone. "What's the point of an emergency police hotline. I could be bleeding to death. I could be a woman about to get raped."

"Trane, you might as well hang up."

"What?" He looked at me like I was crazy.

"I called already. The operator gave me a number, I called it, spoke to a detective Dorsey. He told me that I couldn't even file a missing persons report until after Miles had been missing twenty-four hours."

"You were asleep, probably drugged. He could've easily been missing for more than twenty-four hours," Coltrane said.

"I told the detective almost word for word what you just said."

"And?" Coltrane interrupted.

"He said that if I hadn't heard anything by morning...

"Morning!" Coltrane jumped up from the couch. "My brother could be dead by morning."

"Where are you going," Paradise asked as Coltrane stalked towards the bar.

"To get my keys. Motha' fucka's don't wanna help me find my brother. I need to be on record, when I tell they ass that if I find out some fuck shit done happened, they responsible for what I'm gon' do to whoever done did whatever the fuck they done did to Miles."

Paradise got up and followed Coltrane.

After snatching his keys off the bar, he went behind it, opened the top left hand drawer and pulled out his .45.

Paradise put a hand on his arm.

He gave her a not-right-now look before loading a bullet in the chamber. "Baby," he patted his chest with the nickel plated Grim Reaper. "You my heart. My queen. God knows I'll move heaven and earth for you." A tear crawled out of his eyes. "But, Miles." he closed, opened his eyes, blew out a long breath. "Miles is my baby brother. No questions asked. I'd trade my life, my soul for his safety. And it ain't about him risking his life six years ago, breaking me out of the penitentiary, helping me to expose Senator Jonathon Parker. It's about unconditional love. A love that supersedes safety, understanding, and sometimes even rational." He brushed past his pregnant wife, put his gun in his front jeans pocket.

Trane shot me a what-you-gon'-do-look. I got up and followed him.

"You two aren't just gon' leave me." Paradise stated as fact.

"We have to queen." Coltrane turned at the kitchen door leading to the garage. "Stay here and take care of my baby boy," he rubbed Paradises slightly poofed out belly. "Besides, if Miles is in trouble, you know this is the first place he'll come." He walked out the door.

Paradise grabbed my arm before I could leave. "Cherry?" She looked at Coltrane getting into his beloved Ford F-150 pick up.

"Dammit," He shouted.

"What's wrong baby?"

"Ain't had it a month, and the damn thing won't start." He shook his head in disgust. "I ain't got time for this today. Baby, I gotta take the Nav."

I had one foot out the door, when Paradise put a hand on my shoulder.

Two tears on opposite sides slowly raced down her round, blue-black face. She looked at Coltrane and then back at me.

I grabbed her hand and squeezed. "I'll take care of him."

"Please?" She nodded. "Thank you." She rubbed her five-month poofed out pregnant belly as I walked around to the passengers side. Although Coltrane and Miles were two years, two weeks and two days apart, they couldn't have been more alike. It was uncanny. Their alikeness was the reason Paradise didn't have to say any more than she had. I knew how she felt, I knew what she was thinking. I don't think it's humanly possible for a knowing woman to not fall deeply in love with either Jones brother if they let themselves come to know them.

The twenty minute ride to the Dekalb County police precinct on Memorial Drive was uneventful. Quiet. Trane didn't utter a word about his almost new pick up not starting. I knew how much he hated leaving Paradise without any transportation.

By the death grip Coltrane had on the steering wheel, I imagined that his mind was racing, searching for anyone that might have done this. Just as I was. Miles had no enemies. Hell, he didn't have enough friends to have enemies. I knew everything. I mean everything about him, and his brothers past. The only person that could have, would have done something foul to Miles was Jonathon Parker and he was dead.

Coltrane pulled up to the side of the street behind the prison, across from the courthouse, in front of the building were people came to pay their tickets.

"Trane, you can't park here."

He put the Navigator in park and jumped out.

Fuck it. I shrugged. He knew good and damn well Dekalb County didn't play. It was his SUV. I ran to catch up.

"I need to speak to a detective," Coltrane said to the desk sergeant that was engrossed, working a crossword puzzle.

"Anyone in particular," the old sergeant said, his head still on the page and his half pencil still tapping the desk.

"I don't care. It's an emergency."

The sergeant looked up for the first time. "What kind of emergency?"

Damn. Now, I'm all for senior citizens that wanna work. But this old fuck was way too damn old to be breathing, let alone working the front desk. Just like cheap ass Dekalb County to hire a fuckin' fossil.

"Look, can I just speak to a detective?" Coltrane asked.

"You got homicide, drugs, robbery," he looked off into space, "Let's see, oh yeah, there's vice, no they combined Vice with robbery, or was it...."

"Missing persons," Coltrane said.

"No need to get your britches in a bunch. I ain't deaf," he said handing Coltrane a clipboard with some papers and a little yellow half-pencil attached.

I couldn't believe how much patience Coltrane was showing. Hell. I was two seconds from jumping over the counter and strangling Crispy Attucks.

"Sir, something has happened to my brother. He's been missing for, I don't know, between fourteen to forty hours."

"How old is he?"

"Forty-one," Coltrane said.

The sergeant took the clipboard from Coltrane's hand. "He ain't missing until forty-eight."

I interrupted. "I was told..."

"Young lady, I don't care what you were told." The old man took off his glasses. "He ain't missing until forty-eight hours." The fossil looked over Coltrane and at me. "What you? His baby momma."

My muscles tightened.

Coltrane grabbed my arm. He must of known. Crispy Attucks had no idea that the man he wasn't trying to help had just saved his life. "No, I'm his fiance," I slowly enunciated every syllable in the word.

"Well, good for you. I hope you still his feeeeee-onnnnn-sayyyy when you find him," the man said.

"What do you mean by that?" I bit.

"Then again, he might not wanna be found." Crispy made eye contact with me. "He might've upgraded."

"Man, what is your problem. I'm a tax paying citizen and I'm just trying to do what's right. But you are up here disrespecting my brothers queen, while I'm just trying to speak to a detective."

He put his glasses back on. "And I done already told you," His bald head moved like a pendulum to the rhythm of his intonations, "that your brother ain't missing till forty-eight hours."

"My brother could be..."

"Come on Trane, you tried. Now lets go find Miles."

"Yeah, Trane, listen to the fee-onnnnnn-saaaayyyyy."

I looked at him. He wasn't worth it. Hell, his old ass had to be due to die any minute. Before walking out of the swinging glass double doors, I turned and asked the Sergeant, "How was the after party?"

"What after party?"

"The after party that followed Moses's parting of the Red Sea."

We walked out of the station. I couldn't believe the Navigator was still there. Not for long I thought. "Trane, run, tow truck." I pointed to the black tow truck that was pulling up.

"Call you back baby," he closed the lid on his flip phone and took off running.

The big burly farmer John looking overall wearing tow truck driver knocked on the drivers side front window. "I got orders to tow this vehicle."

Ignoring farmer John, Coltrane put the keys in the ignition, started the SUV, put the gearshift lever in drive and hit the gas. He pushed a couple buttons on the stereo before a twelve inch Ipad like screen emerged from the dash. He used his finger to draw the number 201 on the screen. The channel changed. "Check out CNN, see if... I don't know."

"Where are we going?"

"Downtown to your high-rise. I wanna take a look around, your apartment, the building, Miles's car..."

"STOP!"

Coltrane slammed on the brakes. Looked at me and then at the TV screen that my eyes were glued to.

A car skidded. Swerved. "Stupid ass son of a bitch," the driver of the Camry that barely avoided us said as we stood stock still on the I-285 entrance ramp.

Coltrane was still. Hands frozen on the wheel.

I never seen her face, but If I lived an eternity, I would never forget those dull soulless gray eyes. Eyes that smiled during, and after the arm came down and bashed Miles in the head. "That's the bitch," I cursed.

Chapter 3

Karen Parker Rose

I cursed the day I married Judge Royce Donovan Rose. I swear if there was any other way to get away with my plan, I would've chosen *it* and not married, or slept with the worm I sleep with every night. Well almost every night. A smile began to crease my lips as I imagined the agony... the pain... the hell... that I was about to unleash on Mr. Jones.

A bright light brought me back to my current boring reality. The cameras were now on me and Royce, but the thirty-four journalists microphones were still aimed at the podium in front of us.

Royce let go of my hand. Thank God.

He stood and walked to the podium. Such the media hound.

I glanced at my watch. Oh my God, it seemed like six hours instead of six-minutes since Royce and I took the St. Pius cathedral stage with Ryan and his pet wife, Janet. I was so embarrassed to be sharing the stage with such a weak man. I don't see how anyone could follow such a marshmallow. I turned to Janet. Even she wasn't crying. But her cottony soft husband the great Bishop Ryan Paulk was. What kind of man would break down on national television? It would be different if he were playing the media for sympathy, or if he were the kids' biological father. All the damn homeless kids in America and this peace corps prophet and his pear shaped wife adopts a Rwandan refugee.

Royce cleared his throat, "Good afternoon. My name is Judge Royce Donovan Rose." He put his arm around Ryan. "I've known Bishop Paulk and Janet for over thirty years, and I can tell you that I've never met a man, a person with half the heart," he turned to Ryan, "that this man possesses. And any that know this man and his lovely wife knows that I am telling the truth. St. Pius and the Paulks' have been a Godsend to this community, this city, this country."

Royce looked out at the journalists and cameramen that scribbled, recorded, and listened to his every word. "Hasn't eleven-year old Ezekial Paulk suffered enough. Having been pried from the cold, hard, brittle, dead arms of his refugee mother. Little Ezekial had very little hope of survival. So little, that the mission hospital in Burundi had voted to put him to sleep. There were so many babies, children, women, and men, that needed immediate medical attention and the makeshift hospital was underfunded and ill equipped to handle a new born with what they thought was AIDS, but actually turned out to be Type 2 diabetes. Bishop Paulk, who was in Burundi praying, volunteering, doing whatever was needed of him at the time couldn't let man play God, so he took responsibility for the malnourished, sickly newborn. After nursing him until he was well enough to travel, This man to my right not only adopted the Rwandan baby, but he took out a second mortgage on his home to pay for little Ezekial's immediate medical care."

Royce paused for effect, looked out at all the faces that filled the first two rows of the cathedral.

"I stand before you today, humbled. I never thought I'd live to see the day that I would plead with criminals. But plee, I will." Royce removed his arm from the shoulders of his defeated friend. With praying hands in front of him Royce continued, "Please, I beg you, bring Ezekial home. The governor and the District Attorney have agreed not to prosecute if Ezekial is returned within 24 hours unharmed. Please, time is of the essence. Ezekial will not survive much longer than that without his insulin."

Oh my God. This was way too much drama. Two grown ass men crying over a damn child that probably won't live past twenty-one. A child that wasn't even an American. It was times like these that I needed an onion under my eyes, so I could boo hoo for the cameras. And even then, I'd probably have trouble crying being that I was so excited about tonight.

I'd been watching, listening for three days. And finally, Coltranes' pet wife sealed her husbands fate this morning. I didn't think he would ever finish. Hell, I wouldn't mind going a round or two, or three, with Coltrane myself. All two-hundred and forty-three pounds of pressure, banging my insides from the back. Nine inches of angry, black, hard, fleshy steel, pounding, piston like. Sweat dripping off his chest and face, falling onto my back. Fist full of blonde hair, pulling, stretching my skull. His free hand slapping, leaving red hand prints on my perfectly round pink ass.

Before I knew what was happening I'd bolted out of my seat. I didn't care who was looking. I jerked, closed my eyes, and exhaled as my juices sprayed my inner thighs.

"Karen?" Janet Paulk, loudly whispered.

I responded, only after the two aftershocks from my gargantuan orgasm subsided. "Forgive me," I sat back down, "I just."

"I know." She patted the back of my hand with her liver spotted fingers. "I know," she smiled.

No the fuck you don't. I just had the most excruciatingly wonderful orgasm.

She patted my hand. "We're all saddened by Ezekials disappearance," she whispered.

I glanced at my watch. Thirty-two minutes. The special report was only supposed to be five, seven minutes. "Don't worry Karen, we'll be out of here in fifteen, twenty minutes tops," Royce had said repeatedly this morning and before I left the house. Lying fucker.

After the media left and Royce and I said our hope laced goodbyes, I led the way to Royces Ford Taurus. I waited. He opened my door and before Royce could close his, I let him have it. "You said fifteen, twenty minutes tops. I told you I had shit to do. But noooo, you have to give a state of the union frigging address, a damn church sermon after every question from the reporters. Have you ever heard of speaking in sound bites?"

"Karen? my closest friends' son has been abducted. I would've said or done almost anything if it produced results. Have you no shame. No sympathy."

"Don't shake your head at me like that?"

"What are you talking about?"

"Your balding, dyed head. That's what I'm talking about. Your wrinkled neck turning from side to side, like... Like... I disgust you or something."

With both hands on the wheel and his eyes on the road, Royce drove in silence.

"Aren't you going to say something?"

"What do you want me to say, Karen?"

I crossed my arms, seething.

"You want me to tell you how insensitive you are. You want me to tell you how embarrassed I was when you shot up out of your seat like a rocket and just stood there like a deer caught in the headlights." He shook his head again. "I don't know why I..."

"Married me." I completed for him. "You know good and damn well why. Because you're scared I'll blow the whistle on you if you didn't." I scowled at him. "And you had the audacity to say, that you thought you'd never see the day that you would plee with criminals, when you are a criminal yourself, you kiddie fucker."

"Nineteen! He shouted. "She told me she was nineteen!"

"So, you say. Hmph. Besides, what is an appellate judge doing picking up a Craigslist call girl?"

"I'm not going there Karen."

"You should've thought about not going there before you went there. My entire life is synchronized and today you threw my entire life off."

"Karen, we were there thirty minutes. Ten minutes longer than I had initially stated."

"Thirty-nine minutes, nineteen minutes longer than you initially stated."

Karen, was all I heard Royce say before reclining my seat, closing my eyes and resynchronizing my timing for this evening. By the time I had the plan down to the minute, the black electronic front gates that led to Rose manor opened.

Two hours and eight minutes later, I was in my bedroom getting dressed. Royce was either in his office or his bedroom, probably surfing the web looking for some underage trim.

****

One hour and four minutes later, I was in front of the first of four garage doors. I used the garage door opener I had programmed the other day when I was here. Two minutes later, I turned the spare key in Coltranes' kitchen door lock. After opening the door I turned to the wall on my right and pressed in the same code I watched Coltrane's pet wife use to arm and disarm the alarm.

Three minutes later I was in the master bath laundry closet putting the rubber gloves on before I reached into the dirty clothes hamper. "Bingo!" I said aloud while retrieving the soiled towel. I balled it up, put it to my nose and inhaled the sweet nectar of Coltrane's demise.

A week of watching, listening to their carnal sounds of pleasure. Her legs twisted up like a pretzel. Him being careful not to rest his weight on her pregnant belly. Waiting for his release. Waiting for her to remove the towel from under them. Hoping it would end up in the dirty clothes hamper and not the wash machine as had the other three.

Seven minutes after I disarmed the alarm, I was resetting it. I was in no rush. Coltrane and his pet wife were still at church. Funny, how a little African refugee brought two races, and two religions together. I wonder if Ezekial had been white, would the blacks have been so supportive.

I popped the hood on Coltranes Ford F-150 truck, opened the fuse box and replaced the faulty relay I'd put in late last night, while they were asleep.

I climbed in, hit the garages remote. Waited. Pulled out. Parked. Got out. Walked back into the garage. Got into the stolen twin Black F-150 that I had driven, backed out the garage bay and backed into the bay that Coltranes truck had been in. It was a risk, but as long as I could see and hear everything from my iphone, then I'd know if Coltrane discovered what I'd done.

Thirty-three minutes later, I pulled into the Pleasant Point luxury apartment complex. I pulled the Eagles cap over my head before parking and getting out with the red towel in tow.

"Honey, I'm home," I said after opening the apartment door. "Oh my God!" I shouted. Mile's head was on his chest. I grabbed the nightstick sized baseball bat from the shoe rack next to the door. Eight strides later I was standing right in front of his lifeless body. I pulled the tape from around his head. "Miles." I lifted his head. Looked into his dead face. "No! Please. Oh my God! Miles, please say something?"

He didn't move. I let go. His head dropped back onto his chest.

"Fuck! Fuck! Fuck!" I shouted. Turned. Seven steps later, I was facing the living room wall. "Idiot! Idiot! Idiot! Idiot!" I banged my head against the wall. Again and again.

"Help."

A voice. I froze. Turned.

"Please," Miles whispered.

"Thank you. Thank you. Thank you," I said looking down. I didn't know how much time Miles had left. Determined to beat God, I ran. Mile's was mine. A clowns smile spread across my face before I swung. The first impact made me drop the bat. Blood spurted from the side of his head like a water fountain with gum in the spout.

"My brother had the democratic nomination in his pocket before your brother exposed him. He woulda' been the 44th President. Who he had molested and killed was not Coltrane's business." I picked up the bat. Miles's head lay to the side. Blood dripping from his lips and gushing from his head. His stare was off into space. "Jonathon Parker was thirty-eight, when you and your brother killed his dreams. My dreams. I swung thirty-eight more times.

After catching my breath, I licked the blood that had splattered onto my lips, walked eight steps. Took off my bloody rubber gloves, dropped them into the biohazard wastebasket next to the shoe rack. Reached back down, removed the hand sanitizer from the shoe rack. Poured a generous amount onto my hands, scrubbed. Dropped the bottle in the wastebasket. Removed a fresh pair of yellow rubber gloves from the shoe rack, put them on and took the red towel from the shoe rack and went into the bedroom.

I left the apartment for the last time twenty-nine minutes after I had arrived. I pulled the Eagles cap over my head and casually walked to Coltranes pick up, got in and drove away. I pulled out my iphone to check to see if Coltrane and his pet wife had made it back home. I almost forgot. I placed the iphone on the passengers seat, pressed in the numbers 4869 to unlock the phone that came factory installed in Coltranes truck, before calling the police.

Chapter 4

Cherry

"The police," I said, moving back from the peephole.

"Ding dong. Ding dong," the door bell chimed again.

Coltrane took the blunt from my fingers. "I thought you said these walls were Cush proof."

"They were." I coughed. "They are."

"This is the police. Is anyone home?"

"I'll take care of this." Coltrane said as he took the stainless steel circular stairs. "You better answer that queen," he turned, "It might be about Miles."

If I wasn't stressed the hell out, scared to damn death, and buzzed out of my mind, I would've moved much faster. I wasn't scared about the cops smelling weed in my place. I was scared of what they had to say.

"Ding dong. Ding dong."

"Queen," Coltrane called out, "You gon' get that?"

Miles was the only man that called me queen. I was his queen, just as he was my king. But, what if the police are here to tell me that Miles.... What if Miles is....

"I know someone's there. I hear voices," the scratchy soprano voice said from behind the oak front door. "Please, it's important."

I didn't even hear Coltrane come back down the stairs. "Come on queen, we'll answer it together."

He was so gentle, as he helped me to my feet before half dragging, half carrying me to the front door.

"No!" I shook my head. I pulled back. "Don't answer it." I looked into his eyes. "Please, Coltrane. Don't?"

"You don't wanna find Miles?"

I shook my head no before pushing him into the door and breaking free.

"Is everything okay in there," the voice sounded from the other side of the door.

I ran.

"Yes ma'am, everything's fine," I heard Coltrane say.

I was sitting cross-legged on the floor behind the stairs when her words assaulted my conscious - Assata Shakur was in exile herself, she didn't know me from Eve, but that didn't stop her from taking me in, giving me refuge in the mountains of Cuba, far away from the unseen hands of the F.B.I. For two years, I was safe. In those two years, I grew a lifetime soaking up every lesson that Assata taught me. It's been six years since I seen her, but her words were as clear as if she were right there under the stairs with me.

"If you're deaf, dumb and blind to what's happening in the world, you're under no obligation to do anything. But if you know what's happening and you don't do anything but sit on your ass, then you're nothing but a 'punk'." I never was and never would be a punk.

"Good evening, sorry to disturb you this late, but does Miles Davis Jones reside here?"

I got up and came from under the stairs.

"This is his apartment..."

Back straight, walking forward, I said, "Yes, Miles Davis Jones lives here."

The woman looked more like a 70's revolutionary in a pants suit. Not a detective as her credentials had read.

"I'm Detective Innocence Branch with the Atlanta Police Department."

I was so close to Coltrane I could feel his body heat. I took the detectives extended hand. "I'm Cheryl Sharell, and this is Coltrane Jones."

"Can we step inside?" she asked.

When we didn't move fast enough, Detective Branch said, "I could care less what you've been smoking, or what drugs you may have behind the door. I'm with homicide, not vice."

Homicide? Miles was gone. The frozen look of hopelessness plastered across Coltranes face told me that he must've been thinking the same thing.

I moved to let her in. I searched her empty eyes for whatever message she was there to deliver.

We walked into the den. "I would offer you something to drink, but all we have is water." I extended a hand for her to sit down on one of the barstools in the den.

The detective looked at the Evian, and Fiji bottled water stocked bar. "No thank you, I'm fine." She reached into her white linen pant suit jacket pocket and took out an electronic note pad-recorder and placed it on top of the granite bar top.

She looked at Coltrane, and then at me. "Do both of you live here?"

Although we had moved to the den, Coltrane hadn't left my side. We could've been Siamese twins for all Detective Branch knew.

"No. Miles is my fiance', Coltrane is his brother."

I followed the detectives eyes. She looked at me, then Trane, and then back at me. Coltrane must've been thinking the same thing, because at the same time, we unlocked our hands and took a step away from each other.

Innocence Branch's expression asked the question that her mouth did not. Why was Miles's fiance and his brother sitting in Miles's apartment at midnight, smoking bud, lights dimmed, listening to the Spinner's classic hit, *"Love Don't Love Nobody."* And why had they been holding hands.

"Detective Branch," I began.

"Call me Innocence."

I nodded. "Innocence, I woke up this afternoon alone, which was unusual because Miles and I never slept past seven. His wallet, keys and cell phone were still here. I searched both levels of the condo looking for signs were he might've gone. And when I didn't find anything, I picked up my cell, called Paradise...."

"Who's Paradise?"

I waited for Coltrane to answer. When he didn't, I said, "One of my closest friends, and Coltranes wife,"

Again, Innocence's eyebrows furrowed with confusion.

"After speaking with Paradise for a few minutes, we discovered that I had slept for over thirty-six hours." My voice took on a more somber tone. "That's when I knew that something foul had happened to Miles."

"What time was this?"

"Quarter after three this afternoon. After hanging up I drove over to the offices of EYE technologies."

"Eye technologies?"

"The IT and virtual based private detective agency we own." I paused before asking, "Am I going to fast?"

"No. You're doing fine," Innocence said not looking up.

"Well, our receptionist Ms. Dot, hadn't heard or spoken to Miles since Friday."

"She didn't try to reach either of you Monday when neither of you showed up at the office."

"The office is closed Saturday through Tuesday. And somedays, Miles and I either work from home or we're out in the field. But, when I looked at mine and Miles's phones after waking up, I noticed that we had over twenty missed calls, which I returned during the course of the afternoon and evening."

"Where any of the calls out of the ordinary?"

I shook my head. "No."

"What happened next?"

"After giving Ms. Dot the rest of the week off, I called 911. Tired of being on hold, I hung up and went to Trane's and Paradise's place. From there, Coltrane and I went down to the main Dekalb County precinct. After being told that I couldn't file a missing persons report until Miles had been missing 48 hours we...."

"Who told you 48 hours?" Innocence asked.

"The desk sergeant."

"A police academy cadet learns that in the state of Georgia, the missing persons filing time is 24 hours." Innocence said, before shaking her head in disbelief. "That's good ole Dekalb County for ya. Our tax dollars asleep."

"After leaving the precinct, we went and picked up Paradise."

"Is Paradise your wife's legal name?"

I was beginning to worry about Trane. The zombie eyes and his blank expression, staring at the designs embedded in the white, Italian marbled den floor.

"No. Her legal name is Tameeka Jones," I answered for Trane. "Tameeka Teena Marie Jones.

"So, you two went and got Mrs. Jones and you went where?"

"New Dimensions First church of God to attend the prayer vigil for that poor little boy, Ezekial Paulk."

"Did you attend the service?"

"I just told you...."

"No, you said you went to the church to attend the prayer vigil."

I was about to check Innocence Branch, when her tone softened..

"I don't mean to be rude, but I need you to be precise."

"Tameeka, Coltrane, and I attended the prayer vigil. We arrived around seven and left around nine." I couldn't tell her that we left at eight in order to meet my weed man.

"Okay, you left around nine, and then?"

"Coltrane took Tameeka home, and we came back here."

"Why didn't Tameeka come back with you?"

"She's pregnant."

"Round about what time did you and Mr. Jones walk into the apartment?"

I looked at a catatonic-like Coltrane. He offered nothing.

"I guess it was around eleven, give or take a few minutes."

Innocence removed her tall, slender frame from the barstool. Looked at us. Took a couple steps forward, took Trane's left and then my right hand. "In homicide cases, an officer from special services is usually escorted by a detective to deliver news that a family member has been found."

A glimmer of hope. Innocence was alone. No Police priest with her, so that meant that Miles.

She continued, "The first blue and white had been on the scene less than ten minutes, when me and my partner arrived seconds in front of FOX news. A blue and white on the scene knew Miles. He'd done private surveillance for EYE technologies in the past. He gave me your address. It was obvious that whoever called 911 to report the incident, got in touch with local news agencies. I knew if I didn't move fast, you would've probably found out what had happened from the local media. That is no way to find out that," she looked at me,

"Your fiance'," and then at Coltrane, "and your brother was found in the living room of a near downtown apartment."

What little hope I had left was exerted in the pressure I mustered to squeeze Innocences hand. "Is Miles... Is he okay?"

She shook her head. "I'm afraid not."

Lights out, unconscious, Coltrane crumbled, collapsing to the marble floor.

Surprising even to me, I remained calm, showed no emotion. There was more and I wanted, no I needed to hear everything.

I didn't move or speak. The only reason I knew that Coltrane was still breathing was because after Innocence removed her two fingers from his neck, instead of administering CPR, she took out her cell and called for an ambulance.

While waiting for the paramedics, I asked, "What happened? How did he... How did he die?"

"We won't know for sure, until after the autopsy."

"When will that be? And how long before the results come back?"

"Usually seventy-two hours, but."

"Innocence please," I squeezed her hand. "Miles is... Was my world, what are you not telling me?"

"I googled Miles on my way here, and when I saw your name pop up several times I googled you."

"Okay, and?"

"You've come a long way, Wild Cherry."

"Those days are behind me. Far behind."

"I just don't want you to go back to where you've been, and I'm not talking about prison, but," she shrugged her slender shoulders, "I guess you'll find out soon enough."

"Find out what?" I asked.

"Ezekial Paulk was found naked, bound, gagged and dead in the apartments only bedroom."

"God no," I whispered.

"God ain't had nothing to do with what someone did to that boy and to Mr. Jones."

"What did they do to Miles?" Forgetting who Innocence was, acting on instinct, I grabbed her by the shoulders and started shaking. Spittle flying every which way as I shouted. "What did they do? What did they do to my king?"

She grabbed me, pulled me close. Hugged my waist. "The assailant or assailants stripped Miles naked, before wrapping him up in silver duct tape. He was bound to a wheelchair secured to the apartment floor with anchor hooks."

"Continue."

"Ms. Sharell, I promise, this case will be properly handled."

I pushed her back. "Properly handled. What does that mean? No, I know what it means. N-O-T-H-I-N-G. Now that we got that out of the way, will you please tell me how Miles died."

"I told you...

"The unofficial version. How do you think he died?"

She looked like she was considering whether to tell me.

"In three days, I'll know anyway. Please, Detective Branch. Please."

"He was beaten to death."

"Where?"

"His head."

"With what?"

"A stick, a bat, a pipe. I don't know...

"A smooth edged blunt object." I said.

"Ms. Sharell, I assure you, this case is top priority for the Atlanta Police department. We'll find the responsible party."

My, "Okay," was nonchalant.

"Ms. Sharell, you wouldn't happen to know anyone that might have done this?"

"No."

"You and Miles have any enemies."

"No."

"Ms. Sharell," she put a hand on my shoulder.

"Knock! Knock! Ding dong! Ding dong!" the doorbell chimed. "Paramedics."

"Please let us handle this. Don't do anything crazy. If you do, I promise you will regret it."

Regret my ass. I walked to the door thinking that if this Karen Parker Rose bitch had anything to do with killing Miles, she'd regret the day she popped out of her momma's twat. And after I finished with the tramp, I'd go out blazing, taking two .44 magnums inside the Dekalb County Police precinct and open fire.

Chapter 5

Karen Parker Rose

Fired up was the best way to describe the way I felt. Miles was dead and Coltrane was at Dekalb Medical, suffering from clinical depression, no doubt crying like the punk-bitch that he is. Probably had an IV drip in his arm being pumped with anti-depressants.

It had been two days since I'd used a synthesized voice machine to alert the APD on the whereabouts of Miles's and Ezekial's bodies. I so wish I could watch and listen as Coltrane's wife, Parasite dealt with her husbands state of mind. But duty calls and more important, my cell didn't pick up service in this damn redneckville hick town. After five-years of coming to the prison, you'd think I was use to not having a signal. I was, but it wasn't until recent that I had spyware installed in Coltrane's and Miles's homes. Spywear that allowed me to see everything.

The prison had been built in 1967 and it opened it's cell doors in '68. So why did Jackson State Penitentiary look like a medieval European castle? Maybe because it was home to some of the most mid-evil mother fuckers that ever committed a crime. I was so tired of making the fifty-six minute drive from Atlanta to Butts County every month. They should've named it Butt-fuck County, cause in one way or another that's what was happening to most of the inmates in the Jackson State Pen. In any case that was their problem not mine, dumb asses shouldn't have gotten caught, and the ones that were innocent should've been smart enough to prove it. And don't let me get started on the death row dummies. Idiots committing major crimes with mini minds.

Shit, a bitch liable to have a heat stroke in this hotness, I thought as I wiped my brow with the back of my hand.

"Scue me, Scue me."

I turned.

A zit faced monstrosity was right behind me. I had to be moving slow as shit in this August heat for this blob to have caught up. I was already out of my car when I saw her drive onto the prison grounds, and now, she was right behind me.

"My name Faye," She extended one of her Meathooks.

I wasn't trying to be rude, but I couldn't help but stare. I had never seen spandex on someone that big. Didn't know spandex, expanded that damn far. Ain't no way this cow could get into a one size fits all anything. Clothes so tight, the tramp probably had enough yeast in her cooch to start a bakery.

"Dis my first time visiting. My man on death row."

I bet my life I could guess the trailer park trashes so called man's race, I thought as I entered the prisons main entrance.

If this cow tapped me on my shoulder one more damn time? I turned.

She brandished one of her meathooks. I couldn't believe she had the nerve to show off a ring with a diamond so small.

"Me and my dude gettin' marred."

Bitch, buy a vowel. The word is married I wanted to say. I hated white bitches that tried to speak like they were from some black ghetto. Black's called it sounding Black. I called it sounding stupid. In my case, I was just being me. I guess I'd had so much nigga shit happen to me in my life that I naturally developed a ghetto vernacular. And now I was purposely being rude to Sasquatch.

"You 'ont talk much huh, shawty?"

Shorty. Wasn't nothing short about me, but my patience. I looked at Sasquatch, refused to comment, turned and let her continue talking to my backside. I was five-foot five and a half inches of flawless fineness.

Thirty minutes later, I was sitting in an attorney client room waiting for a black man that came one day short of fooling America into electing him president. A man that had stolen and killed any and everyone that got in his way as he rose to national and international fame as a Baptist church bishop and politician, but like most men he followed his little head instead of his big one. The ultimate reason for his fall from grace.

Seven minutes passed, before two huge guards escorted TJ Money into the room. After removing the shackles from his feet and hands the guards left.

He took a seat facing me, his back to the metal door, arms folded across his chest. A wicked smile creasing his small lips.

I spoke first. "It's working."

"I know," he said.

Smug bastard, I thought. "You mean you know that Miles and the kid are dead."

"I know that too," he put a hand in his mouth and pulled out a small ball of paper.

"For somebody on twenty-three hour a day lockdown with no TV, you sure *think* you know a lot of shit that's going on."

His focus was directed on the chewing gum sized ball of paper he'd taken out of his mouth. After smoothing the paper out with his palm, he said, "I don't *think* I know anything." He pushed the palm sized piece of newspaper across the silver metal table.

I looked at yesterdays Atlanta Journal headlines. "Didn't I just tell you that?"

"Yes, but your first words to me were, *it's working*." He smiled. "You were referring to my plan, which I knew would work. Why, because I came up with it."

"Your plan," I looked at his arrogant ass, "You mean our plan.

"Karen. Karen. Karen."

"TJ. TJ. TJ."

"You've been coming here once a month for over four years. And because of my promise to devise a plan to help you exterminate certain vermin, you made me a promise. And now that my plan is working, I expect you to keep up your end of that deal."

"Did I not become active and donate fifty-thousand to the Innocence Project? Did I not convince the now, Georgia court of appeals chief appellate judge to marry me a little over a year after his wife's sudden death?"

TJ looked down, patted the orange jumpsuit he was wearing, and looked around the room before he spoke. "Karen, Am I still sitting in a prison attorney-client visitation room? Am I still sitting on death row?

"Smart ass."

"Thank you," he responded.

"We still have work to do. Your part is far from over."

"As is yours, babycakes. As is yours."

I scooted forward, reached down in my bag, and came up with my legal pad. Pencil in hand eyes on the yellow paper I asked, "What's next?"

"A formal answer on my last appeal," he said.

"TJ, I can't do anything about the speediness or lack thereof. You been in the system six years, you know the appellate courts are slow."

"Not so slow if you're screwing the chief appellate judge, and I meant screwing in more ways than one."

"Look TJ, I'm on it. Just give it a little more time."

"I'm about out of time. Eight months from now, on March 24th, 2015, I'll be electrocuted," He said. His voice. His entire demeanor calm.

Frustrated I asked, "What do you suggest I do?"

"I don't care. You have enough on Judge Rose to get him to convince at least two of the other four judges to overturn my conviction on the basis of the improperly used forensic evidence as stated in the brief prepared by my Innocence Project attorney?"

"Even if you get a new trial, do you honestly think a jury while acquit you?"

"A jury acquitted OJ," he said, "besides, that's my problem. Now, I am going to go over the next phase of my, I mean *our* plan with you, because I know you will do the right thing. After all who knows what I will say and who I will talk to as my time grows shorter."

"Is that a threat?"

He smiled. "Of course not babycakes. You of all people know that I don't do idle threats."

Did he just threatened me, Karen Elizabeth Parker Rose?

"Now remember Karen, timing is everything."

Thirty-two minutes after TJ began recapping the next phase of *my* plan, with a smile on *my* face and murder in *my* eyes I walked out of the prison and into the late August afternoon sun.

Chapter 6

Cherry

The late August afternoon sun was at it's zenith. The dark tent didn't provide any shelter. And with everyone having on black, it was even hotter under the tent than it was out in the sweltering ninety-three degree Atlanta sun. The way sweat was rolling off of my forehead, you couldn't tell that I was the only one with dry eyes.

I'd cried Monday when I woke up, knowing that the nightmare I'd had was so much more than a dream. I'd cried Tuesday, after Detective Branch delivered the news of Mile's murder. I'd cried Wednesday after seeing one of the last living legends, a lion of black America reduced to a kitten. Twenty-hours lying in a catatonic state, an IV in Tranes arm trying to drip life back into him.

Albert Coltrane Jones was a hero to so many. A modern day vindicated Robin Hood. He'd made millions from his tell all book MVP. He'd donated millions, half his proceeds from his countless speaking engagements over the last several years. Trane singlehandedly forced the house and the senate to repeal

55

the Conspiracy law. With conspiracy, no physical evidence was needed for a conviction, all the prosecution needed where two co-oberating witnesses. Witnesses that were usually convicted felons that had been promised a sentence reduction for their finger-pointing cooperation. This law had been the reason that the feds had boasted a ninety-seven percent conviction rate for almost thirty years.

It was bullshit unconstitutional laws like conspiracy that made me not trust and have very little regard for man's laws. And Miles was the first man that I had known other than my father who shared my passion. After finally finding a man that would gladly put his life on the line for freedom, a man that loved as hard as he fought, and fought as hard as he loved, was taken from me.

The other night at the hospital I remember looking behind me. Paradise had put two chairs together. Half her body on one, the other half on the other. My back would be broke if I slept like that.

I had turned back to the man that was made up of the same DNA as the man God had chosen for and taken from me.

I had walked to Trane's bedside. His eyes had been closed. I gently took his hand. For the first time in twenty-four hours he spoke. "They didn't even have the decency to come and tell us. We had to hear about Miles and that poor kid on TV."

I nodded, understanding that he was still delirious. He didn't remember yesterday with Detective Branch. I wonder how much he did remember. Probably just temporary amnesia.

"Why Miles, and not me?" he asked.

For a second I wondered the same thing. But, that was not for me to answer, maybe not for me to know. But, I did know that crying and mourning wasn't going to solve the mystery behind Miles's death. Somebody had stolen and destroyed what was more precious to me than every life on the planet combined, including mine. I didn't know who, or how that somebody or somebodies were going to pay, but as God as my witness they were going to pay.

****

Four days after Miles's body was found, we were burying him. It had been a small private funeral. And now, twenty-some odd family and friends were under the black tent at the cemetery. The body of Miles Davis Jones may have been forever encased in the shiny black casket in front of me, but his spirit was alive and well within me.

Reverend Solomon One-free was just about to throw dirt on the casket when the small crowd of family and well-wishers turned to where the sirens were coming from.

Four unmarked cars drove through the grass. I was just as shocked as everyone else. And even more shocked when eight similarly dressed dark suited buster brown shoe wearing men came forward with their guns drawn.

"Nobody move! Everybody stay where they're at," the obvious leader said, brandishing a badge and a gun in front of him.

Reverend Solomon One-free stepped forward. "Have you no decency, this is an internment..."

The man and his men completely ignored the reverend.

"Albert Coltrane Jones," the men approached.

Paradise held onto her man as if her life depended on it.

Coltrane met the man's eyes, "What could be so important, that you felt the need to interrupt us putting my brother in the ground?"

"Turn around," the man barked.

"Turn me around!" Coltrane barked back.

The suit swung. Coltrane ducked, came up, elbowed the muscle head cop in the jaw, knocking him into Reverend One-free's wife. In the blink of an eye, twenty some odd friends and family were fighting the police. No one seemed to care that they were armed, including myself. I ran up on the closest suit and hit him as hard as I could with a closed fist.

"Ahhhhh," he screamed, dropped his gun, and put a hand to his bleeding ear.

I scrambled, picked the gun up, and was about to go Columbine on every last one of them blues brother suit wearing cops, until I saw Paradise, lying on top of Miles's casket.

Broken fold up chairs, scattered flowers, one of the poles holding up the tent had fallen.

I dropped the gun, and ran over to Paradise. She was unconscious.

A gun shot was fired.

Everyone froze.

Coltrane was face down on the grass a foot in his back. He couldn't see Paradise.

While tending to my girl, one of the suits hollered, "Albert Coltrane Jones you are under arrest for," the suit roughly slapped handcuffs on Coltrane, "Two counts of first degree murder."

"Murder. I haven't killed.... What?" Coltrane said as two cops pulled him up from the ground.

"That's for a jury to decide, asshole." One of the suits said.

Paradise was groggy, but she seemed to be fine. Just in shock.

I walked up to one of the suits. The black guy. "My name is Cheryl Sharell, I'm Mr. Jones's attorney," I lied, "Can you tell me who Mr. Jones allegedly murdered?"

"Coltrane," Paradise shouted. "My baby." Paradise doubled over in pain.

I turned to her.

"Paradise," Coltrane shouted, right as his head was roughly shoved into one of the unmarked cars. "Cheryl, get my baby to the hospital," he managed to get out before the back door closed.

Twenty minutes later, I was rushing Paradise through the emergency double doors of downtown Atlanta's Crawford Long hospital. I couldn't believe this shit. I mean, why couldn't they have waited until the man at least buried his brother.

An hour later, I was still wondering the same thing as I paced the emergency waiting room floor. I still didn't know who they were saying Coltrane had killed.

"Turn that up," some lady sitting in the visiting room was telling her child.

I looked up at the 42 inch waiting room flat screen. A mug shot of a much younger Coltrane appeared.

"We've got breaking news in a story that's still developing... Atlanta Police now have a suspect in custody in connection with the shocking murders of eleven year old Ezekial Paulk and Forty-one year old, Miles Davis Jones. Miles's elder brother, Albert Coltrane Jones has been arrested and charged in both murders. The bodies were found in an apartment located near downtown Atlanta.

Now, Jones is no stranger to the justice system. You may recall, he escaped from the Atlanta Federal penitentiary in 2007 after serving nine years. While on the run Jones was able to expose corruption in the D.A.'s office that eventually forced Johnathan Parker to abruptly end his 2008 presidential bid. Jones was later exonerated on all charges and was awarded an undisclosed sum by the state of Georgia for his wrongful conviction. Again, the story is still developing, we'll stay on top of it and bring you more information as it becomes available."

Chapter 7

Karen Parker Rose

"Not available? What do you mean not available? Is he in court? Is he in the bathroom? Is he in a meeting?" I asked Royce's buzzard necked, coke bottle glasses wearing secretary.

Royce wanted to wait until after the funeral, but I insisted on him urging the D.A. to make the arrest immediately. I didn't know a fight would've broken out between the special task force officers and the internment attendees. Just like I didn't know someone caught the entire melee on video.

"I-I don't know... I mean I am not at liberty to say Mrs. Rose."

"Which is it, Doris, You don't know, or you can't tell me why *my* husband hasn't been able to take *my* calls or why he hasn't returned *my* calls all day?"

"I apologize Mrs. Rose."

I put the phone on mute to conceal my laughter. I loved to make Royce's pet-secretary squirm. I could care less that Royce was humping the help. Somebody had to do her. She was a basketball with legs and arm."You apologize for what?" The fun part was knowing that Doris knew that I knew. Before she could think of an answer I continued, "Have you done something to me that requires an apology?"

"No. Mrs. Rose."

"Parker Rose."

I'm sorry Mrs. Parker-Rose. I meant, uhm, I was uh-apologizing for your inconvenience?"

I don't see how she stood upright with the spine of a jellyfish. I so hated people like her which was the mass majority of the worlds population. If I wasn't so pressed for time I would go down to the federal building and really make the spineless sperm-bucket squirm. I could care less that Royce was poking Lassie. I just couldn't believe Doris Allibaster Willouby had the nerve to screw someone elses husband.

"Would you like me to leave Judge Rose a message Mrs. Rose, I mean Mrs. Parker-Rose."

I pressed the end button, disconnecting the call, just as Bucky walked up the gravel, weed, and dirt driveway. Elmo and his older brother Bucky Barnes were just two half breed society reject mutts that lived off of a dirt road in Covington, Georgia, about forty-three minutes east of Atlanta. Their house if thats what you wanted to call it would've been condemned by the city if it could've been seen from the road. The roof was made of rusted tin. It was a one level small wood ranch that looked as if it were home to every species of termite known to man. The front and sides of the house were littered with wrecked cars in different stages of repair.

"Bucky, get that damn wet rooster off the hood of my car," I shouted as I got out of my Rover. I hated rain. "And tell your half wit brother to hurry the hell up."

"Ah, he comin'. This bein' his first time and all, he wanna look and smell good for the whore."

I looked at the lean, six-foot pockmarked faced, thirty-something curly haired bumpkin. "I wish you would've followed in your brothers footsteps."

"Hell, I would've, but I can't wash my ass in no cold water. And whats the use of puttin' on clean britches if'n my ass ain't clean."

"Bucky, why don't you have hot water?"

"Just ain't made it down yonder, to get me no stamps, to mail the bill off. We gots the money, thanks to you, the prophet, and the check we get for my brudder every month."

Using the word ignorant to describe the man that was getting in the stolen truck beside me would be an extreme understatement. Bucky Barnes had become one of TJ Money's disciples while serving time in Jackson. And he and his brother Elmo spent at least half of their money on the .99 a minute TJ Money, prison-prophet prayer line.

Moments later, three hundred pound Elmo Barnes came skipping through the weeds in the rain past an old tractor. Elmo was much darker than his brother.

"Hey sister," Elmo said, a mile wide grin on his huge face.

"Boy, whachu got behind yo' back?" Bucky asked.

He thrust out a hand full of dandelions and grass. "I picketed some flowers. I figgered the lady we's goin' to see would like some flowers."

"Dem ain't no flowers, dem weeds. Now, throw 'em down and git your tail in this truck, for we leave your fat ass in the rain," Bucky said.

Bucky may have been dumber than dirt, but he was more obedient and faithful than any dog, despite smelling worse than a wet one. That's why I kept using him. This was the first time I had allowed him to bring his retard brother on an assignment, but the plan was simple and as big as Elmo Barnes was, it would be more fun to have him along.

I reached into my purse and pulled out a can of coke, and a pill bottle.

"I want some," Elmo said.

"Bucky, you and Elmo take these," I handed the two brothers two blue pills each. "You can wash them down with this."

"What kinda pills is they?' Bucky asked.

"Just pills to make you relax."

"I'm already relaxed."

"Me too," Elmo said.

"Take the pills, Bucky. They're from the prophet," I said.

"Prophet Money?" Elmo asked.

"Is there another?" Bucky scolded, taking the pills and the can of coke.

Even with the air on max, I was about to choke. Old Spice and funky-wet-nigga's-ass didn't mix. I tried breathing out of my mouth. I tried taking a breath in ten second increments. Nothing worked.

"Bucky, I don't care if you have to bathe in a swamp, you better never come within a hundred feet of me smelling like that."

He raised his arm, grabbed Elmos head and brought it into his armpits. "Do I stink?"

Elmo shook his head, "Nope, I don't smell nuttin'."

Before I knew what was happening, Elmo palmed the back of my head and my nose was buried under his massive damp armpits.

The truck swerved in the rain.

I heard a slap, "Let her go idiot," Bucky said.

His massive hand released my head, I barely missed hitting a volkswagen bug in the next lane.

"You dumb shit? Whachu trynna do?" Bucky asked, his brother.

I was so stunned, words hadn't formed in my mind yet.

"I was trynna' see if I was the stinky bean."

Bucky, slapped his brother upside the head again. "You coulda' killed us. I swear." He shook his head. "Sometimes I wished I woulda' left you in that nutty farm, fucking retard."

I wanted to kill the jolly black retard, probably would have, if he would have smelled half as bad as his brother. After turning onto Coltrane's street, I pulled out my iphone, put in my passcode, pressed the correct application icon and I was in. "Great, no one's home yet," I said aloud. "Look, you two, do exactly as I say." I looked at both of them as I pulled into an empty garage bay, and took out three stocking caps. "Understood."

"Yes, sister," they both said in unison.

"I'd been making use of Bucky for three years now, and he didn't even know my name. He had never asked anything about me or about whatever he was paid to do. Sister was all either of them knew.

I locked the garage so no one could use the remote before going in through the kitchen door. Now all we had to do was wait. Coltrane was in jail. I looked down at my Movado. 9:00 AM. According to the staff nurse at Crawford Long, Parasite, should be, being released right about now.

Chapter 8

Cherry

"Right about now girl, I just wanna go down to the Fulton County jail with a bomb strapped to my back," Paradise said.

"I know you do girl, but Rhythm's his attorney. She's getting to the bottom of this craziness," I said as I turned the windshield wipers on max before turning out of the hospital grounds.

"I'm just glad the baby's okay," Paradise massaged her pudgy belly, "cause if I woulda lost my baby..." She let the threat hang in the air. "I just can't believe they are trying to say that Coltrane killed Miles. How could they think?"

"Paradise, you have to calm down, before your blood pressure goes haywire again. Remember what the doctor told you about getting too worked up. Please, I'll take care of everything, one way or the other."

"You know how Coltrane feels about Miles," Paradise spoke as if Miles were still alive.

"Yeah, girl," I patted the back of her hand, "I know."

"Who would do something like that to Miles and to a child. And why?"

"I don't know." I shook my head. "I just don't know."

"I'm so sorry," she looked over at me. "I'm being so insensitive. I didn't even ask if you were okay. I can't imagine what you must be going through. You and Miles were so perfect, so in love. I just can't believe he's gone. Everybody loved Miles. Why would someone kill him? After everything Coltrane's been through with the justice system, you'd think the cops would've been more, I don't know, discreet, nah that's not the word I'm looking for. Anyway, you know what I'm saying. The Government already screwed my baby once. Coltrane's a hero. I just can't believe they are accusing him. There's no way Coltrane could've..."

"Paradise!"

She looked over at me.

"Please. Can we just ride in silence. I'm sorry, but I need to think, and you are driving me..."

"Watch out!"

"Shit." I slammed on the brakes, barely missing the garbage truck that was inches in front of me.

"Miles would kill me if he knew I had his 69 cougar out in this rain. Thank God, I didn't hit that truck."

Paradise turned to me, a concerned look on her face.

My eyes were focused on the soaking wet brother on back of the green and white garbage truck. He had the nerve to wink after flashing a smile that displayed a huge gap where at least four teeth were missing in the middle of his mouth.

"Okay, he needs not to smile ever again in life," Paradise remarked.

"No, he needs to be on TV smiling on the back of a garbage truck. A caption running across the screen reading, 'Why America needs Obamacare'," I said.

"So, is Rhythm really a good attorney?" Paradise asked, as I drove around the garbage truck.

"Very good," I replied, hoping she would be quiet and let me think.

"What if she can't get him out? What if the cops planted evidence to make it look like Coltrane killed Miles and that boy? What if they killed Miles because he helped Coltrane expose the system? What if this is a conspiracy to get rid of two strong black men?"

"Paradise!" I screamed. Both of my hands strangling the steering wheel of Miles's convertible.

"What?"

I pulled over to the side of the road up the street from her house. I closed my eyes, breathed, opened them, turned to my girl.

"What?"

"I don't know how you are going to do it, but girl, you are going to have to calm down."

"That's easy for you to say. You're not five months pregnant. Your man is not in jail on some, some, trumped up murder charges."

"You're right. My man is dead."

"Oh God." she put her hand over her mouth, "I'm so... I don't know what to do." She began to cry.

I pulled away from the curb. It was storming outside. I should've been home in bed with Miles instead of out in this mess with crying Carla. She was getting the hell on my last nerve.

I pulled around the cobblestone horseshoe driveway to the front doors.

"You comin' in?"

"Nah, girl. I have to get home to Miles."

A confused look shrouded her face. "You sure you don't wanna come in for a minute?"

"Nah, I told you..."

"Miles is dead?" Paradise said.

"I know that."

"You keep referring to him as if he's still here."

"No, I'm not."

"You just said that you had to get home to Miles." She grabbed my hand. "Come in, just for a few. I'll cook you breakfast. That's the least I can do for all that you've done."

I should really go in with her. Neither of us really needed to be alone, but I couldn't take much more of her manic ass. "No, you get some rest. I'm going to catch up with Rhythm, see how Trane is holding up. And then I have to catch a few hours of sleep, if I still remember how. It's been so long since I slept."

"I still don't see why we can't see him. You think the guards are going to do something to him?"

"No. Tameeka." I called her by her government name. "I'm sure Trane's fine. Physically. The only reason he hasn't seen a judge yet is because they locked him up yesterday and there's no court on weekends. But, you best believe he'll see a judge tomorrow."

"You sure your attorney friend can get him a bond?"

"Yes," I lied. I'd say anything to shut her up, so I could leave and have some semblance of peace. I knew Tranes chances of getting bond were slim to impossible. The only time a black man got a bond after being charged with murder was when the victims were black males, which in this case was his only hope.

Paradise stepped out in to the rain. "Call me as soon as you talk to Rhythm," she said, before running up the five steps to the door.

I know I should've waited for her to get inside. And I hated lying about having to go home and get some sleep, but I had to get out of there. I needed some me time to clear my head.

With the funeral, Coltrane's arrest, the media, mine and Mile's business, I had not had much time to read over everything I had gathered on Karen Parker Rose. What I did know about her was that she was that crazy ass Jonathon Parker's sister. She was fairly attractive. Very rich. She was married to a judge that was old enough to be her father. And if she was behind Mile's death and that childs, she was probably responsible for Coltrane's arrest. "Fuck!" I said aloud. Miles's 60's muscle car fishtailed in the rain as I made a U-turn. If Karen had gone through all this trouble, then she's a sick bitch like her brother had been and anyone close to Coltrane and Miles was probably on her to-do list. Including Paradise.

****

It took me seventeen minutes in the pouring rain to drive less than three miles back to Tranes. I reached in the glove compartment. "Shit!" No gun. I jumped out the car and ran to the door. I didn't even ring the bell. Just took out my key, and stuck it in the top lock and turned. I repeated the procedure for the bottom lock.

What died? I put my hand over my nose. "Paradise," I shouted while running up the stairs, taking two and three at a time. Next thing I knew, I was falling. "Noooo!"

"Yessss!" I heard a woman's voice reply. The same woman's voice that had haunted me in my sleep.

The master bedroom smelled even worst than it had downstairs. Having been in similar situations in the past, I knew not to panic. Dogs sensed fear and by the looks of my girl she'd been mauled by the most vicious species of dog. The human dog.

I couldn't move. There was a knee in my back holding me down, and someone held my arms.

"Pull the bitch to her feet," The woman's voice said.

I still couldn't see who was holding my arms behind my back.

The woman appeared in front of me. a stockinged cap over her face. She wore beige dickie pants and a beige dickie shirt, both several sizes too big.

"Going for the 2010 white-wanna-be-thug-sagging-look?" I said.

"So, you're the infamous Wild Scary," she said. "Don't look so tough to me."

"Tell your goon to let me go and I'll show you just how tough I am."

"Let her go!" The woman said.

I lunged. Tackled the woman. I felt a shock. I convulsed. Flopped around the bedroom floor like a fish out of water. And then the lights went out.

I woke up. My eyelids fluttered. Light. I was on my back. The room was spinning. My head pivoted left, then right. Where were my clothes? My underwear. I frowned. That smell. I gagged, turned my head and threw up at the same time I saw Paradise. My girl. My friend. Bare, bruised and beaten. Her body a few feet from where I lay on the floor.

Hands. I turned my head. Wet fingers, not mine. Prodding. Poking. Rubbing my taught skin. Numb. Couldn't move. Couldn't fight. My ankles. Someone. Something was spreading my legs. No tears. No frown. No smile. Voiceless. Refusing to give him, them the satisfaction of hearing my pain. Even the lump in my throat, I quietly swallowed as it mounted me.

Inside me. Panting. My eyes. Eyes of a zombie staring at the hairless beast that howled and panted with pleasure as he plowed his nature in and out of my once precious womanhood.

Beauty studying the beast, that I am, that I was, that, I will always be as his features are being etched in my mind, my soul. Even more woozy, but alert from drinking in his putrid scent, counting the beats to which the rhythm of his body moved, stroked.

I wanted, needed to remember every detail, down to the brown nylon stocking cap he wore. The clammy, slivery feeling as his slimy slim body crawled across my skin. A moment had become an eternity. Time had no clock. How long had it been going on, had become how long would it last? How many had defiled my body, had become how many would defile my body, Paradises body.

I turned my head again. Lifeless eyes stared back. "Paradise," I managed a silent whisper. No tears. My jaw rested in my own warm vomit. I stared at my friend. My mind called out to her, "Paradise," To Him, "God? Take me God. Take me."

The rapist took my legs off of his shoulders and violently pushed them to the ground. "This whore ain't no good. She ain't like her over there. Now she a screamer. This here whore ain't utter a damn word." He stood up. "I done cum all I can cum. Boy, you give her a try. I'm goin' to the shitter."

I'm going to the shitter, I repeated over and over in my head. Remembering every syllable, every intonation of his southern accent.

"I don't want to." I heard a child like deep voice say.

"What I tell you about actin' like a sissy. Is you a sissy, boy?"

"No. I ain't no sissy."

"Well take this. Put it on your pecker and go be a man."

I laid there, not knowing if I could move. I knew if I did, it would be futile. I didn't know where Karen Parker Rose was. She had been quiet since I had been conscious. Determined footsteps bounded out of the room, as questioning footsteps trudged closer to where I lay. Things were still fuzzy. The room was no longer spinning. I made out a hand. A huge hand. Dark. He was having trouble putting a condom on.

"Don't worry with that," I whispered loud enough for the man to hear. "A real man doesn't wear a condom," I managed to say with extreme difficult. "You do wanna show him that you're a real man."

"Yea ma'am. I ain't no sissy. I'm a real man."

"Show me."

No matter how hard I tried, I couldn't stay awake. The next time I woke up the huge man-child was inside me. I couldn't feel. Didn't know if he was raw or wrapped. I prayed that he had entered me raw.

A toilet flushed.

"You bout finished boy."

The second rapist bucked. He convulsed before his huge flabby body collapsed on top of me.

"Get your fat ass up and come on, boy," my first rapist said.

"See, I'm a man," The rapist said while getting off of me.

My mind smiled before I blacked out.

The next time I came to, Karen Parker Rose stood over me. She had a dust buster like vacuum in her hand. The only thing was that it wasn't a vacuum at all. It was a DNA detector, very similar to the one widely used on crime scenes all over America.

"You better kill me," I said.

"Hmmm, let's see," she slipped off her oversized tennis shoes, exposing her French manicured bare feet. She lifted her leg and went from Paradise to me. "Eeny, meany, miney, hoe," Her big toe momentarily resting on my lips. "Catch a trick off her flow. If she hollers fuck her more, let the silent one live, cause she's such a bore, eeny, meany, miney, hoe." She lifted a bare foot and smashed it into Paradises' face.

"Why?" I asked.

"Albert Coltrane Jones took everything from me," she said. "Now I've taken everything from him."

Chapter 9

Karen Parker Rose

"Him," the prosecutor said, pointing an accusing finger at Coltrane, refusing to address him by name. "He beat his brother to death with a cylindrical blunt object. He kidnapped and suffocated an eleven-year old child. And the state believes that the accused, Albert Coltrane Jones sexually molested..."

"Your honor," Coltrane's Medussa looking dreadlock wearing attorney interrupted.

The judge banged his gavel on the bench. "Mr. Coward, the accused is not on trial here. If you are not bringing further charges against the defendant at this time then the court is not interested in what the state believes...."

"But, your honor, the state is preparing to charge the defendant..."

"Preparing is not charging. Until you have evidence and a grand jury is assembled..."

ADA Clarence J. Coward interrupted, "Your honor it is clearly evident..."

Judge Gamble banged his gavel on the bench and stood up. "Mr. Coward, I will not let you turn this courtroom into a circus. This case will be tried in my courtroom not the media."

Coltranes brown skinned, snake haired attorney stood up again. "Your honor, Mr. Jones has already wrongfully served over nine years in prison before proving his innocence. He's married. Has close ties to the community. His wife is expecting their first child. He's inspired thousands, hundreds of thousands to re-invent themselves, become job makers and job takers. In the last seven years since escaping from prison, my client," she extended a hand toward the tired, sad looking man that I so loathed, "Has been instrumental in helping to right so many wrongs. He's helped us address unconstitutional laws, and he has been a pillar of our community..."

"Mrs. One-Free," The judge interrupted.

No that idiot did not hire one of them racist One-Free cult members to represent him. This should be interesting, I crossed my legs and continued listening.

Judge Gambles geriatric white ass continued, "the court is well aware of Mr. Jones's past. Although, I am sympathetic to your client's plight, he is still being charged with two counts of murder and do to the heinous circumstances of these crimes, I am setting bail..."

The ADA was on his feet, "Your honor, the state staunchly recommends that bail be denied." The ADA thrust an arm toward Coltrane. "He beat his own brother to a bloody pulp."

"Bail is set at five-million," the judge banged his gavel down with finality.

I stood up. I wanted to scream. I could not believe it. I absolutely could not believe that old fuck gave Coltrane a bond. "Bull-fucking-shit." I shouted.

Coltrane and half the court turned their heads.

The judge banged his gavel down. "Order. That language will not be tolerated in my courtroom."

"Excuse me." I stepped on toes and bumped knees trying to get out of the row I was sitting in. For all I care, everyone from the judge to Coltrane could kiss my tanned white ass. I marched out of that kangaroo court and over to the elevator.

I'll be double damned under hell's furnace before I let that wrinkled goat-faced, civil war relic have the last word. There's more than one-way to skin a judge. I should know.

I pressed the number fourteen as the elevator door closed.

There he is. I opened the glass door. "Nathan Dobbs Beckford!" I slammed the door to the District attorney's office, "Why are you not prosecuting Albert Coltrane Jones?"

"Whoa. Whoa. Karen," The DA held an arm out like he was trying to stop traffic. "We are prosecuting Albert Jones."

"I meant you, personally." I stood with my hands on my hips tapping the toes of my Jimmy Choo heels on the marble floor.

"Clarence Coward is my best ADA, he is more... No disrespect Karen, but who I put on any case is not your concern. Why are you so concerned with who prosecutes Mr. Jones?"

I gave him a why-the-hell-do-you-think look before crossing my arms. The foot tapping continued.

"Excuse us Barb," Nathan smiled at his barely legal looking secretary, before putting his hand on my arm. "Karen," he smiled, "would you be so kind to step into my office."

I jerked from his grasp and marched past him into his spacious office.

He softly closed his door. "This case has nothing to do with Jonathon?"

"This case has everything to do with my brother. Coltrane humiliated my brother. Made him look like a criminal, a murderer."

"Jonathon made himself look like a criminal." The DA said. "He framed that man."

75

"That man is a liar and a cold blooded murderer. Look at what he did to his own brother. How could you allow him to get a bond?"

"I didn't *allow* him to get anything. Judge Gamble did that."

Much calmer now, I crossed my arms. "What is taking so long with the DNA results?"

"How did you know about the DNA testing?"

"I have my sources." I said. "Now what about it?"

"Karen, your brother was a friend. And I am a longtime admirer of Judge Roses. And I say this with all due respect," he paused as if I would take whatever shit that was about to roll off of his tongue more seriously, "Stay away from this case."

"I'll stay away from this case after I go talk to Pete Spire over at the Constitution. Or maybe I'll call Bob Herald over at the Post. Maybe they can get the DNA results."

The DA picked up the phone from his desk. "If I make a call to DNA diagnostics, will you leave it alone, Karen."

I smiled. "Of course."

Five minutes later, I walked out of the DA's office with an even bigger smile on my face than the one I had faked before agreeing to stay away from the case.

Chapter 10

Cherry

The case was on top of Reverend One-Free's desk when Rhythm walked into his church office. My back was to her. I was on my knees. I needed strength and God was the only one that could help me navigate the road I was about to travel.

I heard my old friend as she took a seat. I was done praying for now, but I still wasn't quite ready to turn around. Once Rhythm saw my face she would insist on helping me, helping Paradise. But she couldn't. Not this time. Karen had made this personal. And even if I accepted the type of help I knew she'd offer, there was no way she could come back into the church after being a witness to the type of hell I was about to unleash. The hell that I prayed God would bring me back from.

I slowly stood. A pain hit me in the stomach. I bent over.

"Cheryl," Rhythm shouted while rushing to my side.
I turned.

"Oh my God." She put a hand over her mouth. Girl what happened to you?"

"I was..."

Next thing I knew my eyes were fluttering. The voices I heard sounded like movie voices being fast forwarded. My head was ringing. Sounded like sirens. And then silence.

****

My bed was moving. My eyes fluttered open. Who were all these people? And where were they taking me? I was on my back. Bright lights stung my eyes. I squeezed them shut. Still, light was trying to penetrate my wrinkled eyelids. Voices. All I could make out was Mwa, Mwa, Mwa. And then silence. Darkness.

****

My mind awoke to an incessant beeping. Like water slowly dripping. Instead of drip, drop, drip, drop. It was Beep. One second. Beep. One second. Beep.

"Somebody, please turn that damn beeping noise off," I pleaded, refusing to open my eyes for fear of being blinded. Blinded by the light that was fighting to yet again, break through my eyelids. I knew if I succumbed, opened my eyes, saw what was making that horrible beeping sound I'd do everything in my power to kill anyone that stood in my way to destroying the beeping machine. Every second, on the second, Beep. Beep. Beep.

Now, the sound of footsteps accompanied the beeping.

"Cheryl?"

Without thinking, I opened my eyes. The light was blinding. I closed, opened them again. I couldn't see beyond the light. Was this the light that led to the other side? Was Miles behind the light?

"Miles?" I called out.
"Cheryl," he called back to me.
A tingle shot from my toes to my head. "Miles?"
"Cheryl, it's me Rhythm, honey." She took my hand.
"Miles," I called out.
"No honey. It's me, Rhythm."
"Rhythm?"
"Yes, sweetie, I'm here. How do you feel?"
"I don't."
"You don't what, Cheryl?"
"I don't feel. I don't feel anything." I lied. Actually, I did. I was in mortal pain everywhere. But sympathy wasn't going to get me nothing but a worst headache than the one I had.
"Did you get the case from Revs. office at the church?"
"What case?"
"Where am I?"
"The intensive care unit at Crawford Long."
I rose. Winced in pain, and laid back down. "How long?"
"Close to twenty-four hours."
"Beep." One second. "Beep."
"Rhythm? Exactly how long have I been here."
"Let's see?" She pondered. "You called me yesterday around noon. I couldn't answer because I was in court with Coltrane. Once I left, I checked my messages. You said it was an emergency and that you were at New Dimensions. I came straight from the courthouse. I got there about one. You were in Sol's office on your knees praying. Almost as soon as you realized I was there, you passed out. I called an ambulance and you were rushed to the hospital."
"What time was that?"
"I guess it had to be around one thirty."
"What time is it now?"
Rhythm looked at her watch. "Quarter after eight."

"AM?"

"Yes. AM.

I attempted to sit upright. "I have to get out of here."

"Not today. You have two bruised ribs and a nasty concussion. The doctors think." She paused as if she were trying to put the right words together. "They think that you may have been raped."

"I was."

A hand shot to her mouth.

"Beep." One second. "Beep."

"Rhythm," I grabbed her elbow, ant turned to that damn EKG, beeping machine. "My heart is fine. But if you don't unplug that damn thing. I am going to lose what little mind I have left."

Seconds later, she got up off her knees, "Okay, it's unplugged. Now, tell me what happened."

"Did the doctors do a rape kit?" I asked.

"Yes, I believe so."

"Fuck." I grabbed her arm. "Rhythm, listen. I need you to go to the church, and on top of Reverend One-Free's desk, there is a small gray plastic case about the size of a... Hell I don't know. It's a small ass plastic thing with cotton swabs, quips and two clear test tubes inside. I need you to bring it to me."

"What is it?"

"I need you to trust me and please bring it..."

The door opened. "Ms. Sharell, how are we feeling this morning?" A young blonde haired man wearing a starch white doctor's thingy with a stethoscope around his neck walked in.

"I don't know how we feel, but I feel peachy." I made a bad attempt at masking my pain with sarcasm and a fake smile. "Now when can I leave?"

He picked up a chart at the end of my bed. He looked way to young to be reading a medical chart. "Uhm-hmm." he grunted. A few seconds later he grunted again. "Uhm-hmm."

I looked at Rhythm.

She shrugged her shoulders.

Much slower and more dramatic this time the doctor said, "Uhmmmm-hmmmmm."

"Can you please tell us why the hell you keep uhm-hmming. Didn't you learn any patient-bedside etiquette in medical school?"

"I'm sorry Ms. Sharell."

If being a doctor didn't work out for this kid, his teeth had a great chance of starring in a toothpaste commercial.

"You took a pretty bad beating. And it says hear that you were sexually assaulted."

As calm as a still wind, I said, "That's not true."

"It says here that there was an excessive amount of vaginal tearing and bruising." he looked up at me for the first time since picking up my chart. "There are bite marks between your upper thighs and on your chest."

"I don't care what it says. The sex was consensual. I was not raped."

"Ms. Sharell?" He paused. "In my experience, I've seen women just like yourself, in denial until it was too late for the guilty party to pay for their crimes."

"In your experience. Are you serious? You aren't old enough to have experienced a tenth of the shit I've been through. So save that bullshit for someone who gives a flying fuck. Now, I told you I was not raped. And no I don't have a husband, and my fiance is dead. The sex I had was rough, but it wasn't rape and if this hospital doesn't destroy the rape kit that you obviously administered without my permission, I will sue you and this damn hospital. Now if you will kindly take your Uhm-hmming ass out of my room I would thoroughly appreciate it."

"Get some rest. I'll check on you in a couple hours," his radiant smile making me even more upset as he left the room.

"You told me that you were raped, but you told Dr. Tolbert that you weren't."

"It's complicated, I'll explain everything in time. But first, I need you to get that case from the church."

"Not until you tell me what's going on."

"Rhythm please?"

"Cherry, you know how I get down. We've been through a lot together. I love you. Let me help you."

I took her hand. "Rhythm, I was raped. It was horrible, but you have to trust me. I am handling it. That case in Revs office is a rape kit, one that I did on myself." I looked her in the eye. "If you really want to help, you will trust me."

"At least tell me whachu gon' to do with the rape kit."

"I'm going to bribe William into processing the kit and checking the DNA against anyone that's in the system."

"I'll do it. Besides, William wants me to handle his discrimination case against Fulton County."

"All the gay and down low brothers in Atlanta, you would think the APD were more sympathetic to gay officers."

"Apparently not," Rhythm said. "Don't ask, Don't tell obviously just pertains to the military, but trust and believe when I finish suing the city for their treatment of one of it's most decorated officers, William will be able to walk around the station singing Chaka Khan's, *I'm Every Woman*, in high heels and a short dress and no one will dare say a word."

"Thank you, girl. I feel better knowing that you have my back."

"Sisterhood girl. We have to stick together. Speaking of sisterhood, I've been trying to get in touch with Paradise. We got Coltrane a bond. I just need her to sign some papers so we can secure..."

"Paradise! Shit!"

"What happened?"

Chapter 11

Karen Parker Rose

"What happened?" Royce asked. He sat in the study, his eyes glued to the paper, his back turned away from me.

"What the fuck do you mean, what happened?"

"Karen, must you always use such foul language?"

"Must you always ask stupid ass questions Royce?" I marched in front of him, snatched the paper out of his hand. "Don't shake your head at me like I'm the idiot."

He took off his glasses and uncrossed his legs. "Yesterday, I got a call from Nathan Beckford. Can you imagine how embarrassed I was when the DA calls and tells me of the scene you caused in his office after Judge Gamble granted that Jones boy bond." Royce stood. "The DA, a total stranger to me, calls me and tells me my wife has not only made a scene in the courtroom, but you had the audacity to question the DA's tactics. Is there anything more you can do to derail my future prospects at becoming the next Supreme Court justice?"

"Yes, there is so much more I can do, but I won't. At least not yet."

"What do you mean by that?"

"Terrell Joseph Money."

"Who?"

"TJ Money. The former pastor that's due to be executed next April for murdering someone he didn't kill."

"What about him?"

"See Royce," I pointed a finger in his direction. "That's why I curse so much. That's why I make so many unnecessary scenes. I told you that I needed you to make sure the courts decision is overturned and he get's a new trial?"

"On what basis would the court of Appeals throw out the verdict?"

"Oh my God. I've already told you. I gave you a copy of the appeal prepared by the Innocent Project's attorney's I've been working with over the past five years. Do you pay attention to anything I say?"

"Not really. At least not when it comes to anything that could get me thrown off the bench and disbarred."

I put my hands on my hips. "You have one week. One week to reverse the courts decision in the matter of Terrell Joseph Money Vs. The state of Georgia or," I threw several lewd pictures on the studies hardwood floor, "Or these pictures will end up on the desk of the ethics committee and we'll see how fast your ass will be off the bench and out of law."

"Karen, are you insane? There is no way in Sam Hell, I can get the other sitting judges to review the case and the appeal in a week and rule on the appeal, the soonest I can even read over the case and render my opinion is a month."

"Okay, I'll give you one month from today."

"Are you insane?"

"No, but you must be, asking me the same stupid ass question twice and getting the same answer."

"What answer."

"Silence is not an answer," he said.

"The hell if it isn't. Watch," I turned and walked off. For the life of me I couldn't figure out why Royce kept trying me. By now, he had to know that he couldn't win any type of anything with me. He may have been a top judge, but I was his judge, jury and executioner. Deep down inside he had to know this.

A few minutes later, I was upstairs in my home office on my computer. I typed in the name Rhythm One-Free. "Damn," I said aloud. One thousand, six hundred and thirty two hits. This black bitch must be some kind of attorney all-star.

Two hours later, the words began intermingling as my eyes tired. Forty years ago Rhythm One-Free had been Rhythm Azure a law student at Howard University.

She had become politically active in the Moses King rape and double murder case. After she'd exhausted all of his appeals, and in 1982 she organized a huge march where fifty to eighty thousand people came from all over the country to support her in her quest to have Moses's conviction overturned. Not only did super bitch get Moses King, a Chicago gang leader exonerated for the rape and murders of a black Chicago politician and his wife, she also nearly singlehandedly spearheaded the collapse of the 70's and 80's notoriously corrupt Chicago city government.

And after serving as much time as Coltrane had served, Moses King was free. He changed his last name to One-free as did all the members of his brother's One-Free religious cult. Not only did Rhythm follow suit, she married Moses and they were still together after all these years. She might've been a bad bitch then, but she had to be pushing sixty and some change now. The old bitch had skills, but there was no way she was getting Coltrane off and if I even think she has a chance, she'd just come up stinking like the others.

"Knock! Knock!"

"Yes?"

"Can I come in?" Royce asked.

"For what?"

"I am your husband.

"And."

"This is my house Karen."

"And."

"And, I want to have relations with my wife."

"Can you assure me that TJ Money will get a new trial?"

"I can't make any promises."

"Oh well."

He kicked the door. "Dammit Karen."

"Dammit Royce." I stifled a giggle. I'd bet my life he'd taken a Viagra like he'd done last week, when I turned him away holding a petrified hard-on. Most women and almost all men had no idea of the true power of the poo-nanny.

"Karen, please."

"Uhm. Oh. Oh." I wanted him to think I was pleasuring myself.

"Karen?"

"So wet. My palm is resting on my baby ass smooth, Brazilian waxed pussy. My index finger and forefinger are tickling my swollen pink lips. Oh. Oh. Yes. Damn. So wet."

"Okay. Okay."

"Okay what, Royce?"

"I promise, the man will get a new trial."

I opened the door.

Chapter 12

Cherry

I opened the door walked over to Paradise's area. I pulled back the curtain that separated my girl from the others fighting for their lives in intensive care. Paradise looked like a mummy. So much gauze wrapped around her head. A tube ran from the middle of her chest to a machine behind her bed. Her blood looked as if it were being filtered through a machine and back into her body. An IV was attached to one of her wrists.

With each baby step I took closer to her side, the worst I felt about leaving her. If she didn't ever speak to me again, I would be hurt, devastated, but I'd understand. I took a deep breath and took the last two baby steps that put me at her side. I just hoped she allowed me to explain.

"Paradise," in the quietest of tones I spoke her name.

Her eyes slowly opened. A slight smile creased her lips. "It hurts."

"I can't imagine what you must be going through." I shook my head. "I swear I can't."

"They were in the house waiting when you dropped me off."

I nodded.

Her eyes watered. "They beat me."

I nodded.

"They took turns raping me."

I nodded.

"They spit on me."

I nodded.

"They kicked me."

Tears now clouding my vision as I nodded.

"The stockinged capped woman said. She said that, that I could thank my husband for what was happening to me."

I sniffed. "I'm so sorry that I..."

"Don't." She shook her head as I was just about to apologize for leaving her in the house two days ago..

"Please don't." She managed to extend her arm toward me.

I took it.

She squeezed. "You're the strongest woman I've ever met. And if you break down, than what little fight I have left will be gone. I need you Cheryl. You are my hero. My strength. My friend. You and the life I have beating inside me make my life worth fighting for. If it weren't for my baby, I'm sure I'd have given up before the paramedics moved me from my bedroom floor."

I nodded.

"This baby is the future. This baby represents hope in a world full of misery and despair.

I will instill the best of me and the best of Coltrane in her."

"Her. It's a she?"

It was her turn to nod.

"Why Cheryl? Why me? Why now? Am I that bad of a person?"

"No Paradise. You're not."

"Than why has God taken so much from me? Why has He allowed those men, that woman to... to...."

I saved her from saying the words. I slightly squeezed the hand I held. "God didn't have anything to with what happened to you, to Miles, to Coltrane."

"How can you say that when God is master over everything. He gives and takes life. He is the author of life and the editor of death."

"He also created us in His image. Not his physical image but His image to reason, to think, to problem solve. God wants us to work through life as if it's a huge mathematical equation. One that requires thought, application, and reasoning. Although God allows men to do evil, He isn't happy when they do it."

"So why does He allow man to make Him unhappy?"

"His promise," I said not knowing where any of this was coming from.

"What promise?" she asked.

"God's promise to allow man to reason, to choose his own destiny. If God forced mankind to do his will, than we wouldn't have souls. Just hearts and other organs to function like a robot. God gave us dominion over the earth. And it is our choices that separate us from the Humane, the ordained, and the animals. You see Paradise, there has to be chaos in order for us to know what order is."

"It's not fare," she said.

"No one said it was supposed to be. But at the end of the day, this life, order and paradise will be restored to those who have strived to do right."

"How do you know all of this. You don't even go to church that much."

"I don't know how I know, or where what I've said came from. I just know. It's what I feel. And Paradise, I don't have to go into a building to find God." I jabbed a finger into my chest, "He's here." I used the same finger to tap my self on the forehead. "And God is in here."

"I love you Cheryl Wild Cherry Sharell."

"I love you too Tameeka Paradise Jones."

I still felt like a zero leaving her, but she obviously didn't know I'd ever been there, and I sure wasn't going to enlighten her, at least not now.

She tried to cough, but had trouble doing so. I didn't know what to do. It wasn't like I could cough for her. After several tries she managed to get whatever out she had been trying to cough up. Trying to cough seemed to have taken a lot out of her.

She beckoned me to come closer.

I did.

"Closer," she said.

If I came any closer I would be in bed on top of her.

She took a hand and ran it through my shoulder length Hawaiian silk extensions before turning my head so my ear was close to her lips.

"Promise me."

I turned so she could see my eyes and my mouth. "Anything. Anything," I said again. And I meant every consonant and vowel in the word I repeated. After all, I'd left her in the house after I watched the ambulance arrive. I left her not knowing if she were even alive. She could have died alone, like I was going to do when all was said and done. I left her for my own selfish reasons. Selfish reasons that involved revenge and retribution.

She angled my head back so my ear was again near her lips. "If anything should happen to me, I want you to..."

We were like twins. I knew what she was going to say, so I saved her the words. I turned to her. "You don't even have to ask. Of course I will raise and love your baby as if she were my own, but don't even talk like that, girl. The doctors says you're going to pull through."

She smiled, coughed and then smiled again. "Thank you, but there's more."

The look she gave me was as strong and determined as any look that I'd ever seen on anyones face, in anyones eyes.

"There is no greater love than the love I have for my man. I know this is wrong and I pray that I don't break hells doors wide open, but I love that man more than I love God. God, don't make me feel like Coltranes touch makes me feel. God don't make my heart palpitate at the sound of His name. God don't turn my worst hours... into my best days."

I wanted to respond, say something like yes God does. He created Coltrane for you, brought you two together, but right now her and God weren't on the best of terms so I just listened.

"What I'm saying... What I'm asking, begging is if something should happen to me. And I know I'm asking the world, but Coltrane is my world."

I waited.

She just stared into my eyes. The gauze on her face caught the lone tear that escaped her eyes.

"If something should happen to me, Cheryl," she paused. "I need you to take my man."

"You want me to do what?"

"I want you to take him. Love him. Marry him. Take my place."

"Paradise?"

"Cheryl, I'm serious. You said yourself, that any woman who came to know the Jones brothers had no choice but to love them."

Was she losing her mind?

"You said that Miles and Coltrane were so much alike, cut from the same DNA."

"But..."

"You had referred to Miles as God manifest in man. You had attributed your love for him for changing you into a

God fearing, believing woman. Coltrane is but an older version, a little bit rougher around the edges than Miles, but he is still the closest you will ever get to God without dying."

I guess now wasn't the time to tell her that I planned to die as soon as I thoroughly fucked that bitch up that did this to all of us.

"I look up to you. You are my definition of a real woman, and Coltrane needs a real woman, cut from African warrior queens of the past. Coltrane won't live up to his destiny, he won't make it without you, if, if I pass on." She reached out for my hand.

After giving it to her. She said, "You said anything."

"If something should happen to you, and that's a million to one if, how do you know Coltrane will want me."

She smiled. "I know my husband."

I squeezed her hand and smiled. That was all the answer she needed. Although I had no idea how I was going to keep my promise. She just better not die and ruin my plans to join Miles.

"Can I come in?" Rhythm asked pulling the sheet back.

I waved her in.

"You two look like you just finished watching a documentary of all black men in America being shot down by the worlds biggest firing squad," Rhythm said.

"That would be called a dickumentary," I said.

"Okay," Rhythm chorused.

"If you two are trying to make me feel better it is not working?" Paradise said.

Rhythm set her saddlebag brown satchel down in the padded metal folding chair next to Paradises bed. She took out some papers and held them in the air.

"I bet these will cheer you up," she said.

"What are they?" I asked.

"The one on top is a form granting Cherry power of attorney over you and Coltrane's estate."

Paradise looked confused.

I was definitely confused.

"The papers behind the power of attorney form are bank papers and the courts order for bond."

"Coltrane has a bond?" Paradise asked, her voice filled with life.

Rhythm smiled. "Yes he does. It's five million dollars."

"I don't care if they need my heart, kidneys, and a lung, I want him out," Paradise said, before coughing.

"I thought you would say something like that. So over the last couple days I've been putting together the proper paperwork of course with Coltrane's permission, but now I need someone to act as power of attorney for the bank to allocate the funds to secure the bond," she explained.

"Does Coltrane know. About what happened?" Paradise asked.

"I just found out an hour ago?" Rhythm looked at me like I had some explaining to do.

"Please, let me be the one to tell him," Paradise pleaded with Rhythm, before looking to me. "Cheryl, I've asked so much of you already."

"Sign the damn papers girl so we can go get your man," I said.

After we signed the necessary papers and Rhythm notarized them, Paradise looked at me. "You just don't know how much this means to me."

Chapter 13

Karen Parker Rose

"You just don't know how much this means to me," Mercedes Knox said. "God has finally answered my prayers. I done filled out so many applications, I can't even remember applying for this job. But like my momma say, don't kick a gift horse in the mouth. I'm just glad you gave me a chance Ms. Slocumb. Wait 'til I tell momma-an-em that I'm the representative," she paused. "What you say my title was again Ms. Slocumb?"

"Director of Player Personnel," I said crossing my legs, while I sipped a Starbucks Vanilla mocha-latte. Me and Mercedes dingbat-hood-not-so-fabulous Knox sat in the food court of Philips Arena. I had called her this morning, and arranged an interview an hour before she was scheduled to be at work.

Before I met the ghetto-princess-frog in the food court, I picked up a perfect replica of Mercedes's security badge from the same uniform store that I'd gotten the Central cleaning uniform used by the cleaning service that Crawford Long Hospital employed.

"So, what I'm'o be doin' again?" she asked.

"Whatever you're asked to do," I said, uncrossing my legs.

"For fifteen dollars an hour, shit, I'll fuck the basketball team, the coach, and the ball boys. Wait till I tell Quisha, and Ke-ke, I'm a personal player dictator for the Atlanta Hawks, them bitches gon' hate." she put a hand on mine.

A shame. Nah, this woman was a damn shame. She had more money into her gold, glitter fingernails than she did in the clothes she wore.

"I'm sorry Ms. Slocumb. I usually ain't this ghetto, but I'm just so happy. You just don't know how long I been trynna get up out that hospital." She looked at her pink mickey mouse digital watch. "Damn, I gotta leave now so I can catch the bus." She got up. "I'm probably gon' be late but fuck it. I'm movin' up like George and Weasy."

"George and Weasy?"

"The Jefferson's Ms. Slocumb. You ain't never seent the Jeffersons?"

"No," I said with finality. Changing the subject I asked, "So how much do you make in a day at Crawford Long?"

"Seven-fifty times eight minus my lunch hour is," she calculated in her head. "Forty-nine dollars and seventy-five cents."

To say she was dumber than dirt would be an insult to the ground I walked on. I took out three crisp one hundred dollar bills. "Take the rest of the week off. Don't even call in. If Central Cleaning nor Crawford Long respects you enough to pay you more than minimum wage than you shouldn't show them any kind of courtesy or respect."

"Yeah," she nodded. "You right Ms. Slocumb. Fuck them ho's. They don't give a damn about a woman trynna better her damn self," she snatched the money and ran. She didn't even ask me were and what time to report to the fictitious job I had just hired her for.

"Karen Parker," I heard someone behind me, "Is that you?" the mystery soprano voice asked.

I had no idea who was behind me and didn't care. I put my cell phone to my ear and sped up my pace. I had things to do and people to do them to.

An hour later, my brunette wig was wrapped into a bun and the black, plastic frame school teacher glasses had me looking like Peg Bundy on *Married with Children.* The exact look I was hoping for when I picked out my disguise. So much trouble to get into the intensive care unit.

Three years ago in 2011 anyone could have slivered past the minimum security intensive care unit of any hospital in the country. But in 2012, Carl Weebler the Comatose rapist as the crispy half-size man was known had gone on a ten city, twenty seven hospital, thirty-seven man and woman raping spree. Hospitals everywhere where forced to step up hospital security, especially intensive care security, that's why I had gone to so much trouble duplicating Mercedes's fingerprint card and barcode ID.

I looked down into the cleaning cart I had been pushing. The black and white Mercedes Knox name tag stared at me until I lifted it and the smock it was attached to. The battery-acid filled syringe was right were I'd put it ten minutes ago when I took the cleaning cart from the area where the real Mercedes Knox told me they were. I could hardly believe that Parasite had actually survived the rape and beating I had orchestrated.

I'd just used the barcode to access the intensive care unit, when my thoughts were interrupted by the commotion coming from the staff break room in front of me. Curious, I stepped inside.

Everyone was glued to the forty-two inch break room flat screen that hung from the ceiling.

"Whats's going on," I asked the big nosed grizzly bear nurse that was stuffing her face with some type of dessert.

She pointed a whipped cream laced finger at the screen. "It's OJ all over again."

It never ceased to amaze me how fat ass people could gorge themselves in public. If I was the size of this bear standing next to me, I'd be too embarrassed to eat a celery stick in public. And the big bitch was a nurse. Such hypocrisy. She was a heart attack waiting to happen. How the hell was she going to tell an obese patient that they had to lose weight when she was a French fry away from a heart attack her damn self.

"Where is he going?" I asked, referring to the man that had a squadron of flashing light police cars following behind him. As soon as I asked the question a caption flashed across the television screen.

"I don't know, but I wouldn't wanna be the attorney in that truck with him," another fat nasty nurse asked.

"I'm sorry, I just don't believe he molested that little boy, let alone killed his own brother," the grizzly bear said.

"You better believe it. These nigg," some old wicked-witch of the west creature looked at me for the first time, "black men today ain't worth the clothes on their backs."

Because I had walked in, she stopped herself from saying nigga. I was so tired of blacks with their hypocrisy. My skin was white, but I bet my life that I was more black than any of the five witches in the break room. Nigga-nigga-nigga I wanted to scream.

"Ms. Charles, contrary to popular belief, there are way more good black men then there are bad."

How the hell did this Fat nasty know? As big and ugly as she was, ain't no way any type of man had been involved with her. You could tie ten pork chops around her neck and the dog still wouldn't play with her ugly ass. Even when my cooch was covered with red herpes puss bumps, it looked better than her creature feature face.

"Latrice, what you know about men. You ain't been alive long enough to know a good man when you cummin' all over his soul pole."

"Ms. Charles, you so nasty," the grizzly said to the should-be-retired old witch.

"Sweetie, ain't nothin' nasty about non-verbal-extra-carricular-communicable activities. Ain't you seen the memo?" the old nurse asked.

"What memo," several nurses intoned.

"Ain't nothing wrong with a little bump and grind, especially when a nigga make you think he invented sex," she clapped, threw her hands in the air, "hallelujah! Can the church say amen."

"Amen," the nurses replied.

"Look," the old witch said, pointing to the screen, "He right around the corner from here."

No, this fool isn't gon' come here. Murphy's damn law. What can go wrong usually damn does. I left the break room and headed toward the elevator. Oh well, the Parasite bitch will live to breathe another day.

I got off the service elevator to chaos central. I hid behind a clipboard as Coltrane came running through the revolving hospital front doors.

"Tameeka Jones, where is she?" Coltrane asked the attendant working the hospital information desk.

"Coltrane," Rhythm shouted as she came through the doors behind Coltrane.

"Stop right there," a uniformed officer came out of nowhere, his gun out in front of him.

Coltrane looked at the officer and turned back to the information desk attendant. "Tameeka Jones, please, she's my wife."

"Albert Jones, get your hands in the air!" another officer shouted as he came barreling through the front revolving doors. "Now!"

"My wife!" Coltrane shouted at the attendee.

"Intensive care," the young man said before dropping to the floor, behind the desk.

At least eight officers were in the hospital lobby with their guns drawn.

"Nobody move! Everyone stay where they are. The situation is under control, a plain clothes officer announced. He was the only one that didn't have a gun pointed at Coltrane and his female Johnnie Cockroach attorney.

"Everyone just relax, my client is unarmed. He just wants to see his wife."

"Not happening," the closest uniformed police officer said.

Coltrane walked toward the officer that just spoke.

"Freeze asshole," the officer said.

Shoot him. Shoot him. I wanted to say to the officer. Since I couldn't allow anyone to recognize me, I stayed put and kept sending telepathic messages to the nervous looking white cop that Coltrane had walked up on.

"Get back! Get back!" two officers shouted, keeping the media at a distance.

Coltrane put his head up to the butt of Nervous Neds gun.

"In less than two weeks, my brother was murdered, my wife was beaten and raped, I was falsely accused again of murder, and now you're trying to accuse me of molesting and murdering a child. An eleven year old boy."

"Coltrane, that's enough," Rhythm said. "Don't say another word."

Ignoring the advise of his attorney, Coltrane said, "You might as well shoot me, kill me where I stand, cause I'm not going anywhere until I see my wife."

"The hell if you ain't," The officer said trying to grab Coltrane.

A scuffle ensued. In no time, Coltrane was covered in uniformed officers.

The sound of a gun shot exploded in the lobby.

I hoped beyond hope that Coltrane had been shot or even better, he'd managed to take the nervous cop's gun and had killed another officer in the scuffle. As bad as I wanted to stay and find out the outcome I couldn't. I used the gunshot to get back on the elevator and go up to the second floor. There was an exit there.

Chapter 14

Cherry

There is an exit there, and there I pointed to the diagram I'd drawn as I studied the condemned looking cabin. I'd been in the woods all night, studying, looking, planning. The sun was rising which was the cue to make my way back to the car which was parked on the dirt road not too far from the no trespassing signs that were posted at the beginning of the property that I was on.

Twenty minutes later I was on the entrance ramp to 400. I swear, people in Atlanta didn't have a driving idea. It was sunny and the temperature was already pushing eighty and it wasn't even eight o'clock. I couldn't drive two exits before traffic was stop and stop. If there had been a wreck I'd understand but there was nothing. This shit was re-damn-diculous. I couldn't even enjoy the breeze, had to turn on the air. A nine to five was out of the question. Bush and Bin Laden together didn't steal enough money to pay me to deal with Atlanta rush hour morning traffic. Whoever named it rush hour was just as retarded as everyone else on the Atlanta highways in the morning and afternoon. Wasn't no one in a damn rush to get anywhere.

My vibrating cell phone brought me out of my rage.

I looked at the caller ID. RESTRICTED. "Hello?"

"Well good morning to you."

"William?"

"Who the hell else? You expectin' Idris Elba, maybe LL?"

"Either would do," I said.

"I know that's right, Fruit. I'd take both. Double the fun, double the pleasure, and two snaps."

William was so over the top, but I still loved him. Always having to be different. When Rhythm had introduced us a few years ago, I told him to call me Cherry, he called me Fruit.

"Why are you calling me from a blocked number?"

"I'm on the departments phone. You know the police department is the only phones in town that ain't tapped."

"William, I'm so sorry I didn't call you back yesterday. Things have been so out of control lately as I am sure Rhythm has told you."

"Girl, you ain't gotta tell me. Rhythm didn't have to tell me. When I'm not checking in, or checking out evidence my ear is glued to everybody's business, police business and civilian business. The officers may talk about me behind my back, they may have thrown me in the evidence room basement, but trust and believe them bitches with badges always find a reason to come see ole William. They gossip more than me."

"William, you are an angel."

"I know, Fruit."

"How did you get the DNA results so fast?"

"It's all about who you blow, not who you know, and who you know that they had blown."

"William!"

"Don't William me. You think I'm the only loose booty with a badge? Half the badges in the PD are on the down low, and the other half are just low down. The only reason they call themselves alienating me is cause I'm like coke. I was tired of playing the game. The closet I'd lived in for so long just became too damn claustrophobic."

Seeing that I was never going to get an answer, I interrupted, "Thank you so much William. I owe you"

"Well, I wish the hell you'd start paying up."

If I didn't just hang up, I would never get off the phone. William and Rhythm went way back. I'd only known him for about five, six years. And since then, we'd been tight.

I looked at the clock. I couldn't believe it had taken me two and half hours to drive forty miles. Morning slow hour traffic in good ole ATL.

I was at the Fulton County jail trying to find a parking space. This is ridiculous. Visiting hours just began at eight-thirty and visitor parking was already packed. Oh well. I reached in the glove box and pulled out the handicapped sticker I used only for emergencies. While backing in the parking space my phone buzzed again.

I looked at the caller ID. RESTRICTED came up again. I almost didn't answer it. And if William hadn't come through for me in record time I wouldn't have.

"Fruit?"

"Why are you whispering?" I asked.

"I'm so sorry. So sorry," he whispered.

"Sorry about what? William I don't have time for this."

"Tameeka Jones passed away this morning."

I closed my eyes. So much death, so close to me. I was numb. And all I could think about was the man I was going to visit this morning. My heart truly bled for him.

"Fruit? You still there?"

"Paradise," was all I could say. "Paradise."

"Fruit?" he whispered.

It's like the wind of the world had been sucked out of me. I was drained. How was I going to tell Trane? What was I going to tell Trane?

"Fruit, I only got a minute. The official report will probably read something like she died from injuries resulting from blunt force trauma to the head and midsection."

"Whats the unofficial report?" I asked.

"She died of toxic shock, after they did an emergency C section."

"The baby?"

"She was born three and half months premature..."

"Is she alive?"

"Barely." There's no way that baby should be breathing. Probably won't be for long. But for now, she is. And on her own. Gotta go, call you later. Smooches."

I took of my seat belt and opened my car door. I had to tell him.

Forty-five minuets later, I was sitting in a metal fold up chair behind a Plexiglass partition. Coltrane had just sat down. He faked a smile before picking up the black phone. it wasn't really a phone, just a receiver for one of those ancient house phones, the one's with a cord going from the bottom of the receiver to the phones square like base.

We shared a very uncomfortable silence. I didn't know what to say.

"How's my Queen?" he asked.

"I can't believe they locked you back up after we went through all that trouble to bond you out," I said ignoring his question.

"I can't believe any of this. I've been accused of a lot of things, but never anything like this."

I'd cried more in the last ten days than I had in all my life. In fact, I don't think I cried this much as a baby. I don't mean boo hoo crying. I'm talking about that gut wrenching, energy draining howling type of crying. The type of crying that began in the soul and travelled north. And just because I couldn't hardly see because of the water welling up in my eyes didn't mean I was about to break down now.

"Queen?"

No. I was going to be strong. I had to be strong. There was no room for weakness. One weak moment could mean failure and the word failure was not in my vocabulary.

"Queen?"

I heard Trane the first time. Just wasn't ready to respond. Didn't know how to respond. His brother, and now his wife. And him. Innocent. Framed. In jail, helpless to do anything but watch.

"Queen, why are you crying?"

"I'm not crying," I shouted.

"Okay. Okay."

"I'm not," I sniffed.

"Hey, I believe you. But, can you tell me why you have a stream of water running down your face?"

"How do you do it?" I asked, dabbing my eyes and face with a kleenex.

"Do what?"

"Keep fighting?" I asked.

"Excuse me?"

"Your best friend took everything from you. Your money and nine years of your freedom. And yet you kept fighting. Woody Harrelson's father came the closest to escaping from the Atlanta Federal Pen. You're the only one to ever successfully escape. You risked so much to prove your innocence. And after you were exonerated you moved on as if nothing had happened."

"That's what I wanted everyone to think. Queen," his expression became very serious, "not a day goes by that I don't reflect on what I've been through. And not a day goes by that I don't try and help save a young brother or sister from developing and harboring the murderous mentality that I once had."

"What does your mentality have to do with all you've been through. You didn't have a murderous mentality when Jonathon Parker framed you."

"Maybe," he shrugged. "Maybe not, queen. But, when I met Jonathon, I was one of the most ruthless drug dealers in the southeast. No matter how much I've been through, I put so many others through worst. So many kids in the hood grew up without a mother or father because of me. It was either the dope that I poisoned the streets with or the bullets my drug money bought. Bullets and dope that robbed some kid of their father, robbed some mother of her son," he shook his head and blew out a long breath. "Karma is a mother, queen."

"You ain't never lied."

"At least, not in the past ten minutes I haven't," he said, sounding just like Miles.

"And you always keep a cool head. And just like Miles, you're always smiling."

"All the crap that has rained down on my head." He paused. "Queen, I have to smile to keep from frowning." He put his free palm up against the plexiglas that separated us. I put my palm up against the glass where his palm was.

"And the day, the moment I quit fighting is the moment I stop making a difference, and when that happens you better call the morgue to come get me."

"I hear you Trane. Like you, I been fighting all my life. But, I'm tired. I'm just ready to go, end it. Living is so overrated."

"How would you know? What do you have to compare living with?"

"What do you mean?"

"You've never been dead, have you? Don't answer. Let me rephrase that. When you felt as if you were dead, or when you wanted to end your life, how did you feel?"

I had to think about that a minute. "I felt... I felt terrible. And how do you know I've contemplated suicide?" I asked him.

"Anyone who has gone through hell, danced with the devil, and smoked from his pipe has contemplated giving up. Some have. But you Queen, you're still here, strong, beautiful and with more fire than I have ever seen in a woman or man."

"You need to stop drinking that jailhouse juice."

"I wish. You know I don't even drink, but right about now I'd love a fifth of anything. You just don't know?"

"No I don't, but I'm learning. And lately, I learned that Karen Parker Rose has been very busy."

His eyes lit up at my change of subject.

I was happy to have something to share that would hopefully give him hope. I began, "In the wee hours of the morning a couple days ago, I swept the condo and I found nine cameras and six listening devices. I went to your house and reprogrammed the twelve cameras I found there and I didn't bother the nine listening devices."

"Unreal," he said.

"No, this bitch is very real and very disturbed. I don't think she wants you dead, just everyone in your immediate circle."

"She's accomplishing what she set out to do," he said. "Does Rhythm know?"

"Some, but not everything. Trane, Karen Parker Rose is a fruitcake on steroids. She been hovering over the cuckoos nest for some time now. What she has done to you, to us, has taken years of planning."

"Why? Why is she so obsessed?" Coltrane asked.

"Her brother. Although she was the youngest of the two, she was a mother figure to Jonathon. And most likely a wifely figure. I'd be surprised if she and Jonathon weren't sleeping together."

"That's sick."

"Very, but so is she. And Trane, I bet her IQ is off the charts. People like her are usually so intelligent that they go insane. They see the world as it is, not as it is projected to be. Their sense of right and wrong is determined by them. In their eyes everyone else is inferior to them. They are analytical to the nth degree. They also tend to be extremely sociopathic which is the most dangerous thing about them. Social scientists believe that socio-pathology is untreatable. When a sociopath with a genius IQ, like Karen, is locked onto a cause, there is no stopping them and the time it takes to accomplish their mission is irrelevant although they are obsessed with time."

"If time is not relevant than why are they obsessed with it?" he asked.

"The hands on a clock or watch is the only thing that ties them with reality. Time is their barometer for success. Everything is always *now* and *now* never ends, so it's time that puts parameters on their, *now*."

"How do you know all of this?"

I smiled. "Six years in several different mental institutions. I was very much like Karen." My facial expression became serious. "I am very much like Karen. I've even shown sociopathic tendencies in the past, but by no means am I a sociopath. I just do what I have to do."

"Queen, I want you to tell Rhythm everything. The cameras, wire tapping...

"No Trane. I can't. This bitch will never stop. A prison cell won't stop her, she has too many resources. She has to die. But, you have to trust me. If I don't know how to do anything else, I know how to kill. Don't worry Trane, before she dies I will hand over enough evidence to get your charges dropped, evidence that will prove that she did everything your are being accused of."

He shook his head. "I can't let you do this."

"Let?"

"What I meant was, I can't let you risk your life for me."

"First of all, Trane you ain't letting me do anything. No one lets me do shit." I stood up. "And I ain't risking shit for you," I exploded. "That bitch killed the man I love. That woman watched and laughed as two men, animals raped and beat me. Because of her Paradise is dead."

He dropped the phone and dropped his head.

I sat back down. I couldn't believe I had just lost it. Watching his heart shatter into a million pieces broke me. I didn't care anymore. I cried. He cried. We cried together.

Several minutes passed before he wrapped his huge hand around the phone. He nodded, motioning for me to do the same. His palm was no longer touching the plexiglas. "She won. I give up." he shook his head, dropped the phone got up and walked away.

For at least two minutes I just sat there with the phone to my ear. Waiting. Waiting for someone. A sign. I didn't know what to do. I just knew how I felt. For over two thousand years, over four hundred in this country, black people had been done any old way by white people. Most times we didn't have a choice but to accept being lynched, raped, robbed, and beaten. But now we had a choice. I had a choice and there was no way in Sam Damn hell that I was going to let this small town, funky white, rich, psycho bitch win. I be damned if I let her take one more good black man away from society, away from me. She had me all the way fucked up, if she thought I was going to lay down, fetch, rollover and play dead.

Chapter 15

Karen Parker Rose

"You will lay down, fetch, roll over and play dead if that's what I tell you to do Karen?" TJ Money said, as he sat behind the desk in the attorney-client visitation room.

I'd been under the table five-minutes before TJ exploded into my mouth. After spitting into a kleenex I came up from under the table, wiped off the short hookers skirt I agreed to wear and took a seat across from him.

"That wasn't so bad, now was it, Karen?"

I didn't so much mind, blowing his short ass. The smug look on his dark, wrinkled mug is what made me daydream about pressing a hot iron up against his face.

"Earth to Karen." TJ snapped his fingers. "Earth to Karen."

"Let me tell you something, you little midget fuck," I growled. "You're in the safest place in the world right now, but once you get a new trial and you beat your case you won't have this steel, concrete and all these guards to protect you." I sat back and crossed my legs, my control slowly returning. "Trust, you'd rather run through a cave full of hungry grizzly bears with honey basted all over your ass than to fuck with me."

He smiled, reared back in the metal folding chair, and locked his fingers behind his balding head. "I don't wanna fuck with you Karen. I just want to fuck you, you know, from time to time. And maybe a little head when I'm in a rush."

"TJ, I'm not going to pretend I like you. You know that I don't. But, I do respect what you have been able to do over the last three decades. I respect you for being able to still fool so many, even after you've been on death row for several years. Your prison-prophet ninety-nine cent a minute prayer line, ingenious. You are a master of deception. I respect that. But, I hate you. You're short. Old. Ornery. And your wittle eency weency peter won't even get hard anymore. I was surprised you were able to ejaculate. Yep, I respect and hate you at the same time.

"Hate is such a strong word my dear. It is the evil twin of love," he said.

"I got your evil twin."

"Oh really, now."

What I wouldn't give to knock every tooth out in his forever smiling mouth. "Yes, really now."

"I sense a little trepidation. A little nervousness. Are you nervous Karen?"

"About what?"

"Holding up your end of the deal."

"Look you geriatric Katt Williams, you have fulfilled your end of the deal," I stood up. "I have fulfilled mine."

"Not so fast my white knight with shining puffy pink lips," he said. "I am not back in court. Nor have I been informed by the courts that my conviction has ben thrown out."

"I told you that Royce is finishing up the brief now, maybe as we speak," I said. "I'm a woman of my word. Your conviction *will* be overturned."

"Until then, until I receive the order from the court you *will* continue coming once a month, and making me cum once a month, babycakes."

"Who do you think you're talking to?" I remained standing.

"To a white woman with the best set of deep throat sista' girl lips this side of heaven. To the woman that will continue to do as I say until I say different."

Not his words, they were empty. It was the smile on his face that had just signed his death warrant.

"Do we understand each other, Karen Parker Rose, because if we don't, I'm sure I can find someone to come see me every month, maybe Nathan Beckford, the district attorney. Of course he isn't nearly as gorgeous as you are, but he's a blow hard and can probably suck a golf ball through a straw. But then again, I may not even be interested. I will have fucked you so hard and so deep by then, I'll probably be too exhausted to do anything but talk about what you have done."

"Are you threatening me?" I asked while thinking of creative and fun ways to permanently wipe the smile off of his face.

"I believe we've had this conversation," he said. "Do you not remember what I said about threats?"

"Don't let your mouth write a check, your ass can't cash."

"I won't, my dear." He leaned forward and took his hands from behind his head, "You just don't let your thoughts drive you into trying to cash any of my checks. In laymans terms," he smiled, "Don't even think about fucking me. I'm older than you, I'm smarter than you, and I'm stronger than you. And please understand, my dear. I fuck much harder than you."

Two hours later, I was still steaming. That midget fucking TJ Money. I couldn't wait for Royce to get home so I grabbed my keys and drove downtown. When I pulled into a space next to Royce's I checked the time. Two-forty five. In two hours and fifteen minutes Royce would be out out of court. twenty minutes after that, he should be in the parking garage. I just waited in my SUV. "Shit." TJ had me so mad, I couldn't even focus on how I was going to make him suffer, after I got his case overturned. "Fuck. Shit. Damn," I shouted. If I was a man. If I was a fucking man. I swear I would kill a fucking judge or something, just to get on death row so I could kill that little black fuck. "Fuck."

"Karen?" Royce knocked on my window.

I opened the door and jumped out.

"Ow. You hit me with the door," he said rubbing his knee.

"Royce, do what the fuck ever you have to do. I don't care. Get that midget fuck's case overturned."

"Karen." He looked around the parking garage. "Keep your voice down."

"Royce." I closed my eyes, tried to relax, but that midget fuck's smiling face popped into my head. My eyes popped open. "Fuck you Royce. Fuck everything you stand for. Fuck everything you have tried to build. I am going to ruin you. I am going to make you wish your daddy flushed the sperm that spawned you down the toilet if TJ fucking Money doesn't win his appeal." I opened the door and got back into my Rover.

"Karen!" he shouted.

I started my SUV and pulled out of the space.

Royce was saying something. Fussing, but I couldn't hear a damn thing. Wasn't interested in anything he had to say. TJ Money was a dead man. Oh, he was going to get out alright. I'd spend every dollar, call in any favor, fuck whoever I had to to get him out. Just the thought of torturing his ass made me wanna.... made me wanna cum. TJ Money's ass was mine and he didn't even know it.

Chapter 16

Cherry

His ass was mine and he didn't even know it. I stood over Bernard's snoring figure. I didn't know people lived like this, could live like this. At first I thought I was standing on a dirt floor until I scraped my shoe across it trying to remove a candy bar wrapper that had stuck to the bottom of one of my two inch heels.

Now that I saw that Bernard Barnes was exactly where I'd hoped he'd be, I backtracked through the maze of filthy clothes, beer cans, discarded Heath bar candy wrappers, and roaches until I was back in the front room.

I unzipped my black leather surgeons case. It had been years since I had done anything like this. Years since I used the tools of death that my father had taught me to use. I Held the scalpel in front of my face admiring the stainless steel blade's diamond sparkle. A diamond blade scalpel was so sharp that it could cut through steel.

I stood over the old worn couch that Elmer Barnes was sound asleep on. He slept naked, just as his brother did. Elmer slept with his thumb in his mouth and his arm wrapped around a picture frame. Curious, I bent down to try and get a better look at who was in the eight by ten picture.

With the grace of cat, I moved just as one of Elmer's hairy leg dropped to the floor. I squeezed the blades shiny steel handle. I was poiscd, rcady to strike at the first sign of trouble. I just knew he'd wake up as hard as his leg had hit the ground, but he didn't. Just made a smacking sound with his mouth and went back to snoring. Which I couldn't understand. How could someone snore out of their nose. His thumb was stopping up his mouth. A yellow stained white sheet half covered his huge body.

The picture he held was of two little boys standing between a huge overall wearing white hillbilly and a petite light skinned black woman.

I knew Elmer was slow before he had gotten on top of me. I just didn't know he had the mind of a ten year old, until I read up on his family a couple days ago after I received the results of my rape kit.

His mother had shot his father and ten year old Bernard had shot their mother. The Barnes family tragedy had made the front page in the June 1988 Covington Gazette.

I placed my surgeons case on top of the silver metal trash can lid, the cleanest place in the two room shack. I knew Elmer didn't know that he'd done anything wrong to me. Just like I knew no one, human or animal should live in such filth and decay.

Careful not to cut his arm, I removed his thumb from his mouth. And before he could put it back in, I crisscrossed the scalpels across his neck, instantly killing the manchild. Instant and painless death was my gift to him for releasing his seed into me so I could learn the identity of my rapists.

Although I hadn't seen his or his brothers faces I had no doubt that the lanky long curly haired light skinned man snoring in the next room was my rapist.

I stepped over more clothes, sidestepped more garbage as I walked into the kitchen. There was a metal tub full of dirty dishes on the floor, next to a fireplace. No stove. No sink. But there was a buzzing dirty off white ancient ice box looking refrigerator in the corner. Next to it was a tap with a green water hose attached. The other end of the hose was inside the metal dish filled tub.

I searched for a towel in the dark kitchen. When I didn't find one, I went back into the front room where I saw a pile of dirty clothes. I prayed that a rat or something worst wouldn't jump out of the pile while I moved things around with the blades of the bloody scalpels I held. I don't know why I hadn't worn gloves. I used one of the curved scalpel blades to remove a T-shirt from the pile. The T-shirt would have to be my towel. Moments later I was back in the kitchen washing my blades off. I dried them with the shirt before I walked out of the kitchen and into Bernard's room. I pushed the button on the naked lady lamp next to his bed, illuminating the bedroom. It took a minute for my eyes to readjust to the light.

"Bernard Barnes," I shouted. He still didn't wake up, so I reached down beside the twin bed, pulled the belt from his muddy jeans and, "Whap."

"Gotdamn," his body convulsed. He grabbed his pimply red butt cheeks, before turning and looking at me. "Bitch."

"Nah, that would be you."

"What?"

"You were referring to yourself as a bitch," I said.

"Fuck you," he spat.

"I plan to."

He lunged. I sidestepped, and sliced the back of his hand.

"Gotdamn it," he shouted.

"God didn't have anything to do with your damnation. That's all you playa."

"Elmo! Elmo!" he shouted.

"Your brother is a little busy bleeding. I seriously doubt if he hears you."

He picked up a shirt and began wrapping his hand. "You lucky you got them things in your hands."

"These things are called scalpels."

"Likc I givc a good gotdamn." Hc got up off thc bcd and grabbed his penis. "I'm glad you cut me. Now, when I get them things out your hands, I'm gon' take that pussy again, and this time I'm goin' in raw and through the back door bitch."

I walked over to the window in the bedroom and placed both scalpels on the termite infested wooden ledge.

"Whachu think you doin'?" he asked.

I pulled my dress over my head, folded it up and put it on the ledge.

"You liked ole Peter Piper up in you, huh? He grabbed his penis. "That ass can't wait for my peter to put this here pipe to ya."

I slipped out of my red thong and my matching bra. "I bet taking pussy is the only way you've been able to get a woman. Did you also rape your mother before you shot her or did she give it up to you and your daddy freely?"

"Why you so close to the window. Come over here and talk that shit."

There was no way I was taking off my heels. There was no telling how many viruses and diseases were breeding on the floor. I walked over to the end of the bed.

Without warning he lifted the thin mattress and his hand came out with an old .38 police special. "Ain't no fun when the dick got the gun." he sang.

I started walking around the bed to where he stood. "I'm going to fuck you up real good. And when I finish, I'm going to fuck you," I said.

"Click." He pulled the trigger.

"I took the bullets out last night when you were asleep."

He threw the gun on the bed. "I don't need a gun," he lunged.

I caught him with a right to the jaw and a knee to the groin.

"Ahhhhhhhh, fuck. I can't breathe." he bent over and grabbed his family jewels.

I didn't have enough space to do a full roundhouse, so I did the best I could. I kicked and most of the heel of my shoe got stuck in his ear. A second later I yanked and my shoe came out of his ear.

"Ahhhhhhhh," he wailed, grabbing his bloody ear, while still bent over with one hand holding his family jewels.

"At least make this interesting." I shook my head.

He waved a hand in the air. "I give. I give. You win. I'm sorry."

"You ain't even close to being sorry. But you will be." I stepped into each swing. My fists tap danced all over his face and head. I don't know how long I was hitting him nor did I know how long he'd been out before I stopped to catch my breath. He was half on the bed and half on the floor as I stood over him. My knees were killing me. The only reason I knew that he was alive was because I still smelled his beer and puke flavored breath.

Fifteen minutes later, I stood over the bed admiring my work. My father would be proud. I had to be creative, because of course Bernard 'Bucky' Barnes didn't have bed posts. After I dragged his skinny ass back onto the bed and turned him on his back, I'd used the beds frame to tie his hands and neck to. I probably dulled the blade on my scalpel cutting up the bed sheet to use it as rope, but it was what it was.

Now for the fun part, I thought as I left the room, went to the flimsy front door opened it and picked up the end of the board that didn't have splinters sticking out of it. The man that worked in the wood section of Home Depot asked what I was going to do with the two by four that I had him cut and reshape

118

into something that resembled a splintery triangular baseball bat with a screw shaped head. The two and a half foot plank was a half inch in diameter at the tip and its diameter increased to almost six inches in diameter at the smooth end, the end I grabbed. With my free hand I grabbed the rubber mallet that was next to the plank.

I barely had the tip in, when I swung the mallet.

"DUHHHHHHHHHHHHHHHHHHHHHHHH!"

I swear, I'd never heard anyone scream so loud.

"DUHHHHHHHHHHHHHHHHHHHHHHHHHHHHHH HHH!"

He screamed even louder when I pulled the plank out of his ass.

"Please? Please? Please? Don't! No more! No more! Please don't kill me? Please don't kill me? I'm so sorry," he whimpered.

"Did you have mercy on Tameeka Teena Marie Jones when you beat and raped her?"

This time I jammed the plank in with my hands. No longer caring about getting splinters.

"DUHHHHHHHHHHHHHHHHHHHHHHHHHHHHHH HHH!"

I pulled it out. Oh, God. I had to hurry up. The blood and feces that gushed out began to turn my stomach.

"She made me do it," he cried.

"Who is she?"

"Sister. The prophets, apostle."

"Prophet?"

"Prophet TJ Money's apostle."

"Keep talking." TJ Money was in prison on death row. What did he have to do with Karen? How did they even know each other?

"I heard about the prophet while doing a stint in Jackson. He was on death row so, I never saw him, but the cons said he was the real deal and like Jesus, he was sacrificing his life for the sins of man, and that any man no matter what he did or what he'd done could get to the kingdom of heaven through the prophet."

"You got to be bullshitting me."

"No, swear ta God. He got a prayer line. 976-GOD-TALK. Every day, there's a ten minute message of redemption, and it's only ninety-nine cents a minute to listen."

"Get to the point. What's TJ Money have to do with what you did to me and my girl?"

"He sent Sister to me. She promised us money and salvation if I helped her do Gods work."

"God's work. You call what you did to me and my girl God's work."

"Sister said that all of you were evil. The little kid we stole..."

"And raped."

"We didn't touch that boy. I mean we didn't have sex with him. Homosexuality is a sin. We didn't touch the man we took to that apartment either. We just wrapped him up with duct tape."

I dropped the plank, and climbed onto the bed stepping over him.

"What are you doing?" he asked. Where are you going?"

I stepped off on the other side and walked over to the ledge and picked up my scalpels. My hands were bleeding but I didn't care. They were just splinter cuts. What Bernard 'Bucky' Barnes had just said had cut me much deeper than anything I could ever do to him. I cut his right arm loose, his neck and his right foot. "Roll over or die," I said not thinking. It was like I had traveled outside of my body. Like I was possessed by his referring to what he'd done to the man that I would die for, the man that I was going to die for.

"You still have my left arm and leg tied up."

I criss crossed the two scalpels carving an X onto his back.

Again he screamed, arched his back and turned over.

And before I knew what I was doing, I had crisscrossed my blades again. Bernard 'Bucky Barnes' had died screaming and as a Eunuch.

Afterwards I screamed. Just lost it, right there in that cabin like home. I couldn't believe what I'd done. When he referred to Miles and what he had done I had just blacked out. "Fuck." Bucky Barnes's testimony would've freed Trane and convicted Karen. Dammit. I didn't even ask him how she looked, if she was white. And TJ Money, how did he know Karen. I don't know what the hell is going on, but you best believe I was going to find out.

Chapter 17

Karen Parker Rose

"**Find out** what?" I asked. "The man's been on death row for six years."

"Did you? Were you and him?"

"Fucking." I screamed into the phone. "Can't you say the word, Royce. Do you wanna know if me and that black half-a man midget bishop were fucking? Huh Royce? You think someone like myself would lower herself to screw someone like him? His age. The only decrepit Viagara enhanced dick that has ever been up in this is yours." I looked down at my crotch as the rare mid-day Atlanta summer breeze blew the Victoria Secrets silky material against my creamy waxed skin.

"So, you're saying that you have never had relations with, cause if you had...."

"I could've sworn I was speaking English."

"Don't get smart Karen. I'm doing what you asked. I just need to know, because if it gets out that you and him.... And I was the chief appellate judge when his case..."

I pressed the END button and put my phone on silent. My idiot meter was registering full and couldn't take anymore idiot conversation. I placed my cell phone in my bag and pulled out my high powered black binoculars.

I stood next to some dead rich fuck's mausoleum watching as the funeral procession crept through the cemetery, followed by an unmarked black Chevy Suburban.

I was dressed for the occasion. Not because I had planned to, but because black had been my favorite color for as long as I could remember. My Rover was black, most of my clothes were black. I liked my coffee, black. I even liked my men black, although I was white and had married white. Even my kid was black. My kid. I hadn't seen Karl in six, seven years and hadn't talked to him since Jonathon died. The only reason I knew that the kid was still living in Houston with his aunt Reshonda was because none of my court ordered child support checks had gone uncashed.

I turned my attention back to the internment. Beautiful. It was absolutely beautiful. Four officers dressed in black suits escorted Coltrane through the grass to the internment. Coltrane had been given one of three choices. He had chosen to attend the internment instead of the wake or the funeral. He too had on a black suit accentuated by silver shackles on his ankles and matching handcuffs on his wrists. How humiliating. So perfect.

Ah, ain't that sweet. His snake head attorney took his hand as she stood next to him. There were twenty-nine people... No, a white sixties muscle car was pulling up. It was Wild Scary. Where had she been? And why hadn't she been part of the procession of cars that followed behind one another. The tramp emerged from the convertible, smoothed her black dress out and turned. She seemed to look right at me, but that was impossible. I was almost a football field away from the internment, and the six foot mausoleum I stood behind provided perfect cover.

Although she couldn't see me, I saw everything. Even the smile on her face before she turned and walked through the grass.

For nineteen glorious minutes, I enjoyed the suffering on Coltrane's face as they laid Parasite to rest. I can't even begin to explain the joy that encompassed my very being when I'd been informed that Parasite had passed away.

I wonder if knowing Coltrane resisted re-arrest and had been on the way to see her had killed her or the additional child molestation charges that were brought against him. I'd bet it was the child molestation charges. Maybe it was the news that I had leaked to FOX. During the chase to the hospital, FOX and every other network had reported that Coltrane's DNA was found around and inside the kids mouth. I'm sure the bitch was smart enough to know that the DNA that the media were referring to was her husbands semen. The semen that I had stolen from the red towel in their dirty clothes hamper. The semen that I had wiped around and had put in the mouth of that kid. Hell, I even used the same towel to smother the kid with.

After everyone had pulled off, I walked out of the Cemetery and down a couple blocks where I parked the Rover. I clicked the chirper to unlock the doors and disarm the alarm. After opening the door I sat down on something wet and mushy.

"Shit!" I jumped out of my seat, scraping my leg on the front door. I turned around, looked at what I had sat on. "Bitch! Fucking bitch." My black Vera Wang dress was ruined. I used the tips of my fingernails to remove the note from under the bloody penis and balls I had just sat on.

BUCKY SENDS HIS LOVE FROM HELL. WHAT HAPPENED TO HIM WAS A BLESSED GIFT COMPARED TO WHAT IS GOING TO HAPPEN TO YOU.

"Bitch, you have no idea who you are fucking with," I said aloud as if Wild Scary could hear me.

Chapter 18

Cherry

"Do you hear me, Cheryl?"

"I'm listening Rev," I said as I sat in the church office at New Dimensions.

"That's not what I asked, Cheryl."

"What do you want me to say, Rev." I shook my head. "I've already gone there. There's no coming back until I finish what *she* started."

"Cheryl." Rev got out of his seat and walked around his desk. He took a seat next to me. "Karen Parker is evil." He took my hand. "You're not like her. You have compassion. You love. You feel. God is love. God is compassion. God feels your pain. It is the God in you that has sent you to me. Deep down inside you know that God does not approve of what you have done to those men, what you are planning to do to Karen."

"What would you have me do Rev? Get on my knees and pray. Ask God to show me the way. Ask God to deal with Karen. Ask God to save Trane."

He got up and took my hand. "Come with me."

I followed him over to an open space in his office. "What are you doing?"

"We are going to do exactly what you guessed I would have you do."

He knelt down and gestured for me to do the same. "Talk to Him. Tell Him how you feel. Ask Him for guidance. Talk to Him like you have never spoken to Him before." Rev stood back up.

"Where are you goin' Rev?"

"This is between you and God. I'm leaving you two alone." He threw me the keys. "Lock up when you leave."

I sat there on my knees thinking, reflecting on all the shit I had been through in my thirty-six years. I don't know how long I'd sat there before I spoke.

"God, we haven't spoken in a while, at least not directly. Yeah, I been to church, and I feel you in my heart. I guess I wouldn't have made it this far without your guidance. But, lately, you have to admit, my life has been real fucked up. No disrespect, but I might as well say it like I think it. You know what I'm thinking any damn way. I quit questioning you long ago. I know some things are just not for me to understand in this life. Things like, why would you let that white bitch take Miles. I been living halfway right since I met him. He brought me back to you. I just don't get it. And Paradise, what did she do? What did that little boy do? What did Coltrane do? Hasn't he been through enough? I ain't never died, but I truly believe that sometimes dying is better than living. Yeah, I know that's a fucked up thing to say, but it's real talk. It's the way I feel.

"And don't think I don't know how you set me up. If I knew that you were going to call Paradise home, than I wouldn't have promised her I'd get with Trane. You know I would have walked into that police station after I wiped Karen off the map, and you know I would have made them kill me. But, because of that promise, the one I had made to Paradise, I can't do that now.

When you took her life, and spared mine and the baby's I knew you had your hand on me. I love you, you know that, just like you know what I'm going to do before I do it. I know it might not be all the way right, maybe not even half right, but I gotta do the bitch in a very special way. And I know that Vengeance is yours and it'll still be yours, I just ask you to let me be the tool that you use to exact that vengeance. So what's it gon' be. Don't answer that, it ain't like you would anyway. But, can you just guide my steps and my scalpels."

An idea suddenly popped into my head. I knew what I had to do to save Trane. I knew how to make him see the light. He'd saved so many, now it was time for him to be saved.

I got up from the rug and almost ran out of the church. As bad as I wanted to go the hospital and check on Trane I couldn't. I doubt that just my words could save him, so I stopped at the condo, grabbed Miles's Platinum American Express and headed to the airport. On the way, I called Rhythm and Rev, told them my plan to save Trane and they too went into action. I looked up and said aloud as if he could hear me, "Don't worry Trane, I got you king."

****

I hadn't seen Trane since he'd tried to take his life, the night after Paradise's funeral. I had told Rhythm that I needed two-weeks to pull off the miracle that I had in mind. And because of Trane, my two weeks had been cut down to nine days. I had until Tuesday, three days before Trane would be moved from Grady Hospital's psych ward back to the South side of hell as inmates referred to the hole at the Fulton County jail.

Coltrane had planned on finishing what he'd attempted a week ago. No one in their right or left mind would insist on returning to hell unless they had a death wish. And the only way for Trane to get to Paradise was to die. And the quickest way to die was to take your own life, like Trane had already tried.

And after I had explained all of this to Rhythm she had reluctantly changed her strategy. At first, she had argued that shooting for an insanity plea would damage Trane's credibility. When I asked her what was more important, Coltrane's life today, or the way you choose to fight for his life tomorrow.

"Besides, I just need a couple weeks," I had pleaded.

Rhythm had rushed a motion to the judge and had Coltrane's stay at Grady Hospital's psych ward extended. Rhythm knew she was taking a huge gamble, but she had known I was right. Changing his plea to guilty by insanity was the only way to protect him from himself while I fought to save his life and prove his innocence.

After his first twenty-four hours secured to a bed, being fed anti-depressants through an IV, Trane had been moved to an area where he underwent a battery of tests to determine if he was mentally competent enough to stand trial. Psych evaluations, especially in capital offenses could take anywhere from two weeks to two months, but in six days Coltrane had convinced the states and the defenses experts that he was in complete control of his mental faculties. Hence, he was being returned to Hell on Tuesday the day after Labor Day.

The hole, special housing unit, segregation, whatever the politically correct term of the day was, it was all the same. The six by eight dull concrete gray cells were reserved for government informants, inmates that feared for their lives, escape artists, inmates that caused trouble in general population, and the most hated inmate, ones that had been accused of sexual misconduct. The latter were housed in the hole for their own protection. Murderers, thieves, drug dealers, they all salivated at the prospect of raping and killing any sexual deviant that was allowed to share their air in general population.

And when I served six months in the hole on the female side of the Fulton County Jail back in '08, after taking down that anti-Christ, TJ Money, we renamed the solitary confinement to Hell.

Showers, three times a week, and in the summer when the sadistic guards played games with the heat and air, the residents of Hell developed heat rashes, bad colds and even mild cases of Dementia.

Bag lunches that consisted of a thin slice of bologna between two pieces of half stale white bread, a peanut butter sandwich, a bag of plain salty potato chips and a piece of fruit, either a soft apple or a hairy orange was lunch and lunch was the best and most nutritious meal of the day. Breakfast and dinner meat was often unidentifiable. The cold breakfast and dinner trays could have and should have been added to tests of how far contestants were willing to go to win on the show Fear Factor.

The only thing that Coltrane had done to earn his permanent stay in the segregation unit at Fulton county, was escape from Atlanta's maximum security Federal penitentiary, seven years ago in '07. The same escape that technically didn't count because a year later, Coltrane had proven his innocence and had been exonerated for the drug kingpin charges that he'd been falsely convicted of nine years prior.

That's why I couldn't understand why he had been classified as an escape risk. I guess Trane's escape risk classification didn't make a difference now that the charge of aggravated sexual assault on a child had been added to the double murder charges he already faced.

My phone rang.

"Cherry, where are you?" Rhythm asked. "You were supposed to be here an hour ago. Everybody's waiting. And soon, the media will be here and you know the police will follow and we'll be ordered to disperse."

"I know. I'm sorry, girl. I'm right around the corner. I'll be there in a few."

"You said that thirty minutes ago."

I could hear the frustration in her voice. "I promise, this time I really will be there in a few minutes," I said before hanging up. I was literally, right around the corner from the hospital.

I looked at my watch for the umpteenth time. Where was he? I was just about to drive off from the Atlanta Zoo parking area when my guy pulled up in a black van with an Atlanta Zoo logo on each side of the vehicle. I jumped out of the car and climbed into the passenger seat.

"Have you heard of a courtesy call. Negro, I been waiting on you for over an hour."

"You didn't get my text, Cherry?"

"Yeah, I got it, but you didn't give me a reason."

"You don't wanna know, trust me. The good news is that I got the package you ordered."

"Where," I asked.

"Right behind your seat."

I couldn't get out of the van fast enough. "Negro, I will kill you," I said, putting my hand over my heart.

He laughed. "You don't wanna see what you paid for."

"Hell no." I got the jitters just thinking about what he had in that van.

"Can a nigga at least get half the bread you promised."

"Not, if it means I have to come anywhere near that van." I stood a comfortable distance away on the passengers' side of my Lexus.

"Don't be afraid. I'm a zoologist and I can assure you that it's safe. I'd get out and come to you, but I really ain't trynna attract no attention."

"The five grand, the alarm code, the address, and the door keys are in this envelope," I placed the priority mailing envelope on the blacktop parking lot, before I jumped in my

Lexus, climbed over the passengers seat before putting the key in and taking off. After this experience I don't think I will be buying weed from him anymore.

A few minutes later, I jumped out of the Lexus and shivered at the thought of what was in that van, right behind the seat I was sitting in.

I should've been at Grady Hospital an hour ago. In the last nine days, I had been to five cities, done radio, TV, you name it. I sent out the call and by the looks of Marietta, Peachtree, and Decatur Street, black men all over had responded. And now, I was over an hour late for my own event. I felt really bad about it, but, I couldn't let Karen think that I had forgotten about her. After all she sure hadn't forgotten about me, and if I hadn't had her under twenty-four hour surveillance I would've been a memory. That bitch had planted enough C-4 explosives under my car to blow up half of the Atlanta Airport parking lot a couple days ago. By the time my plane had landed back in the ATL, a couple days ago Friday night, thanks to my surveillance of her ass, my folks had disarmed and removed the bomb. It was shit like that that made me do what I just did with my weed man.

Because of the crowd in front of Grady, I had to park in the Grady Homes projects six blacks from the hospital. I met Rhythm at the hospitals Emergency entrance.

"You have two hours before visitation is over," Rhythm said as we hurried through two security checkpoints at the hospital. "Here take this," she handed me a wallet.

"What's all this?"

"Your credentials. You're my legal investigator."

"What?"

"It was the only way to get you in to see him."

In the prison system the attorney always awaited the client, but in the hospital psych ward it was the opposite. Trane was waiting on me. He wore a clean white jump suit. He was clean shaven. His skin was well moisturized. He looked terrible.

"What's up Queen." He spoke in a somber, melancholy tone. "Rhythm said you wanted to see me."

I grabbed a seat and rolled it over to the corner where he sat. I plopped down on the black office chair. "You talkin' to me or the to the carpet?"

"If I said the carpet, than you'd think I was crazy," he said.

"When you were arrested three weeks ago, I thought you might be a little crazy. But after Rhythm told me that you'd tried to hang yourself with a bunch of plastic straws hogtied together, I knew it was only a matter of time before you were snacking on you own diapers."

"I'm not wearing diapers."

"Not yet. But at the rate you're going, it won't be long."

"At the rate I'm going, I'll be dead and everyone will be safe."

"Safe! Are you kidding? Karen Parker Rose is Rosemary's baby all grown up. That bitch is the exorcist. She probably ate the priests that came to exorcise her demons. She's the Blair Witch project on speed."

"Stop it," he laughed. "I'm depressed, I don't wanna laugh."

"Stop what. I'm telling the truth." I put my hand on his leg. "Trane, I got that bitch's number," I whispered. "I've already started ringin' her bell."

"Cherry, you see what she did to...." he shook his head. "She will not stop until you're dead. You see how crazy she is."

"Yeah, I see. But she ain't seen how crazy I can be."

"Cherry?"

I jumped up. "Don't Cherry me. This whore done robbed me of the best thing that ever happened to me. She done robbed you of Paradise and you wanna just take a flying leap of realities cliff. You wanna give the funky bitch the satisfaction of being able to smile. I thought you were a soldier. A hero."

"That's what you get for thinking. I am no hero. If I was, I would have been able to save Miles, Paradise," he extended his arm, "You."

"I don't need saving."

"Yes you did. Yes you do. And if I was a hero, I'd show you that you need saving."

"You know what Trane?"

"What!"

"I don't want you to be no damn hero. Just be a fucking man." I punched him in the chest. "You just like all these bitch-ass no count..."

"Be careful," he interrupted.

"Or what." I hit him in the chest again. Tears rained from my eyes. "You ain't gon' do shit, but find a way to take your own life." I looked him up and down. Disgust registering on my face. "I'm out here killing concrete and burning water, doing every and anything to prove your innocence."

"Didn't nobody ask you to prove anything. Help the bear."

"I am helping the fuckin' bear. You just too busy feeling sorry for yourself to see."

"What am I supposed to see Cherry? What am I supposed to do? I'm on lockdown twenty-three hours a day seven days a week. My family has been killed by the same sick individual that has framed me for the rape and murder of a child and the murder of my own brother."

"And?" I said.

"And what?"

"You forgot the part about you lying down and rolling over like a hungry ten cent whore."

"What would you have me do Cherry? Huh? What do you want from me?"

"I want you to do what you preach."

"What are you talking about?"

"The 2014 commencement ceremonies at the Jihad Uhuru Academy for young Kings. The Boy's and Girl's clubs all around the country. The juvenile centers and foster homes you've spoken at. Do what you tell everyone else to do. Your life story MVP has saved so many young men from being victims. What is it you say. Be a victor not a victim. After all your work, after all of their work trying to become like the man that you are. The man they look up to. I look up to."

He shook his head from left to right.

"Don't shake your bald head at me." I walked up and grabbed his shoulders with both of my hands. "Trane, I need you. Do you hear me," I cried. "I need you. You define what a black man is. Proud, strong, loyal. A man that says what he means and means what he says. A man that can freely use the forbidden word of freedom, because you have already died for it a thousand times. And the more you die for freedom, the more you will resurrect the soul of black men everywhere in this country. What is that poem you recite at every school, juvenile, prison, shelter, everywhere you go to speak."

"If," he said before I could turn on my transmitter.

I turned the transmitter on, so Rev and Rhythm could relay the signal when Trane repeated what he'd just said. "What was that?" I asked again, this time louder.

"The poem is entitled If by Rudyard Kipling."

Twenty thousand some odd black males crowding the streets outside of the hospital began on cue. **"If you can keep your head when all about you are losing theirs and blaming it on you."**

"What is... Who is that?" Coltrane walked over to the window. His mouth dropped open. He was speechless as they continued.

"If you can trust yourself when all men doubt you, But make allowance for their doubting too."

Men, Black and Hispanic filled the streets and the hospital grounds. It was the Million Man March in front of Grady Hospital. Young and old stood at attention as they recited the poem.

"If you can wait and not be tired by waiting, or being lied about, don't deal in lies, Or being hated don't give way to hating, And yet don't look too good, nor talk too wise. If you can dream-and not make dreams your master; If you can think-and not make thoughts your aim. If you can meet with Triumph and Disaster, And treat those two impostors just the same."

Tears raced down the sides of Coltrane's beautiful face.

"If you can bear to hear the truth you've spoken twisted by knaves to make a trap for fools, or watch the things you gave your life to, broken, And stoop and build 'em up with worn-out tools."

Coltrane arched his back and stood up straight. He recited the poem with them.

"If you can make one heap of all your winnings, And risk it on one turn of pitch-and-toss, and lose, and start again at your beginnings, And never breathe a word about your loss: If you can force your heart and nerve and sinew, To serve your turn long after they are gone, and so hold on when there is nothing in you, Except the Will which says to them: "Hold on!""

Coltrane took my hand and squeezed ever so gently.

"If you can talk with crowds and keep your virtue, Or walk with Kings---nor lose the common touch, If neither foes nor loving friends can hurt you, If all men count with you, but none too much."

Coltrane turned to me. "Queen, you did this? You made this happen?"

"If you can fill the unforgiving minute with sixty seconds' worth of distance run, yours is the Earth and everything that's in it, And---which is more---you'll be a Man, my son!"

"No, You did this. These kings are a product of what you have done over the past six years. I just called. They came together to show you how important you are."

"Coltrane Jones. Coltrane Jones. Coltrane Jones," the crowd chanted with their fists in the air."

We stepped away from the window.

"Why aren't they saying Free Coltrane Jones?" I asked.

He smiled. "Because, I taught them that you can't free a man that can't be enslaved."

Before I knew what I was doing, my lips were on his. Before I'm sure he knew it, his tongue was exploring my mouth. We were one. In sync with each other. Our souls touching. It was a passion, a yearning, a needing. We were healing each other. Loving again, something neither of us imagined ever possible.

I was able to breathe for the first time in almost four weeks. Determined not to ever lose my breath again I got into the rental I had arranged to be left in the hospitals parking garage and I put in the coordinates to Rome, Georgia where Karen Parker Rose grew up.

Chapter 19

Karen Parker Rose

"Karen Parker Rose, grow up," Royce said.

We'd just walked into the house, having just come from a charity function in support of Andre Frazier, the Georgia Senator that had been shot last week by a Tea Party member. And after an incredibly boring evening of fake smiles and false promises by politicians that really didn't give a damn if Congressman Frazier lived or died, Royce and I left. On the way home, Royce had done what he does best, piss me the hell off.

I grabbed hold of the wrought iron foyer railing to balance myself as I took off my heels.

Royce grabbed my arm. "Seriously Karen."

I looked down at his hand.

"You need to just leave it alone. Besides, you don't know and more important, you can't prove that this Cheryl woman broke into your Rover and..."

"She left animal entrails on my seat." I lied. "She ruined an eight hundred dollar Vera Wang dress."

"What makes you think it was her?"

I looked down at his arm again. "Do you want that hand?"

He let go.

"It is obvious, that you don't give a damn about me, just like it's obvious that you put less than zero stock in anything that I say."

He loudly exhaled, before closing the front door. "Not again. How many times must I hear this."

"How many times are you going to discount what I say?"

"Look Karen," he reached out to grab my arm.

I shot him a death look.

He pulled back. "You already blackmailed me into abusing my power with your boyfriend. I will not use my influence to have a woman arrested. A woman that you have no proof that she vandalized your truck."

"One, TJ Money is not my boyfriend. He's just another innocent black man falsely convicted in this white imperialistic good ole boy slave injustice system."

"When did you become Karen X?"

"I'm going to ignore that." I paused trying to remember where I was going. "Oh yeah, I don't have proof, but I know for a fact the that black psycho bitch, vandalized my truck."

He crossed his arms. "Okay, convince me."

"Suck my dick Royce," I said storming off towards the stairs.

"Where do you think you're going?"

"I turned at the bottom stair. "To bed!"

"I'll be up in a few to tuck you in."

No he didn't. And he had the nerve to wink one of his beady little eyes at me. "Come into my room a man and I promise tonight you will leave as a woman."

"What does that mean?"

"Come try and tuck me in and I'll show you." I said before marching up the hardwood stairs.

"I guess that means, I'll be sleeping in my bedroom tonight."

I opened both French doors leading into my private space, stripped off my clothes and went into my bathroom and turned on the hot water. I wanted to burn. Burn my skin until it turned red. Blood red.

How did she know? Or did she know? Was it a faulty detonator? A bad wire? A dead cell in the battery. In any case that bitch should be history not a fucking hero. Her face was all over the internet. In les than two weeks, with the use of twitter, Facebook and a last minute appearance on the Victoria Christopher Murray Show, Wild Scary brought over twenty thousand black men together to recite a dead white man's poem out in front of Grady fucking hospital. For what. Albert Coltrane Jones, a criminal.

The water was hot, scalding. I stepped into the steamy shower stall. It felt good as it burned my skin. Burned it raw. It hurt oh so good.

Eight minutes later, I got out. No towel, the three ceiling fans circulating in my bedroom would have to do. A towel would only irritate the areas where the water burnt my skin raw.

All those mud monkeys in front of and around Grady hospital, swaying as they recited a white man's poem. Rudyard Kipling didn't even like niggas and the mud monkeys still memorized his words. Words that weren't meant for them. Fuck.

I tied my hair into a ponytail. I didn't wanna bother with moving all the pillows that decorated my queen sized bed, so I just grabbed hold of my black comforter and yanked.

"AHHHHHHHHHHHHHHHHHHHHHHHHHHHHHHHHH HHHHHHH?" I turned and ran full speed into my bedroom door. I fell, got up turned and screamed again.

"AHHHHHHHHHHHHHHHHHHHH." I couldn't get my fucking door open. "Royce." I banged on the door. "ROOOOOOYYYYCCCEEEE!" I screamed.

He opened the door. "What..."

I ran him over. He fell. I crawled over him and slipped and fell down the stairs.

"Dammit, Karen what is wrong with you?"

I looked back. My keys and my phone were in my bedroom. Oh well. I scrambled to the kitchen. "Yes!" Royce had left his keys and his phone on the granite counter top. I took both and ran into the garage, jumped in his Ford Taurus and tore up the garage door backing out. I drove through the grass and would have driven through the privacy gate if it weren't broken.

"Ring! Ring!"

"AHHHHHHHHHHHHHHHHHHHHHHHHHHHHH!" Royce's cell phone scared me so bad, I hit the gas and drove right into someone else's car. "Shit!"

I jumped out of the car and ran over to the car I had blindsided.

"Wow! Both of the teenage looking boys shouted. Their eyes were about to pop out of their head. "Wow!" they said again.

"Are you two okay?" I asked.

They nodded before onc of the teens smiled and said, "Now we are."

The two boys were staring at me like I was naked.

"Damn," one of the boys said, still staring.

I looked down. I was naked. "Fuck!"

"I won't tell my dad, you hit his Infiniti if we can...

"You'd never be the same if I gave you a taste," I said as I casually strutted back to the Taurus and got in. Now that I had located my mind, I pressed send and redialed the house phone.

"What in God's name?" was the first thing that came out of Royces mouth. Not, are you okay. Not, are you hurt.

"Did you see it?"

"Damn near scared the crap out of me," Royce said. "I think it's dead?"

"I don't care if it's alive or dead, get it the fuck out of the house."

"How did a South American Anaconda get into your bed?"

"Royce, ask me that again and I swear to God, I will come back to the house, get one of your hunting rifles out of the gun cabinet and shoot you in the head. How the fuck do I know how the biggest snake I ever seen got into *your* bed."

"You mean *your* bed," he corrected.

"No, it's *your* bed and *your* room, we just traded."

"I've called the police," he said.

"They're pulling up now. And you might want to get out here. I'm right outside the front gate. I think I just totaled your car. And bring me a robe and some slippers."

Two hours later, I was tucked away in a suite on the twenty-seventh floor of the W hotel at Perimeter Mall. I had never been so embarrassed and so scared in my life. A fucking snake. The one thing I was terrified of. I still can't believe I ran out of the house and drove off with no clothes on. I wasn't ashamed of my body, by no means. But my ass was not meant to be on public display. Them stupid kids couldn't stop staring and when I got back into Royce's car, I could see them laughing. I would've went back to the house and put on some clothes if the police hadn't popped up so fast. No, I wouldn't have. There was no way I was going back in that house with that serpent. I had never seen a snake that big. I shivered just thinking about it.

The best thing that Royce had ever done for me was bring me some clothes, and my purse before handing me his black card so I could come and get this room. He knew without asking, that I wasn't coming back in that house, or on that street until that monster was gone. And those officers. As soon as they saw Royce they wiped the smirks off their faces. Everyone seemed to know the honorable Judge Royce Rose.

My cell rang. I looked at the time. It was 3:57 AM.

"Hello?"

"It's gone. Funny thing is, the snake was drugged. Seventeen feet, and it was still not finished growing."

"I do not care how big it is, what color it was, or how much it weighed."

"I was just wondering how big it would have grown with you inside it's walls," Royce laughed.

I pressed the end button. And I was actually considering giving him some for all his efforts.

My phone buzzed in my hand. I clicked the screen and a text popped up. I sighed. It was from Royce.

The police found a typed written note under the snakes belly. Do you have any idea what it means or who could have done something like this. The police want us to come down to the station tomorrow. They have some questions. Anyway, here is what the note read.

 A SNAKE FOR A SNAKE IT WAS THE LEAST I COULD DO FOR THE "BOMB" GIFT YOU GAVE ME THE OTHER DAY.

Chapter 20

Cherry

"**The other day a bomb** was placed under my car." My head swiveled in the direction of another lonely looking old man walking into the small OK Coral like double doors of the small bar before I continued. "Six weeks ago, my man was tortured to death. A week later, my best friend and I were beaten and raped. I survived. She didn't. Karen Parker was behind everything, I really need your help. No one will talk to me."

Nonchalantly, Bumper Pines nodded his head before turning up the second whiskey and coke I'd bought him in twenty-minutes. I knew it was a long shot, but I'd been in Rome two days and hadn't made any progress. And, I thought that renting a car would help keep me from under Karen's stooges radar.

And from my research, I found out that Bumper Pines was the father of Jonathon Parker's ex-wife. The ex-wife who mysteriously disappeared seven years ago after Jonathon had been charged with his father's murder.

I was just about out of chips. I'd been in Rome two days, shoveled out over three hundred dollars for a bunch of worthless information that anyone could get off the net. Bumper Pines an old broken down drunk was not only my best bet, he was my only bet.

It was as if the town were scared to say anything good or bad about the Parker family. I felt like the outsider in a "Twilight" movie.

Were the Parkers beautiful vampires or something? Karen was definitely something, A vampire was much higher on the food chain than whatever Karen Parker was.

Bumper just sipped and nodded as I prodded. I'd learned from him what I had from the others. Nothing. But, one thing I did sense, was fear. His eyes never in one place, constantly shifting from left to right as if looking for someone. "Sorry to bother you Mr. Pines, thank you for your time," I got up from the worn and torn barstool.

"317 Richard B. Russell Drive."

This was the most he had said in the twenty-minutes I'd been sitting next to him at Billy Bob's Tavern.

"Tonight at nine," he barely said above a whisper, before walking past me as if he'd never seen me.

I pulled out a twenty.

"Gimme a minute sweetie," a gray haired, elderly, toothless waitress said.

"No rush, keep the change," I said before dropping the twenty on the table.

I walked out of the old west double swinging bar doors. I couldn't get over how much the town really looked like that town in those Twilight movies. It was eerie. So eerie, I'd decided to check out of the bed and breakfast I was staying at and hit the road before dark. I had a bad feeling.

"Sweetie," the old waitress moved ten times faster than I thought possible for a woman her age and size.

I turned, "Yes ma'am."

She was right next to me. Her hip was touching my rental car.

"In fifteen minutes come back into the bar. Ask someone, anyone but me if they'd found some keys."

She waved a hand and shook her head before I got the chance to ask why.

"Girlie, I know you ain't lost no keys," the old lady said. "The last person that left me a tip as big as the one you had was Earl Lee Morning and I married him, fifth husband," she looked up, "God rest his soul. Now sweetie fifteen minutes, and oh yeah, after you don't find the keys go into the ladies restroom. Ignore the out of order sign."

I did as I was told and twenty minutes later I walked into the ladies bathroom.

I coughed, while fanning smoke.

"I take it you don't smoke," she said, taking a long drag on the camel that dangled from her pinkish, purple lips.

"No ma'am."

"Call me Momma Jean. I ain't got no problem with your kind like the rest of this hick town do. I done been with a couple of, of..."

"Black men," I said.

"Yeah. Just didn't wanna use the wrong term. You people change what you wanna be called every twenty, t'irty years. I spent t'irty-five years hating until my fourth husband came along. Danny Johnson. Now he was a good 'un. I might even give him another chance after he get out in a couple years."

I could care less about this woman and her past, but she was talking which was more than I could say for anyone else in this town. "What did he do to change your feelings towards black folk?" I continued waving the smoke and coughing.

"He introduced me to Thomas Jefferson."

I frowned.

"Not the president, Thomas Jefferson."

I hoped not.

"One night, my my husband Danny brought Thomas home for dinner, and he never left. At least not until Danny shot him dead five years later."

"Why'd he shoot him."

"Jealous I guess," she shrugged her linebacker shoulders. "I ain't never been no loose woman like most thank. I had Thomas for dessert after Danny went on a beer run that first night, way back when. I don't know, me and Thomas just hitted it off. Good God almighty in heaven above, whenever I recollect on Poor Thomas, my gander rises. That boy was hunged like a swolled up mule. Woulda' married him if he wasn't colored, after all, I divorceded Danny imme'jetlywhen he killeded Thomas.

"I don't mean to be rude Mamma Jean, but," I coughed and fanned more smoke, "Why did you ask me to meet you?"

"Oh, sweetie I'm sorry. Just goin' on about my life, and my seven husbands and two almost husbands. I'm divorced now. See," she waved both ringless hands in my face, while that same Camel dangled from her lips. "I decided to take some time off. You know, do me and maybe a couple women." She winked.

I wanted to gag, but I was too busy fighting cigarette smoke.

"I heared you aksin' old Bumpy 'bout them there Parker's."

The way she said "them there Parker's" gave me the impression that they weren't her favorite family.

She looked around the bathroom, opened the two stall doors before walking back to the rusty old porcelain sink I stood in front of. She leaned against the cracked and stained bathroom wall before taking the longest pull on a cigarette that I'd ever seen.

I just wished she'd get to the point before I died of smoke inhalation.

"You ain't old enough to remember movies like Carrie, the Exorcist, and the Omen."

"I'm a horror movie buff." I said. "I've seen all of the above."

She put a clammy, fat, liver spotted hand on my arm. "That Karen Parker is worst than every devil in any of those movies, and that Jonathon, he was just as screwed up. He was her lacky.

"Hell, I knoweded Blake Parker, the grandpappy, and the worstest of 'em all. After the Great Depression, old man Blake bought up most of the bank notes in Rome, snatching the land right from under the towns' people.

"Almost er'one was forced to sharecrop his land or work in his mines. And those who refused to work for him, he killed. Didn't even give 'em the choice to leave Rome. Word had it that he'd forceded the Sheriff and the judge to kill, to show their loyalty.

"Blake also had an inkling for young girls. He didn't give a flying' fart who 'da young'ns belongeded to. And if'n the father or mother of the young'ns stirred up some dirt, well hell, they'd end up six feet under the dirt. Any ole way two men, fathers started raisin' Cain 'bout what Blake had done to their barely teenage daughters. Right in public, smack dab in the middle of the prize pig judging at the state fair, back in '51," she looked off into space, "or was it '52." She pointed a finger, "nah, it t'was '52. Blake and the two fellers got to scufflin'. Blake got to his knife. And right there in front of man, woman, and chil'len, he gutted them poor bastards right there in public. I tell ya, it was a site. Blood and entrails made a fifty-yard line in the dirt. Come to think of it, I can't 'member anybody else rattlin' Blakes chain 'til one of his illegitimate sons showed up in town twenty years later. Steve Nash. Killeded old Blake dead. Days later he too was dead. Mining accident, they say."

"Can you tell me more about Karen Parker?"

She dropped the butt of her cigarette on the worn and torn black and white checkerboard linoleum bathroom floor. "I'm gettin' to that," she reached into her gargantuan bosom and pulled out a bent and damp looking cigarette.

Oh God, not another one.

She reached back inside her bosom and came out with a huge lighter in the shape of a man's penis. A logo on the side that read, "suck my Bic." She inhaled, swallowed and released a plume of smoke from her lungs. "Ole, Jonathon Parker followed in his grandpappy's footstep. He began preying on young girls when he was a young'n, knee high to a grasshopper himself.

Er'one in Rome knoweded the boy was crazy as a shithouse rat on crack."

So, why didn't anyone come forward, I wanted to ask, but decided against it, that information not important.

"I don't reckon there was a wet eye at the funeral, except for Karen and hell she the one that stabbed him to death."

"I thought he died from pneumonia."

Momma Jean coughed, while waving a hand. "Hell nah, sho' as wet shit stink on a stick, she stabbed the boy in the heart. Her own flesh and blood."

"So why does the world think differently?" I asked.

"Money. The Parkers have mo' money than God, and they will not spare any expense to ruin anyone that has a bad word to say about them."

"What about the autopsy, the death certificate?"

"What about 'em?"

"I just can't believe the whole town covered up a murder."

"Not the whole town sweetie. Just the one's that run things. Don't think you the first that done come askin' about them Parker's."

"Who were the others?"

"Don't matter, they all died of unfortunate accidents, if you catch my drift. Just me talkin' to ya will get me killeded quicker than you can blink, but you's a nice lady and to tell you the truth, I been had my eye on old Bumpy. He ain't been right since one of them crazies, either Jonathon or Karen killeded his daughter Sue Ann. Wouldn't want something bad to happen to old Bumpy for I get the chance to test drive him. Hate to see him come up missin', or you for that matter sweetie."

"Bang, Bang, Bang! someone knocked on the bathroom door. "Bettye Jean Parker, put them cigarettes out and get your tail out front. Break is over."

"You're related to the Parker's," I asked.

She opened the bathroom door. "Honey," she put a hand on my shoulder, "how do you think I knew so much about their history." Her tone was ice cold and gone was the backwoods hillbilly accent. Her diction was perfect. It was as if I were speaking with a completely difference person. She laughed as she flicked the butt of the cigarette in my face before smiling and walking out of the bathroom door.

Anybody else woulda been picking their teeth up after flicking a lit cigarette in my face. But this ole bitch didn't have any teeth and she was a different kind of crazy. I couldn't get out of that smoke pit bathroom and the hillbilly bar fast enough. I was so confused after our conversation. I didn't understand the purpose. I'd seen enough horror movies, been involved with more than my share of horrifying experiences, and been in enough mental institutions to know the look that Mama Jean had shot me after asking her if she was related to the Parkers. It was the devil's smile. It could not be imitated or duplicated. Only Satan could put that look on someone's face.

Shit, the sun was going down. I looked up at the clear blue sky after hitting the chirper unlocking my door. I planned to be out of there by dark. After speaking with Momma Jean, I decided to get in my car and keep it moving. I didn't think twice about leaving the few toiletries and clothes at the Bed and

Breakfast I'd slept at the last two nights. Something about that ole woman sent chills up my spine.

I got in my rental and hit the gas. I'd driven a good hour. The I-75 interstate was right up the street when I thought back to how Bumpy Pines had looked each time I brought up the Parker name. He knew something and was willing to give up what he knew, if I met him at 317 Richard B. Russell Drive, wherever that was.

I made an illegal U turn. I was there for information and I be damned if some woman older than time was going to scare me off. I pulled over to the side of the road and prayed as I put in the address that Bumper Pines had given me. Thank God.

"You will arrive at your destination in forty-seven minutes," the mustangs navigation voice said.

Around forty minutes later I turned on a dirt road. I'd been driving ten miles an hour down the dark road, when five minutes later I saw lights. I look at my watch. It was 8:30. I was a half hour early. The lights I saw from the dirt and gravel road were from a doublewide trailer that had seen better days. I didn't see an address, but it was the only residence on the street. I pulled up put the car in park, reached in my glove compartment. Shit, I left my .45 under my pillow at the bed and breakfast.

At least I had my scalpels, I thought as I opened the door and got out.

Chapter 21

Karen Parker Rose

I opened the door and got out of my Rover. Mad that I couldn't enjoy my dessert. Mad because I had to deal with more bullshit. After leaving the gas station, I marched over to the wall of pay phones. I picked up the receiver and keyed in the numbers on the back of the stupid prepaid card I'd just purchased.

"Niece, that you?"

"Yes," I answered.

"We have a problem," my great aunt said.

"Okay."

"First off, I had a run in with that colored gal."

"Scary?"

"Who'n hell else. Anyways, I called myself havin' a little fun with the gal."

"What did you do?"

"You ain't gotta be soundin' like your dog died. All I did was give her a little history lesson on the family."

"What did you say?"

"Little bit a this. A little bit of that. Told her you killed Jonathon."

"You did what?"

"Get your panties out your ass. If you woulda' done like I said, she'd be fish food by now."

I was so mad I had to grit my teeth. "I told you that she was special. I want her buried alive."

"That's the problem," she said. "That damn useless Roger didn't get the new hydraulic pump on the grave digger until late last night. Now the good news is, him and Charlie got the hole dug before morning."

"So, you had me stop everything I was doing, go to a pay phone so you could tell me everything was under control?"

"Where in hell did you get all that outta what I said?"

"Well, what are you trying to say?" I asked feeling myself getting hot although the temperature was a breezy sixty nine degrees.

"I ain't tryin' ta say a dog gone thang. I'm flat out saying that she didn't go back to the room she was rentin' from Smitty."

"So the tramp still drawin' air?" I didn't give her time to respond with one of her smart ass comments. "As much as it's costin' me, them retards should've dug the damn grave the old fashioned way, with a couple of shovels."

"You ain't seen Charlie and Roger lately. Charlie gotta be three hundred pounds. All he do is sit behind his desk drinking coke, eating Twinkies and watching cop dramas."

"If he messes this up, I'll make sure that he won't be able to get a job as an elementary school crossing guard. His twenty-eight year reign as sheriff of Floyd County will be over. And I want you to tell his fat ass just that."

"Already did," she said, "And Roger got one foot in the grave with his cancer and all. Hell, can't rightly put fear in a widowers heart that's dying from the big C."

"So, let me get this straight. Wild Scary done checked out of Smitty's and you don't know where she is?"

"Now, I ain't said nothing of the sorts. I said she ain't go back after she left me at Billy Bob's."

"Where the hell is she? And why the fuck ain't she in that hole fat ass and Roger finally dug?"

"You better watch your tone. Don't think cause I'm seventy-five I won't put my foot up your ass gal."

Mamma Jean has been handling the family affairs since I killed daddy eight years six months and nineteen days ago. I knew I needed to do something about her, I just hadn't. Mamma Jean was my heart, but with age comes senility and dementia. It was about that time for her to be put to rest.

"You hear me talkin' to you?"

I spoke slow. Careful to over enunciate my words, "No, I did not. What did you say?"

"I said, I think she might be up at Bumper's." She spoke just as slow, mocking me.

I gritted my teeth. Balled and unballed my fists. "I thought I told you to take care of Bumper."

"You ain't told me a damn thang Missy. You asked. And, I passed the message on to Charlie."

"And?" I asked.

"He said it would be easier if we took care of Bumper when they got the grave digger fixed."

"It's fucking fixed," I screamed.

"I swear for God, you raise your voice at me one more 'gain," she scolded, "I told you they just got the damn thing fixed early this morning."

I tried to relax, but it was hard standing outside at a pay phone at 9:30 at night. Wind shooting up my ass. "So, why in the hell isn't Charles at the Pines residence with a couple of body bags?"

"If he ain't there yet, he oughta be damn close."

"Get the fat fuck on the phone, please?" I asked.

"For what?"

"Because I said," I paused to collect myself, "Because I asked you to."

"Hold on," she huffed.

I was getting more excited by the second. I had no idea what I was going to do, but whatever I decided it would be a lot of drawn out suffering involved. The black amazon gorilla is going to pay. I still couldn't believe she'd killed Bucky and Elmo, and my Rover, my Vera Wang dress, my bed, that snake, the bloody balls and..."

"Make it quick KP, I ain't on a secure phone," the sheriff came on the line.

"You fat, useless son of a bitch. Why in the hell is that black..."

"KP, tread lightly."

"Who the fuck..."

"Karen Elizabeth Parker," Momma Jean scolded.

"Where are you?" I asked.

"Where is who?" he asked.

"Forrest Fucking Gump, who in the hell do you think I'm talking to you worthless..."

"Karen, don't make me warn you again," Momma Jean scolded.

"Shut the fuck up, you old witch," I exploded. "I'm on my way. I don't care what you do, but do not, and I fucking repeat, do not harm a hair on the black whores head."

"And the other?" the Sheriff asked.

"Nothing has changed as it pertains to Bumper," I said before hanging up.

Was every fucking body in creation stuck on stupid except me? I always said, if you wanted something done right, kill them yourself.

I marched back to my Rover, got in and reached over what was supposed to be my dessert.

"Is everything alright, my piece of ass asked?"

I reached in the glove compartment and pulled out my 9mm Browning.

"Hey, Hey, Hey," my hundred dollar craigslist dick panicked.

"Get the fuck out." I pointed my cannon at him.

"Shawty, I ain't into that kinky gun play shit."

I pulled the hammer back, "Do I look like I'm playing?"

"Nah, but..."

I swung.

"Got damn," he put a hand to his head, where I just opened up a gash.

"Get out! Now!"

Chapter 22

Cherry

"Get out! Now!" Bumper shouted.

Why? What's wrong?" I asked.

"You don't hear that?"

"Hear what?" By the scared look on his face, I don't think he was asking about the chirping crickets or the rustling pre-autumn night wind. I even turned and looked down the dark road, I'd come down a couple hours ago. Nothing but darkness stared back at me.

Bumper Pines and I were sitting outside his doublewide at a homemade picnic table. I couldn't be sure that Karen hadn't bugged his trailer. And if it was bugged, it ain't like I could do a damn thing about it. I could just kick myself for leaving my gun and my wiretap detector back at Smitty's Bed and Breakfast. Lucky for me, I had another one at the office back home. Good that would do me now.

He grabbed my arm, "Cheryl, you have to go now."

I looked off in the distance. I could just barely, see lights.

"Not without you. You said yourself, that you were as good as dead, if Karen or Betty Jean knew you'd talked to me."

Bumper looked off into the distance. "They gettin' close, go on now," he prodded.

"I'm not leaving you," I said. And it wasn't because he had risked his life recounting the details of the twisted and sordid Parker clan to me. My instincts told me that Bumper Pines was a good man that deserved closure. He'd been a drunken shell wallowing in sorrow since his daughter went missing seven years ago. I wanted justice for him, Coltrane, Paradise, Miles, and myself. Karen and her twisted family had been pissing on people and flushing them down the toilet for far too long.

Bumper had turned and began walking toward the green and white metal trailer front door.

"Where are you going?"

"Can't leave my double wide unlocked."

"Hurry!" I shouted, running over to my rental.

Seconds later from behind his front door Bumper shouted, "Go on now, I'm not coming."

I looked behind me. If I didn't leave now, it was a good chance I would never leave. I turned to the mustang and then back to Bumpers doublewide. "Shit!" I ran to the door and banged. "Bumper I swear, I'm going to get justice for your daughter. And you should be there."

"No!" he shouted.

Bright blue lights lit up the night around Bumper's property.

"I am not leaving you."

"Go on now, I'll be fine."

"I am not going to let them kill you."

"Nice and slow," the bull horn amplified the man's voice over the siren, "Back away from the front door."

The voice sounded like it was ten, fifteen yards away.

"Back down them stairs, Missy. Slow now."

157

"Do as he says. He's the best shot in the county," Bumper said from behind the door.

I raised my hands, backed down the wooden stairs, and took six steps back before bumping into someone. I felt a beefy, grimy hand climb down the back of my jeans.

Without thinking I turned and brought a knee up. "Shit," I screamed, after my knee connected with his service revolver.

"I'm sorry, did that hurt, honeybun?" the sheriff asked, looking as if he were going to hit me again with his service revolver.

I thought the pig had a rifle. Damn it. If I'd known he just had a handgun, I would've made a run for it.

"How's about you and old Charlie have us a little fun honeybun, put on a show for old Bumper," he held the gun to my left ear while he stuck his tongue in my right.

I pushed his face away and wiped my ear.

"A feisty little buggar, huh?"

"Leave her alone Charlie." Bumper shouted. "I'm calling the state trooper."

"Don't see how you gon' do that Bump, seein' as you don't have a house phone and not even Verizon's cell service picks up way out here in the boonies." The blown up Rush Limbaugh looking sheriff turned his attention back to me, "Now little lady we can do this my way or my way." He unzipped his pants.

Now, I couldn't run. He was too close and his police cruiser had more lights on it than a Christmas tree. And everyone of them was fire bright.

"You'll have to kill me."

He shrugged his shoulders. "Either way, cold or warm I'm gon' have me a little taste of chocolate tonight."

I couldn't help but think, how many times had I been on the wrong end of someone's gun? How many times had I escaped death?

He pulled the hammer back.

My stare didn't waver from my would be killer's cold eyes.

The night exploded. There was a loud ringing in my ears. My equilibrium was askew. My head was spinning. I was falling. I'm sorry. So sorry Trane. And then I felt damp leaves and earth.

Moments later, I felt myself being pulled. My ears. The ringing.

"Cheryl," I heard him say.

"Trane?" My eyes popped open.

"Cheryl, can you walk," Bumper asked helping me to my feet.

"Yeah, I think.... Did I get shot?" I began patting myself down. Still a little disoriented. Ears still ringing.

"No, but he did," he pointed to where the sheriff laid in a growing pool of his own blood.

I hugged the elderly white man. "Thank you. Thank you Bumper Pines." I held on until the world stopped spinning.

"No," he said. "Thank you. I wish I'da had the courage," he spit on the dying sheriff, "to do that long ago." Bumper turned back to me. "Now what?"

"Now, you come with me."

"Where we goin'?"

"Bumper, you ask way too many questions."

******

It was close to four in the morning. Rhythm and I sat at the kitchen table. She had a coffee cup of green tea in her hand. I sipped on a coffee cup of Gin and OJ, and I didn't even drink.

"So let me get this straight." Rhythm said. "You been in Rome for two days talking to people about Karen Parker Rose."

"*Trying* to find people willing to talk."

"Sorry," Rhythm continued, "You were *trying* to talk to people living in the town her family more or less built. You ended up buying drinks for Karen Parker Roses', brother's, ex-wife's, father."

"Uhm-hm," I nodded.

Rhythm held up two fingers. "Two things that don't make sense. Betty Jean Parker, the current matriarch of the remaining Parker clan, a millionaire a few times over, is waitressing in a run down honky tonk bar. She lures you into the ladies restroom where she proceeds to tell you about her last seven husbands before she tells you that her niece, whom she is extremely close to stabbed Jonathon Parker to death."

"Uhm-hmm."

"And then Betty Jean tells you that the M.E., the sheriff, and the mortician were all in cahoots to cover up the stabbing. My mistake," she held up three fingers. "Three things that don't make sense."

"She didn't exactly tell me that, but the three had to be involved in the cover up. How else could the autopsy report, state that the official cause of death was complications arising from Pneumonia, when the man had to have a knife wound in his chest."

Rhythm took a sip of her hot tea. "And you believe all of this."

"Yes. I do."

"Uhm-hm," it was Rhythms turn to nod. "You don't find this story just a little fantastic?"

"A little fantastic. Bumpers story is super fantastic, and way too fabulous not to be true."

"So, why is that you believe an old white alcoholic that you just met?"

"That old white man is a historian, when it comes to the Parker family. He has a long documented history with the Parker's, and when you talk to him you'll believe him too."

"I hope so. Because if he doesn't convince me," she let the thought linger in the air.

"Oh, you'll be convinced. I have no doubt about that."

"So, you say Mr. Pines was outside on the Parker's property when Jonathon Parker died?"

"Yes."

"And he saw Karen run out of the house and bury a hunting knife in the backyard?"

I nodded.

"And this all happened before the medical examiner and the sheriff arrived?"

"That's what I was told."

"Mr. Pines thinks that Karen or Jonathon killed his daughter, right?"

"Yes."

"And he never went to the authorities with the buried knife story?"

"Nope."

"And you don't find that just a little strange, as much as he seems to despise the Parkers."

"Not at all. I was in Rome. I'm telling you, everyone is scared to death of the Parker's. You should've seen how they reacted after I asked anything about Karen. For at least three generations, the Parker's have terrorized the small mining and farming town."

"What's the use of spying on them for all these years, if Bumper didn't plan to use the information he'd acquired?"

"You have to ask him that."

"But you do understand my trepidation."

"Of course I do. And if I wasn't completely convinced I wouldn't have brought him here at three in the morning." I reached across the table and put my hand on top of Rhythm's. "In less than a month, Karen killed Trane's wife, brother, a child, and she almost killed me. And Trane is sitting in prison, charge with almost everything she has done. Now how fantastic does that sound?"

"If I could only figure out how Coltrane's semen got into the mouth of that child," she shook her head from left to right before standing. "Maybe the DA's discovery motion will give me some ideas."

"When do you get that?"

"Later on today. Let's just hope, no let's just pray that this Bumper Pines is the real deal. Because right now it's not looking good for Coltrane."

"I know. But he's innocent, and I'm determined to prove it. That's the only reason Karen in still..."

"Don't say it Cherry."

I stood up. I was a little dizzy. "The sheriff of Rome trying to kill me was more than enough to convince me that he was in bed with the Parker's. And even if I didn't believe Bumper's story, he saved my life Rhythm. I owe it to him to at least try and piece together the puzzle of murder and corruption that Karen and the Parker clan had reigned down on him."

"None of this proves Coltrane's innocence," she reminded me.

"Maybe not, but I'm a firm believer, and history has proven that the beginning is the key to the ending. Professor Dorsey, over at Atlanta Metro always says, that every civilization contains the seeds of it's own destruction. The Parker's are a civilization inside a civilization, and if I collect enough seeds and continue to pour water on them, the evidence against Karen will grow into a weed that will strangle her."

"Let's just hope so," Rhythm said. "You think Mr. Pines is comfortable sleeping on the air mattress in the guest room?"

"If you see where he lives and what he lives in, you wouldn't ask."

"I'll take that as a yes," she said. "Look, we need to get some sleep. I told Mr. Pines I'd wake him at eleven so I could get his story, before I march him down to the DA's office at one."

"I hope they don't lock that poor man up."

"Even if Mr. Pines convinces the DA of everything you told me, and you explain that Mr. Pines acted in your defense, the fact still remains that he shot and killed an officer of the law and fled the scene."

"So, what you're saying is that he's going to jail, at least until the DA sorts everything out."

"I'm afraid so," Rhythm said. "Now can we please get some sleep?"

"You go ahead. I'm going to take a nap on your couch."

"Why? Moses got up and prepared the other guest room for you."

"Tell your husband I said thank you. But, I don't wanna oversleep. I'm leaving in a couple hours before morning rush hour traffic. Don't worry, I'll meet you and Bumper at the DA's office at one. I just have something to do this morning."

"Keep your phone close," Rhythm said. "If Mr. Pines's story proves convincing as you say it will, or if I'm not convinced, either way I'll call you."

Chapter 23

Karen Parker Rose

"**I'll call you** back in a few. Gotta wash my ass and put on some clothes. Shit! Right there baby. Right got damn there."

I know her old ass wasn't doing what it sounded like she was doing. After hanging up, I sat in my car five minutes. Five fucking minutes in the woods on the other side of my parents house, which I let her live in. Did one light come on? No. My life was on the line and my own aunt, the woman I entrusted to handle things in my town had been slipping badly. It was 2:06 AM, she knew I was on my way. But did she care? Was she up? Was she even worrying?

I finished screwing the four inch silencer onto my .380 Beretta before getting out of the Rover.

I told Momma Jean that Charlie wasn't answering his fucking phone, the phone that I had paid for. The one that I'd footed the monthly bill for, for over seven years. Charlie should've been at the graveyard way before now putting Bumper in the hole. But was he there? Hell no. Roger was at

Myrtle Hill Cemetery waiting and he hadn't been able to reach Charlie either, but did Momma Jean care?

I moved fast, walking through brush and weeds. I couldn't see two feet in front of me, but my hearing was very acute. So acute, that I jumped at every sound as I walked through the woods to the backyard.

That damn Wild Scary had me on edge. I couldn't help but think of snakes. Big snakes. Just the thought made me speed up. I hadn't been the same since Scary put that damn snake in my bed a couple weeks back. Momma Jean knew what Scary had done. She knew how I felt. She knew how important it was for me to put my hands on the black bitch. Yet, she could care less. That's exactly why I had parked where I had and was going through all this trouble sneaking into my own house. See what she had to say when I ran in on her.

I was just about to walk up the back steps to the deck when I hear, "Burrr! rarararara!"

Two pit bulls where running right at me.

"Psk! Psk!" Psk! Psk!" the .380 kicked in my hand.

I stared at the fallen beasts. Momma Jean loved them damn dogs. She'd brought them with her when she moved into the Parker Estate, seven years ago.

Now I know she heard her precious dogs barking, but had she turned on a light, or got up to see what all the fuss was about?

I walked up the backstairs, around the decks Jacuzzi to the first set of French doors. I put my key in. I shook my head after walking through the door. Incompetent was the word that came to mind. She lived alone in this huge seven bedroom seven bath five million dollar Antebellum estate home, and she didn't even set the alarm.

I slipped off my shoes so I wouldn't make any noise as I walked up the hardwood stairs and down the long hall leading to the east wing where she slept. One of the two bedroom doors was cracked.

I cringed as I heard her disgusting moaning. I reached in and flipped the light switch.

"What the...." I put a bullet in the middle of his forehead before he could finish his question.

"Got damn. What in hell you do that fer?" Momma Jean shouted. " I was just about to bust a huge one." she pushed him to the side and rolled off of the bed. "Damn your time. I ain't had me no twenty year old dick since I don't know when. Shit."

"This is my house. I let you live here." I waved my gun at her. "I've given you money, and control of this damn town. I don't care who you screw, until you start screwing me."

"What the hell you talkin' 'bout Karen?" Momma Jean stood on the side of the bed with her arms crossed. "And put that damn gun down."

"What the hell am I talking about? What the hell kind of question is that. I should've known you were up here getting your rocks off while my whole world was being turned upside down."

"Stop being so fucking dramatic Karen."

"Bumper Pines can put me, us away for good. Two days ago, I told you to have him put down."

"He's a friggin' drunk. No one's gon' take him serious. Don't you think if he could've put you away, us away, he woulda' done so a long time ago."

"No, I don't. He's scared to death of what I will do to him if he starts running his mouth. He's seen the results of my work." I continued waving the gun.

"Then why in Sam hell, do you think he'll go running his kitty licker now?"

"That Scary Cherry bitch." I shook my head from side to side. "Hold on. I don't have to justify a damn thing to you. I pay you. I pay Charlie. You know what," I lifted my gun. "Fuck it."

166

Her body jerked right, left, blood oozed and gushed from everywhere my bullets penetrated her liver spotted wrinkled skin.

I turned out the bedroom lights before leaving. Charlie's fat ass had been wanting to run the show ever since I put her in charge. He reported on Momma Jeans sexual proclivities, as he called it. I don't know if that was the right word to describe her fucking anything with a pole that she could ride. But as I had told him, that's how you know she's a Parker.

After wiping the doorknob down, I left the same way I had come in. Maybe me killing my own aunt would motivate Charlie to do exactly as I said from now on, or until I could find a replacement for him and Momma Jean.

While walking back to the Rover, I dialed Roger.

"Yo' dime," he answered on the first ring.

"Roger, I need you to go over to Parker Road. You'll need your saws and a lot of plastic."

"Why you have me dig this hole, if we were gon' do Bump and that colored gal the hard way."

"Don't question me. Just do it."

"I'm jus' sayin'."

"Park in the woods."

"Karen, you don't have to tell me where to park or how to do my job. Just let me know how many garbage disposals I gotta pick up."

"Four, the one under the kitchen sink is almost new. It hasn't been used since the last time. Oh yeah, you have two to do, both are already at the spot, master bedroom."

"It's gon' take me a good twelve hours to drag 'em down and cut 'em up small enough to put down the disposals," Roger said. "I'd prefer to do this by myself. I don't mind splitting the money with Charlie, but he talks too dog gone much."

"That's no problem. I remember the last time, you damn near cut your own finger off because of Charlie." I said. "Speaking of, have you heard from him yet?"

"Nah, I thought you had."

"I'm goin' up to Bumper's now. This other job is extra. I'm still paying for Bumper. But as far as Scary is concerned, I'll handle her. Don't worry I'm still paying you and Charlie for her as I'd agreed. Instead of twenty-five each, I'm paying you double on the job at the house. The upstairs alarm is off and the first set of French doors on the rear deck is unlocked."

"What about them damn dogs your auntie got?"

"They've already been taken care of. Matter fact, I'm gon' need you to get rid of the dogs between now and tomorrow night."

"Where they at?"

"The back yard. You can't miss them." I hung up the phone and set my ipod to my favorite song, the classic Snoop Dogg 90's hit, '*Murder Was The Case'*.

Thirty one minutes later, at 3:41 AM I was standing over Charlie's body, shining a flashlight in his face. First thing that came to mind, was that I'd killed Momma Jean too soon. Way too soon. Second thing was that I had underestimated Scary. I knew the bitch was bold, but she was also good. Damn good. Had to be, to get the drop on Charlie. He was a fat fuck, but he was an expert marksman, a former Army Ranger.

Shoulda' killed her when I had the chance. I thought back to the double rape and beating.

After doing a quick search of Bumper's filthy, stinking, cluttered trailer home, I walked out into the forest fresh air and dialed his cell again. No signal. Fucking Christ.

After getting in my Rover and driving back up the road, I redialed his number until it began ringing.

"Bumpy Pines," I said as soon as he picked up.

"I'm not scared of you Karen Parker," he whispered.

"Didn't say you were."

He continued whispering, "I might not ever find out what you or your twisted, hell rotting brother did to my Sue Ann, but you can bet the farm that you gon' pay."

"Pay for what? I don't owe anyone anything," I said. "Tell you what. You come on back home. I'll tell you what happened to your half breed whore daughter."

"Don't you talk about my baby like that," he whispered.

"As a matter of fact, I got a better idea. You do what you have to do, and I will tell the world how your daughter was screwing your old best friend when she was in high school. How she came home from lunch everyday, to get some dessert."

"Shut up."

"How she gave you the money that old Joe the mailman gave her for her young, not so precious, not so tight, pussy."

"Shut your filthy mouth Karen Parker."

"I still have the video footage that Jonathon shot way back then. And guess what else?" I paused. "I have footage of Jonathon and his associates taking turns on your baby."

"Please stop! Please!"

"Let's make a deal. Your silence in return for closure on Sue Ann. No one has to know the whore that your daughter was. And I'll tell you the truth of what happened to her and I'll even take you to her. Don't worry Bump, I'm all by my lonesome sitting outside at your picnic table."

"How I know you won't be armed. How I know this ain't a trick?"

"I'll be naked as the day I was born, so you will see that I won't have a weapon on me. As far as this being a trick, you just have to trust me. I think you know that I will not be calling the police about Charlie."

"Give me a coupla' hours. I'm in the city."

"What city?"

"Hell, I don't know. Somewhere near Atlanta."

"Come alone, Bumpy. You know what I am capable of."

I thought the phone had gone dead, until I heard breathing on the other end. "Bumpy?"

"I heard ya'," he said. "Just thinkin'. I ain't quite got my own transportation. I rode up here with someone."

"Scary. I mean Cherry."

"Who?" he questioned.

"Cheryl Sharell," I said.

"Yep. I mean no."

"Don't lie. I know all about her. I know she came to your trailer this evening."

"I ain't told her nothin' yet," he whispered.

"Are you at Scary's Condo near downtown Atlanta?"

Silence.

"Look, I can come and get you. I could care less about Scary, I mean Cherry."

"Who?"

"Cheryl. Like you said, she doesn't know anything."

I heard what sounded like papers rustling in the background.

"You got a pen?" he asked.

"Yes," I lied as I sped toward the expressway.

"I have a bill in my hand, let's see here. The address is," again he paused. "I'll be at the quick trip gas station in Stone Mountain."

"There are a lot of Quik Trip gas stations in Stone Mountain." I racked my mind trying to think of who lived in Stone Mountain that Scary new. Coltrane's snake head attorney. "You're in the Greenridge subdivision. 1619 Brandy Oaks Lane."

His silence was all the verification I needed.

"You can't come here."

"I'll call you when I'm close. Give me an hour."

Chapter 24

Cherry

Give me an hour. I typed into my phone before
pressing the send button, and throwing it on the seat of my
Range Rover. I told Rhythm I had things to do. Besides it was
only nine, Bumper wouldn't be up until eleven. But then again,
what if he couldn't sleep? What if they'd talked and she didn't
believe him? What if she did believe him? I guess it wouldn't
make much difference either way. Whatever it was, it would
have to be what it was gon' be. I needed to see Trane. I needed
to know what was going on with me. Why was I thinking of
him? Was he thinking of me? Of course not, he was Miles's
brother. I was a lot of things, but I had never been the type of
woman to jump from brother to brother, except for Jordan and
Jevon, they were twins and I was tricked so that don't count.

I could hardly believe how long the visitation line was.
It was Thursday morning. I knew unemployment was up, but
damn. And all these crying ass babies. As God is my witness, if
this little bad behind boy behind me hits me in the leg one more
time.

"Number one six four, booth seventeen. Number one six four, booth seventeen."

It was about time, I thought as I walked up to the front and turned in my ticket to the deputy that had called my number.

I wasn't nervous, the hour and a half I had stood in the waiting area to see Trane. So, why was my stomach doing cartwheels as I walked past sixteen occupied Plexiglas booths. Once I reached booth number seventeen I took a seat in the metal folding chair. Of course the guards hadn't brought Trane in yet. That would be too much like right.

I fumbled in my purse before taking out a small mirror. Oh my God, I was a hot mess. I looked like Night of the Living Dead. My eyes were red from lack of sleep and I had more bags under them than a homeless woman pushing a shopping cart. I fumbled some more until I found my Visine. No telling how long it had been in my purse. After squirting a couple drops in each eye, I stood up and straightened my dress. This was the first time I'd worn the form fitting white summer dress. My hair. It wasn't bad, but I could make it better. Again I went in my purse and pulled out a brush. Damn Stevie. He convinced me to let him fuse some Hawaiian Silk extensions in my already long hair. He said it would give me a fuller, more vibrant look. And it did six weeks ago, when I'd flown all the way to Kansas City just so I could give him six-hundred dollars for what should have lasted three months. I brushed, hoping that Trane couldn't tell I had extensions. Shit. Here he comes. I jammed everything back into my purse.

"Good morning, Queen."

I read his lips as he took a seat. "Good morning to you, King," I replied before picking up the phone.

He nodded his clean shaven butter pecan bald head. "I loved Miles more than I love myself," he said after putting the black receiver to his ear.

"I did too."

172

"I had never been unfaithful to Paradise. I loved my wife."

"Paradise was one of my closest friends. I loved her too Trane."

"This is wrong. I feel," he paused. "I feel like I'm dishonoring their memory. He put his palm against the glass. "Miles is my little brother." Water puddled in his eyes.

I put my palm against the window where Trane's was. "Miles was my everything,"

"Paradise was my everything." A tear overflowed from the puddle in his eyes.

"She and I were like sisters."

"Queen, thank you for saving my life. I was going to hang myself you know. This time I was going to take my time and do it right. At least that was before you showed me how important I was too so many.

"You're welcome king. I know how you feel. I was going to do the suicide thing too until Paradise saved my life, before she..."

"How do you mean?"

Should I tell him? Would he believe Paradise made me promise to love and take care of him and the baby, if she died?

"Queen?" His voice interrupted my train of thought.

"Like all those kings did for you. Paradise gave me hope."

"How?"

Why couldn't he just leave it at that? Why did I even tell him that Paradise had saved my life?

"You okay Queen?"

"I'm fine. Just thinking about us."

"You're thinking about us?"

"No, I meant I was thinking about you and I. How we couldn't... How this was..."

"Bad. Wrong. Forbidden. Crazy. Sleazy."

After sleazy, I got up and ran down the long corridor to where I came in at.

"Ma'am, are you okay. Did inmate Jones do something?" The deputy asked. "Did he threaten you?"

"No," I cried, pushing past him and the crowd of nosy ass onlookers.

As soon as I got into my car, my cell phone rang. "Hello?"

"Cheryl, is everything okay."

"No. I mean yes Rev."

"You don't sound okay."

"Allergies," I lied. "At the beginning of spring and fall, my allergies start acting up.

"We have a couple more days before Autumn."

I sniffed. "Tell my allergies that."

"Cheryl, I called to ask if you could meet me at my home. I have someone I want you to meet."

"When?"

"Immediately, if not sooner." Reverend One-free said. "It's extremely important."

I removed my cell phone from my ear and checked the time. "Can I call you right back?"

"Please do," he said before hanging up.

It was 11:30 AM I had to meet Rhythm and Bumper at one. I was about to scroll through my contacts, when I saw that I had six missed calls, all from Rhythm, whom I was just about to call anyway. I pressed the send button.

"I've been calling you since nine," she said.

"I'm sorry. I went to see Trane. Just got back into the car. What's up?"

"Bumper's gone."

"What?"

"I checked in on him at a little before nine. He was gone."

"How did he get out. I mean he had to be on foot. Why would he leave? That's crazy."

"Do you have a number for him Cheryl?"

"Yeah, let me call you back," I hung up and dialed Bumper's cell phone. It just rang and rang. Who doesn't have voicemail in 2014? I called two more times. Same thing.

I called Rhythm back. "He's not answering and he doesn't even have voicemail."

"Did you try texting?"

"If he doesn't have voicemail..."

"Can you at least try?" she asked.

"Okay, but what if he doesn't call or respond?"

"We just have to move on. Do what we can do," she said.

"Okay, I'm going home to change real quick. I'll still meet you downtown at one. Love you bye." I hung up before I broke down. Her words, *we just have to move on* reminded me of what Coltrane had said.

I put my phone on silent, pulled up my middle console and removed a thumb drive from my gangsta-conscious rap section. I needed some old school Rakim to get me back focused on crushing Karen. I inserted the thumb drive as I entered the I-75/85 expressway.

"Silhouettes of a perfect face. Shadows of your smile will always remain."

I pulled out the wrong thumb drive.

"As long as I live you will be my first love and my only love."

Angela and Renee's old school classic, 'My First Love'.

"I miss you so much Miles. Why did you leave me?" I banged a fist on the steering wheel.

"Memories of you when you were mine. A tarnished dream."

"Please forgive me Miles. I didn't try to love him. Didn't mean to love him. But, I lost you. And when I did, I lost

175

me. It may be wrong and if it is, I swear I don't wanna be right, maybe it's the you in Trane. I don't know. I just know that I need that man."

"Time keeps changing," the song continued.

"Coltrane Jones," I said aloud. "I know you feel the same way. Why can't you admit it? Why can't you accept it?"

Richard, my favorite parking attendant, knocked on my window.

I had no idea how long I had been sitting in the valet parking area in front of my building. Nor did I know how many times the song had replayed. Hell, I didn't even remember getting off of the exit.

"I'm sorry King," I said to Richard as I exited my Lexus, "I'm having one of those days."

"I have those quite frequently myself queen," the young black king said.

"I'll be about ten minutes." I handed him a twenty, and kept it moving.

"Good afternoon Queen,"the concierge said as I walked through the revolving doors and into the art deco lobby.

"Good afternoon to you King," I replied.

Miles had instructed the staff at our building to address me as queen at all times. He'd said, that's the least we as men can do to honor a black queen, that graces our space.

No matter how bad I felt, there was nothing like a black king addressing me as queen. How could I keep a frown on my face when I was addressed as queen. Just another reason I loved Miles, and always would. No matter what happened with Trane and I, there would always be a place in my heart reserved for the man that made me realize, recognize and believe that I was truly a queen.

Shit! I forgot all about Rev. I reached inside my purse for the phone. I must've left it in the car. I wonder who Rev wanted me to meet? I got off the elevator, keys in hand.

A minute later I was taking the wrap around piano key colored stairs two at a time. I ran down the hall and into the bedroom. Wiggling out of the white summer dress I'd worn to see Trane was like shedding skin. It was totally not suitable for a meeting with the DA. I ran into my closet and slipped on a conservative blue pinstripe pants suit. Next, I picked up my matching blue, three inch heels, and some lotion. I went and took a seat on the corner of the bed where I massaged lotion onto my ashy ankles, feet and face, not in that order of course.

While bending down to slip on my heels I noticed a watch sized gift wrapped box in the middle of my bed.

I reached for my phone. Shit, that's right I left it in the car. This was the last time she was going to invade my space.

Five Fingers Floyd was expensive, but I had to have that locking system he created and was installing in homes behind the governments back. Floyd was the best B and E man I knew. While serving a dime piece in Attica for six museum heists, he invented the BRICK, a lock that couldn't be broken or opened without the proper encoded retina scan. Not many knew of this technology, because the federal government purchased the technology and patent from Floyd for more money than he'd stolen in his illustrious thirty year career.

I was a little nervous, only because I knew Karen had yet again gotten past all the security measures I had put in place. As I stared at the watch sized box, I wondered if I should open it or take it downtown and let the DA see what I was talking about. But, then again who knows what was in the box. It was too small for a bomb, too small for a snake, but not too small for a poisonous spider, centipede or lizard. Maybe there was a Death Starker scorpion in the box. One sting could kill twenty men.

I ran downstairs and got some tongs out of the kitchen before returning to the bedroom. I used the tongs to pick up the box. I shook it. Nothing rattled. I slowly brought it to my ear. Still nothing. I dropped the box back onto the bed.

I could call someone up from maintenance, but what if it was something in the box that could incriminate me.

I looked at my watch. It was 12:30, already. If I was lucky there would be no traffic. I only lived fifteen minutes from the state building. Fuck it, if she really wanted me dead I would be. I picked up the box and opened it. "Shit." I dropped it on the bed. Blood, two human eyes and a human tongue ruined my silk comforter. there was a laminated type written note on the bed. I used the tongs to pick up the bloody piece of paper.

HE CAN NEVER *TELL* ANYONE ELSE WHAT HE THINKS HE MAY HAVE *SEEN*.
HIS EYES SEE NO MORE. HIS VOICE SPEAKS NO MORE. NOW THERE ARE LESS *BUMPS* IN THE ROAD, BUT STILL I HAVE MORE *MILES* TO TRAVEL, MORE *TRANES* TO CATCH. I'VE BEEN TO *PARADISE* , HAD HER IN MY GRASP. NOW I JUST NEED TO RIDE THE *TRANE* A LITTLE LONGER LET IT LEAD ME TO A *WILD CHERRY* ORCHID IN NEED OF EXTERMINATING. UNTIL I DECIDE WHEN AND HOW WE MEET MY DEAR I HAVE MY EYE ON YOU.

Chapter 25

Karen Parker Rose

"I have my eye on you Shawty," one of the teenage boys said holding up the wall in front of the main entrance at South Dekalb Mall.

I stopped, thought a second. Shook my head. Nah, if he and his future cell mates couldn't even pick out clothes that fit, than it wasn't worth me using my vocal chords to respond.

"Shawty, you just gon' keep steppin', disrespecting' a nigga."

I opened the door to enter the mall.

"Well, fuck you then, Snow White ass bitch."

I let the door handle go and turned around. "Which one of you disrespectful dick breath bastards addressed me."

"Damn," the signifier of the group said, "Kilo, you gon' let shawty disrespect your gangsta' like that."

"You better watch your mouth Snow White before I put something in it," a skinny black kid that barely looked old enough to drive said.

I wasn't racist. Most whites weren't. We were just anti-ignorant. And young black's all over the nation wondered why the white man wouldn't hire them. I walked over to the four bobble heads. Stood in front of the kid with the big mouth. "Little boy, you wouldn't know what to do with," I grabbed my crotch area, "*this*, if I bent over and pulled my dress up right now. I'll have your skinny black ass robbing banks trying to get another shot at," I grabbed his hand and put it up my dress, "some more of this pussy."

The four juveniles were stunned into silence.

"Now, why don't you boys go play on the expressway," I pulled a twenty out of my purse. I let it float to the ground. "Better yet, go buy a gallon of antifreeze and some paper cups. See who can drink the most. Free up some air for someone worthy of breathing it." I turned around and walked into the mall unabated.

A little girl jammed an order form in my face. "Would you like to order some girl scout cookies?"

I bent down. "Little girl do I look like I eat cookies?"

She shrugged, "I 'on't know."

"See how pretty I am." I stood up and twirled around.

She nodded. "Uhm-hmm."

In a gruff deep voice, sort of satanic, I said, "If you eat cookies, you will grow up to be big and fat. You'll turn green and look like what Shrek might leave behind in the toilet after he uses it."

"Mommy! Mommy!" the little girl ran off crying.

A stringy white woman looked up from the crying child. "I ought'..."

"Keep it moving and keep your damn child outta my face," I said, before I kept stepping.

I was too tired and I didn't have time for nigga shit. Girl scout's and disrespectful cat-calling baggie clothed tatted up future black inmates.

****

I hadn't slept in, I looked at my watch, twenty-three hours and forty-one minutes. I'd been running like a racehorse since this time yesterday. And talking about a busy morning. And how about Bumpy's dumb ass. Another one that should have long ago drank a cup of antifreeze. No way anyone with half a brain would get into a vehicle at 6 AM with someone they knew wanted them dead, someone that had no problem making them dead. We hadn't pulled out of the Quik Trip gas station parking lot before Bumper asked why the Rovers passenger seat and floor were covered with plastic. And I answered, right before the bullet to his heart stopped him from asking another stupid ass question.

I had drove all the way back to Rome with my window down. Wind blowing my hair every which way. His dumb, dead ass, stinking up my Rover.

After arriving at the Parker Estate, in my dad's old office, I had typed a note and laminated it, while Roger plucked out Bumpy's eyes and cut out his tongue. Wild Scary had taken me there. The bitch was a walking memory and she didn't even know it. She put a fucking snake in my bed. No more depending on anyone else to kill the bitch, I thought as I made my way out of Macy's.

****

Twenty-two minutes after entering the mall, I left wearing something a little more suitable for meeting the bitch. Something that definitely smelled better than the dress I had worn for twenty-two hours and thirty-six minutes.

And when I stepped back into the September sun at 12:42 posted up in the exact same place were the same four future prison inmates. Not one of them looked my way or said anything to me as I crossed the street and walked to my Rover. Speaking of, I so wish I had time to get it detailed. There wasn't any blood splatter or any other physical remnants that would suggest Bumper had at any time been a passenger. It was the smell of death that I wanted to get rid of.

"12:47," I said aloud before turning onto the expressway. I picked up my cell and dialed 212-364-5340.

"You've reached the Innocence Project, if you know your party's extension..."

I pressed 3124.

"Nicole Kyle."

"Hey Nicole, this is Karen Parker Rose."

"Hey, Karen. You got my message?"

"All five of them," I said.

"I'm sorry. I am just so excited. Just finished speaking with Reverend Money. He wants to see you. He says he hasn't been able to reach you. Karen, I am just so giddy. We all are. And right now, I'm getting dizzy, spinning around in my chair holding the Georgia appellate courts decision," TJ's Innocence Project attorney said. "I'm putting you on speaker, everybody's here in the conference room."

"Karrrrr-en. Karrrrrr-en. Karrrrr-en," the team of attorneys, paralegals, and investigators chanted, before Attorney Kyle took me off of speaker.

"We've been working on Reverend Money's appeal almost six years," she said. "Wow. It's almost over. I am still stunned at the decision to remand the case back to the state court."

"Remand? What does that mean?" I asked.

"It means that there were too many inconsistencies during the trial. Usually, the lower courts would have to go back and forth with the appellate courts, explaining these inconsistencies, but because of the severity of the crimes he was charged and convicted of, TJ's conviction has been thrown out and he will receive a new trial."

"Will he be eligible for bond?" Please say yes. Please say yes.

"Unfortunately No. In the state of Georgia there is no bond in capital offenses. Not to worry though, we're going to trial soon. All praises do to the almighty for you Karen, we couldn't have done it without your philanthropic efforts. You are truly a godsend."

Why did so many people worship something they couldn't see. And people had the nerve to call me insane. All praises were due to my need for TJ's expertise planning.

Before I killed, I proved to my victims that God didn't exist. I would say, "If there is a God, than save this poor son of a bitch's life. Of course that had never happened.

"Hello? Karen?"

"I'm sorry, I'm still here, just lost you for a minute."

Attorney Kyle continued, "This is by far the highest profile case we've ever been involved with."

"Reverend Money is a good man," I lied. "He wouldn't hurt a roach."

"That's what we're going to prove at January's re-trial."

"January? That's less than four months away."

"I wish it were quicker. We've already..."

"Sorry, I have to take this call," I interrupted. "Keep me abreast of any changes," I said before clicking over to my other line.

"Are you close?"

"I'm pulling into the parking garage across the street. Where are you?"

"In the ladies room. That attorney with the dreadlocks walked in my bosses office with another woman about three minutes ago."

I pulled out my other iphone. I pressed a button and I was in. "You did good Doris. I can hear everything."

"When do I get the other half of the money?"

"The day after never."

"What?"

"I don't stutter, so I know you heard me, Doris. And before you have any dumb ideas, bugging the DA's office is a federal offense, you will go to jail, so don't do anything more utterly stupid than the thoughts circulating through your small mind.

"But, my son?"

"Don't blame me. You passed them bad ass genes down to the little bastard. Now why would I give you ten thousand dollars for some Leukemia trial."

"Because that's what we agreed on Karen. You said if I placed hat device inside the D.A.'s desk…"

"So sad, too bad." I hung up so I could listen in to what was being said inside the DA's office.

I put my headphones on and got out of the Rover.

****

"Rhythm, You and I have fought some helluva battles over the years, but this case stinks. This is the kind of case that can make or break a DA's career," Nathan Beckford said.

Scary voice came over loud and clear. "You mean it could destroy your political future."

"It's all political, young lady," The sixty-year old silver haired DA said. "Tell her Rhythm."

"Unfortunately, he's right."

"I'm here not because I want to be, but out of respect for you and Mr. Jones. I am well aware of everything Mr. Jones has endured. The time he's served, and the losses he's suffered over the last couple months. Personally, I didn't believe he hurt anyone. I thought the details of this case were just a little too convenient," he paused before pointing to the brief ADA Clarence Coward held, "Clarence, please give Attorney One-free the motion of discovery."

After Rhythm opened the manilla envelope, the ADA began, "If you will open to page three. In the top left hand corner you will see that we tested the DNA six times at four different labs. That's what took so long for us to hand over the motion."

"Oh my God," Snakehead said.

"What's wrong?" Scary asked.

"Traces of Coltranc's semen were found inside and around Ezekial Paulk's mouth."

"If Mr. Jones didn't sexually assault and suffocate Ezekial Paulk, than how can you explain this?"

"Clarence, we are not in court. She doesn't have to explain anything to us," District Attorney Beckford said to the ADA he'd assigned to the case.

"I don't know how much you know about Karen Parker Rose," Scary said. "I can't prove it yet, but she's behind everything."

****

That whore-bitch.

"Ma'am, you have to take your headphones off and camera phones are not allowed in the building," the tall strong-voiced, dark, deeply fine black man said. "Are you going to be long?"

"Are you?" I batted my eyes. "I love it, long and hard."

He blushed. "No, I mean are you going to be in the building long?"

"No, I'll just be a few minutes. Why, you gon' be my early Christmas present?"

"I'm married, ma'am."

"I am too." I said watching Wild Scary and Snakehead get off of the elevator. I snatched my phone and the other metal belongings I had put in the plastic security tray before stepping back outside of the State building.

One minute and forty seven seconds later, Scary and Snakehead stepped out into the afternoon sun.

185

I tapped Scary on the shoulder.

"Yes," she turned.

"Let me cordially introduce myself." I hauled off and slapped the fire out of her. "Pow."

She grabbed her cheek, turned back to me and smiled.

I turned so that she was facing my back. I slapped a hand on my hips before saying, "I'm Karen Parker Rose, bitch."

Chapter 26

Cherry

"Karen Parker Rose," I grabbed a handful of blond hair. "I got your bitch alright," I spun her around and buried my fist into her mouth, again and again and again.

It took four security guards to get me off her nutty ass. And when they did, I said, "If you had any question, now you know," I slapped a hand on my all natural hips, "I'm Wild Cherry, bitch," and then I spit in her face.

"No thank you," she said, denying the tissue one of the security officers tried to give her." She looked at me seductively, took four fingers and wiped the spit from her face, before putting the same four fingers into her mouth."

"Nasty ass bitch."

"Do you wanna press charges ma'am?" the head of security asked Karen.

"I wish she would," Rhythm said. "I'm sure all these witnesses saw who hit who first."

"Of course I don't wanna press charges, not for such a little misunderstanding," Karen smiled, showing a mouth full of blood stained teeth. "I'll just handle the situation on my own."

"Please handle the situation yourself. Matter of fact, come handle the situation right now," I said. "Or just get back to handling the situation. So, I can continue whipping that white ass. Silicone body, nip-tuck, fake, funky, wanna-be black queen." I pointed. "You paid for that ass, them breasts, those lips, and that nose and you still ain't even close to looking like me."

"I don't wanna be you. I hate you."

"No, you *hate* that you *ain't* me," I turned, "Come on Rhythm let's go. I need to wash my hands. No telling what or who her mouth has been on."

Rhythm and I were in the parking garage elevator when we spoke again.

"Don't let her get to you."

"I ain't no more thinking about her than I am the man on the moon."

"There's a man on the moon?"

"I don't know. Haven't thought about it." We shared a rare moment of laughter.

"No, seriously," Rhythm said. "How do you..."

"I don't know. But, I do know that Miles wouldn't... couldn't... Didn't..."

"Coltrane," she said.

"Huh?"

"You said Miles."

"No, I said Trane." I shook my head in confusion. "Anyway, I don't know what to say."

"Me either. I am so confused."

"What time you got?" I asked. "Never mind." I pulled my phone out of my purse. "Shit!"

"What?" Rhythm asked.

"I completely forgot."

"Forgot what?"

"Hold on. Gimme a sec," I said retrieving one of the many missed calls in my cell phone before pressing send.

"Rev, I'm so sorry. I don't have an excuse. I just forgot."

"I was worried Cheryl. I called you at least a dozen times," Reverend One-Free said.

"I know Rev. I had my phone on silent. You still wanna see me?"

"Can you come now?"

"I'm on my way. Is it okay if Rhythm comes?"

"Put me on speaker, please," he said.

I took the phone away from my ear.

"How do you know I don't have anything to do?" Rhythm mouthed.

Reverend Solomon One-Free continued, "You're with my favorite sister-in-law?"

"I'm your only sister in law Sol."

"You're still my favorite though. And since I only see you at church, I'd be honored if you came with Cheryl. As a matter of fact, I should have called you. You really need to be here. See you two in a few," he said before hanging up.

****

"Nothing in Atlanta is just five, ten minutes away," I said as Rhythm and I walked to Rev's front door in the historical Kirkwood district of Atlanta.

"The drive wasn't too bad, it only took us a half hour to get here from downtown," Rhythm said.

The front door opened.

I smiled. Rev looked like a more mature distinguished Delroy Lindo.

"My favorite superhero crime fighting team," Rev said, his arms spread wide.

I hugged him. "Rev, I am so far from being a hero, let alone a superhero."

"Go tell that to your kajillion fans on webbook, facebook, and youtube. After you appeared on the *Victoria Christopher Murray Show* a few weeks ago, and especially after you brought twenty-thousand black men together in support of Coltrane your popularity seems as high as it was when we took TJ Money and his co-conspirators down." He waved. "Enough about the past, you two come in. "I have someone eager to meet you Cheryl."

Chapter 27

Karen Parker Rose

Cheryl "Wild Scary" Sharell, it is so wonderful to have finally met you. I stared at the finished product in my hand. And if I say so myself, It's a masterpiece worthy of a Pullitzer. Anyone viewing the video would never even imagine that I had hit her first or that I had anything to do with instigating the state building melee.

Best twenty dollars I've spent in a while. I promised the kid a hundred to record us. And now that the edited version was finished, it was time for me to drop off my masterpiece.

One hour and eleven minutes later, I clicked the Rovers unlock button. A popular producer over at FOX news jumped into the passengers seat.

"What is wrong with you, Neil? Are you on crack?"

He kept looking around, moving his head in an erky jerky motion. "I could lose my job if anyone finds out about this."

If he didn't calm down, he might spot the private dick I had just hired to take pictures. "Relax Neil," I put my hand on his crotch. "We're in a crowded movie theatre parking lot. My windows are tinted so no one can see in. We are fine. And no one is going to find out about our little transaction."

"Okay, let me see what you got," he held a shaky hand out.

I stuck my hand down my shirt and pulled out a thumb drive, stuck it into the allotted slot on the dash and pushed play.

Fourteen minutes and thirty-eight seconds later Neil closed his mouth, which had been wide open while he watched my Pulitzer masterpiece.

"Wow. Wow. You have documented her entire life. Where did you get the footage. The interviews. Wow. The doctors. It wasn't what they said on the video, it's what they didn't say. Wow. And the footage earlier today at the state building. Wow."

"Will you stop saying wow?"

"I can't help it. This is big. Cherry is like a modern-day Joan of Arc to women all over this country. And this video will sink her arc. Wow."

I pulled the thumb drive out and gave it to him. "How soon can you air it?" I put my hand back on his crotch.

He placed an index finger to a corner of his mouth. His blue eyes stared straight ahead. "I can cancel Josh Beaman's special report tomorrow and put this in on the six o-clock news." He gently lifted my hand from his crotch. "There is nothing you can do for me in that department, Mrs. Rose."

"Parker-Rose," I corrected. "Please, don't tell me you're gay."

"No, I'm mo-nay." He held out his hand. "I never mix business with sex."

"But, you were just raving about how great the video was, is."

"It is."

"So, why do you have your hand out?"

"Because we had a deal," the forty-something year old news producer said.

"I just agreed to give you the money so you would actually see what I had to offer. After all, you owe me Neil. Or did you forget about the call a couple months ago. Miles Davis Jones, the kid. You got to the scene the same time the cops did."

He pulled the door handle and was about to step out.

"Come on Neil, you might win a Pulitzer or some other coveted journalistic award with this story."

"I might and then," he shrugged. "I might not."

He had one foot out of the Rover.

"Okay. Okay," I opened the middle console and pulled out an envelope. "Fucking leach."

"You offered me twenty grand to run your story," he said before getting out of the Rover with my money.

I smiled. "Oh yeah, Neil, if that feed doesn't play by tomorrow night, you may not live to see the following day."

He looked at the thick envelope filled with hundred dollar bills, and then the thumb drive. Next, he looked up at me and said, "Wow."

Chapter 28

Cherry

"Wow," I looked at the decorative hardwood, flooring, the hardwood ceilings and the faux painted walls. "Amazing. Last time I was here this place looked so bad that a homeless crackhead high on LSD wouldn't flop here. "Wow," I said again.

"Thank you. I'll show you the second level in a few," Rev said, stepping down into a circular, sunken in den.

"That's right, this was a single level home when you bought it," I said as I slipped and fell while stepping down into the den.

"This is my white room," he extended a hand to the walls, "as you can see, the only thing not white is the floors and the Africentric paintings on the wall."

"This is absolutely beautiful," I said before turning to Rhythm. "Girl, why didn't you tell me your brother-in-law, made this place into an art museum?"

"I am just as amazed as you," Rhythm said. "I haven't been here since..."

"Sunflower and I moved in last year around this time."

"The way this place looked, can you blame me Sol?"

"It was jacked up Rev," I said checking out the Gordon Parks, and Charles Hamilton black and white, Jim Crow era still shots hanging on the circular white walls. "What you have done with this house puts every home makeover show on the web to shame."

"Okay Cheryl, don't go giving him the big head. He already has to buy his hats custom made." She turned to Rev. "Just joking brother-in-law. This house is remarkable. I'll definitely be over here more often."

A man that looked to be somewhere in his late sixties, early to mid seventies bounced on his toes as he walked down into the den wearing a priests get up.

After taking his place beside Rev, Rev put his arm around the man. "Rhythm, Cheryl, I want you to meet, Father Shepherd."

"Hello Father," Rhythm and I greeted the priest.

"Afternoon ladies."

Rev, gestured toward two saddlebag brown, leather loungers. "You ladies will definitely want to take a seat."

After Rhythm and I were seated, Rev and the priest did the same before continuing, "Father Sheppard is the Parish priest in Rome, Georgia. The towns people of Rome have been confessing their sins to him since 1966. And in that time he has learned more about the small town's sordid history than probably any other living soul." Rev looked to his left, "Gene, you wanna take it from here."

The tall, shoestring thin Dracula pale priest stood up from the lounge chair. "Thank you Sol." He turned his iron clad blue eyed stare toward Rhythm.

"Canon law strictly forbids me from revealing in any way what a confessor discloses." He began undoing his priests collar. "After today, after the next few moments I will no longer be of the priesthood. "He put his collar in his pocket. "Canon

195

law also states that violation of the seal of confession results in immediate excommunication."

If he didn't have my full attention before, he definitely had it now.

"When I was sent to watch over Rome, I often wondered why I was given this assignment. Before being assigned to Rome, Georgia, I taught demonology, human sacrifice, and exorcism, at the Vatican."

It only took me being in Rome a week before I saw the reason why I was there."

I swear, if this white man says the Parkers are possessed or some such nonsense.

"There were supernatural forces at work in the small town," Father Shepherd continued. "Most don't believe in the supernatural. But if you look at the word, it just means things in nature that have been superimposed in some way. Now as far as the Parkers," he stuck a finger to his lips and looked up as if deep in thought, "How should I say this?"

Oh, lord here it comes.

"I knew that Blake Parker was being guided by an incubus after being in Rome, a week."

Guided, mentored, possessed it was all the same. I saw the exorcist, I knew what an incubus and a succubus was. I stood.

Like a crossing guard, the priest extended his arm, "Hold on, please Cheryl."

Rhythm and Rev were looking at me like I was crazy. I could care less what anyone thought. Father Shepherd was an authority on some shit I just didn't mess with.

Satan's working with some evilness that I just couldn't fade. I mean, he's a spirit, he's already dead. What can I do to him and any of his kinfolk?"

"Please." Father Shepherd walked behind me.

I was out the den and down the hall and at the front door. I didn't look back until my hand was on the doorknob.

"Karen Parker is a socio-pathic serial killer, and I have proof."

I turned.

"Please," the priest ushered me back towards the den. "Come."

"So, I'm at war with Buffy the fucking psycho killer." I looked around the room. "Oops, did I just say that out loud?"

"I don't know if I could have described your situation, your war any better." Father Shepherd smiled.

Maybe, I'll give Shepherd a chance. Maybe he's really not a crackpot ghost whisperer, demon catcher or any of the other crazies that communicate with the dead. I sat back down. "I'm sorry all. I lead a rated R, sometimes X existence, but please believe my mentality is strictly PG. I don't go for the devil, demon talk. Some things, you just don't mess with. If Knives, guns, and sticks don't fade an enemy of mine, than I'm gon' keep it moving as far away from them as I can."

"No shit." Father Shepherd looked around the room. "Did I just say that?"

We all laughed.

"Seriously," Father Shepherd said. "Blake Parker was a rapist and a murderer with sociopathic tendencies. His son, Dalton was a rapist and a murderer with sociopathic tendencies. Dalton's son, Jonathon and his sister Karen are and were..."

I interrupted. "Rapists and murderers with sociopathic tendencies."

"Parker money has always been acquired at the expense of other's lives." Father Shepherd continued. "The Parker's kill for recreation." He pointed a finger in the air, "And not one Parker has ever served time for so much as petty theft. The mind of a sociopath works differently than the mind of a normal person. A sociopath's mind processes information at a much higher speed than a normal person. Their IQ usually registers in the genius level."

"Okay, Father, I am not trying to be rude, but can we kind of fast forward the story?"

Father Shepherd looked over at Rev and then back to me. Both of them smiled my way.

"There's no reason for you to worry."

"Are you serious? No reason to worry."

"Very serious."

I heard him, but kept going. "You tell me I'm dealing with some crazy demon possessed sociopath, that comes from a long line of fruity pebble serial killers," I crossed my arms. "Father, I probably know just as much if not more about sociopaths and serial killers than you do."

"I'm sure you do," he said, "and I am very serious. *We* know all about you."

"Who is *we*?"

"Oh, just a few old fogies that study how history is the key to understanding scripture and controlling the future."

"I'm confused, we were talking about sociopaths a second ago and now we're talking about old men, scripture, and controlling the future. What does any of this have to do with me and our mission?"

"Everything," the priest said. "We use our knowledge of the past to predict the future. And we've made trillions over the last couple hundred years. Money that we used to do everything from helping to topple corrupt regimes, to feeding ravaged war torn people, to building God centered communities."

"You're some kind of secret order like the Illuminati?"

"The Illuminati are of the Luciferian theology. One that believes money and earthly power are God. This religion actually pretends to deify it's followers."

"Follow my way to Hell and I'll make you God on Earth," I said.

"Exactly. Well maybe not that blunt but you get the idea. And this religion is growing at an alarming pace."

"I've never heard of this Luciferian religion."

"I wouldn't refer to it as a religion. More of a school of thought, a theology. And, you've heard of it, you just didn't recognize it. The Luciferian theology is the marriage of two emotions, greed and envy."

"Greed and envy?"

"Greed is an Incubus, meaning a male demon. It doesn't care about anyone but his or herself. Greed is the preferred opiate of the five percent that control ninety-five percent of the world's wealth and information. And then there is Envy, the Succubus, the female counterpart. The mother of all evil. Coveting others husbands, wives, and personal possessions to the point were lives have been lost. Envy is the opiate of the poor. Both are highly addictive. Demonic in their manifestation, evil in their conceptualization. Whereas the body of man is natural. The human mind in it's inception and pure state is super natural, created in the spiritual image of the father and creator of all thought and action. Mankind expresses their supernatural ability through action and thought spurred by love and understanding of righteousness. God has embedded righteousness into all of mankind, even the mind of the sociopath."

"You're saying that," I paused to get my thought together. "Satan is Gold, and Envy and Greed are his tools that guide people into doing evil."

"Close," Father Sheppard said. "Satan is the offspring of Envy and Greed. You can say that he represents money and Gold. He's a narcissistic, covetous devil that subscribes to the theory of individuality. A theory opposite of the truth that *we*, subscribe to. Love, brotherhood, and commonality.

"Who is this *We*?" I asked. "What is the name of your order?"

"We are the Truth Commission. We move quietly and swiftly. Our energies are dedicated to the aiding and preparation of the resurrection of man."

"If all you've done and are doing is so secretive, than why are you telling us about it?"

"It's time you knew."

"Knew what?" I looked at Rhythm and Rev for answers. They looked as clueless as I felt.

"I've seen so much love and hate over the years. Come into contact with many revolutionaries in my time, but I have never followed anyone with close to the passion you have for protecting the God given rights of others. Time and time again, you've risked your life for others. Women that had been raped, and beaten.

"While you were among America's most wanted fugitives, with little to no regard for your own mortality, you came out of exile to help take down and expose a plot to make the mortally evil Bishop TJ Money, the president of this country."

"That's my past. I don't go after crooked pastors, and men who get away with abusing women anymore. My castrating days are over. I spent close to seven years, living in and escaping from mental institutions. Psychologists, Psychoanalysts, Psychiatrists, every type of Psych you can think of tried to figure me out. Hell, I couldn't figure me out, so you know I was no help to them. I didn't even know who I was until I became a fugitive and had to flee to Cuba. There, a queen named Assata Shakur, just didn't educate me, she showed me who I was."

Father Shepherd's face lit up at the mention of Assata. "*We* are, and always have been behind Ms. Shakur. How do you think she's been so well protected and taken care of all these years."

"So again, what does all this have to do with me?"

"The spirit of justice resides deep within you. Right always overpowers wrong."

I don't know how, but I knew he was telling the truth. I had always been driven by justice. Wanting to protect the weak.

"You can defeat the mother of evil," Father Shepherd said.

"Hold on Father, I told you I don't do ghosts."

"You've felt her punch, you watched her bleed from your retaliation. If she's a ghost, than so are you?"

"But, earlier you said..."

"I said nothing and yet everything. Never confirming or denying. But, what I am saying is that evil has nested inside several generations of Parkers. Karen, being the first female-much stronger than the men. But inside you, Ms. Sharell, is the heart and soul of a leader, a fighter for right, even if everyone else is doing wrong. You are anointed. The matriarch of righteousness dwells inside your soul. You are a warrior in God's army."

"Really, I am honored. But can you please tell me how you can help me save Albert Coltrane Jones?"

"Roger Naismith, the chief caretaker at Myrtle Hill Cemetery in Rome, has been coming to mass his entire life. He's been confessing his sins for over forty years. Nothing out of the ordinary, up until six months ago. That's when he confessed and asked for absolution for the twelve bodies he's buried and helped to dispose of. All murdered, all covered up."

"Karen Parker?" I asked.

"Every last one of them."

"How were they disposed of?"

"Karen paid Roger and the town Sheriff huge sums of money to bury the bodies on top of civil war confederate soldiers at Myrtle Hill Cemetery. Three years ago in 2011, Karen had two huge industrial metal sinks installed in the basement at the Parker Estate. Both of them were equipped with large wide mouthed garbage disposals. Since then, bodies were brought to the Parker Estate basement. After lining the floor and work benches with plastic, Roger Naismith and the town sheriff used electric saws to cut the bodies into small enough pieces to go into the garbage disposals."

"Why is Roger confessing this to you now?"

"He's dying. Prostate cancer. Stage four."

I picked up my purse. "Where can I find this Roger Naismith?"

Chapter 29

Karen Parker Rose

"**Roger Naismith** speaking."

"Roger? I was at my Pilates class at LA Fitness this morning when I remembered that you hadn't called."

"Karen, I didn't call because...

"I'm not finished." I crossed my legs and continued speaking in a calm detached tone. "As I was saying, I am sitting outside of Starbucks on a sixty degree sunless autumn morning sipping on an iced vanilla mocha latte trying to cool off, and I don't mean from my work out. Now, I want to know why in the hell did you not call me as instructed?"

"Last night, I didn't get the chance to uhm, to go out to Bumper's and...

"Where the fuck are you?"

After a bout of coughing and hawking he said, "Good morning to you too Karen."

"What's so good about it?"

"The good lord woke you..."

"I am so tired of this good God garbage. If one more person tells me about the good Lord. If one more person tells me how blessed they are," I paused to collect myself. No need to get upset. "I've known you all my life and you didn't start feeding into the God garbage until you found out you had prostate cancer."

"It's not garbage. God is real Karen."

"Bullshit. You know it and I know it. You're just covering all angles, just in case there is a God and a Heaven. You're dying. Hell, I'm surprised you've lived this damn long. But, let me tell you something Roger Naismith. If there is a God, and there isn't, your first class ticket and your own personal lake of fire is awaiting you in Hell. I don't think your invisible God would take too kindly to you being a human body butcher."

"That is what I do. Not, who I am. They are already dead when you send me and Charlie to get 'em."

"Idiot. I pay you for a service that allows me to keep order and justice in my life. A service that according to this invisible God, is a violation of His rules."

"My lord is a forgiving God."

"Stop it before I throw up my morning Latte. You cut human bodies into small pieces and put them down garbage disposals. You think your God is going to forgive you for doing that over and over. You better hope there isn't a God."

"Why do you say that?"

"Are you serious. I mean, are you seriously wanting a response. Because if you are, you win the dumbest-question-asked-in-2014 award. And I am not going to answer such an obvious idiotic question. So, back to my original question, Where.... Are... You?"

"Home."

"What?"

"I'm not feeling to well. The chemo."

"Roger, you have to go get Charlie before someone finds the body if they already haven't."

"I finished with Bumper before I went to chemo yesterday, that's probably why I'm under the weather this morning. After taking care of your aunt and her friend by myself, I had to do Bumper. I'm exhausted and besides, I can't move Charlie by myself."

"I don't give a fuck if you have to rent a friggin' tow truck. Just get his fat ass back to the house and do what you do."

"I don't see why we can't just wait until someone discovers the body. It's not like you had anything to do with what happened to him."

"I don't pay you to see. I pay you to do. Leave the seeing and thinking to me. Now just do what I pay you to do. And, I need you to dig my brother up and the other five you buried before we got the sinks and the garbage disposals installed."

"Karen, there is no way I can exhume the bodies by myself. I'm not the man I used to be."

"You know what, forget it. I'll be out there tomorrow night. I'll help. I'll even bring one of my dresses and some high heels for you to wear, so you can look like a bitch, when you bitch to me about what you can't do and how you're not the man you used to be. For now, Just go get Charlies fat ass." I pressed the end button and a text message popped up. Shit.

TERRELL REALLY NEEDS TO SPEAK WITH YOU. HE SAYS YOU WON'T TAKE HIS CALLS.

I upheld my part of the bargain, so why won't the little fuck stop trying to get me to come see him. The last time, I felt so humiliated. Never again.

You would think after umpteenth messages and texts, and no response from me, he would have gotten the message. I don't know why TJ thought, having his attorney text me would make the slightest difference. And it wasn't like he could blow the whistle on me. That would be incriminating himself, ruining all chances he had at an acquittal in January. And by then the basement sinks and disposals will be cleaned and under a heap of trash at a recycling center or city dump. The basement would be bleached and most importantly, all evidence will have been dug up, cut up, and would be at the bottom of wherever the Floyd county sewer let out.

I pulled out of the Starbucks parking lot. I couldn't wait until tonight. I had to go to Rome now, make sure that shit got done right.

My phone vibrated in my hand. I pressed the answer button on my ear piece. "Hello?"

"Mrs. Rose?"

"Hi Tom."

"Thomas," the private dick I had just hired corrected me.

A week ago, I began searching for private detectives that had backgrounds in surveillance. And after discovering that Thomas George had done surveillance for the US government on several occasions, in the states and abroad I figured he was my man.

"What do you have for me Tom?"

"I'd really appreciate it, if you would address me as Thomas, Mrs. Rose."

"Sure."

"I'm calling with an update, is this a good time?"

"Yes, it is." I could hear paper rattling in the background.

"By the way, I got some great photo's of that news producer getting into and out of your SUV yesterday. After leaving the theatre parking area, I caught up with Ms. Sharell just as she left Solomon One-Free's residence in Kirkwood."

"Isn't that a ghetto side of Atlanta?"

"Used to be, sort of still is. Anyway, I followed her to St. Judes Children's Research Hospital."

"Who was she visiting at a children's hospital?"

"Hold on."

Who still used paper? I wondered, as I listened to more papers being rustled in the background.

"Here it is," he continued, "she visited a five week old infant, born three and a half months premature to a Tameeka Jones."

"Thank you Tom. I have an emergency situation on my hands, I'll call you later to settle up."

"But."

"That will be all," I pressed end. And it was the end, at least for five people. Coltrane Jones, Wild Scary, Roger Naismith, one little sick baby, and now Thomas George. Kill all the loose ends and nothing will get out.

Then again, Parasites little baby was innocent, she hadn't done anything to me, but be the daughter of Coltrane Jones. Yep. I took a deep breath. A smile creased my face. I wonder how Coltrane would react when he found out that his baby daughters throat was cut.

Chapter 31

Cherry

"**His only daughter's throat was cut**, jugular vein gushing blood everywhere, Dooney Bug bout lost it."

The woman behind me was gossiping a mile a minute.

"Girl stop," her friend said. "What happened, next?"

"Number forty-seven."

Thank God. I marched to the front and handed my ticket to the officer. This time Coltrane was already waiting. I sat down picked up the phone and said, "Trane, I know it doesn't seem right, you know the kiss, the way we feel for each other, but I don't think either of us is an authority on love. And for the record, I didn't try to fall in love with you. And, please believe I wouldn't have if Miles were still here. And yes, he ain't been in the ground a season yet."

"Neither has Paradise," he interrupted.

"I know that, just like I know that what I feel is real. And I know you feel it. Don't deny it Albert Coltrane Jones. You love me. You probably feel bad about it, just as I do."

"Probably?"

"Yes, probably. And I wasn't going to tell you this." I exhaled loudly. "The last conversation Paradise and I had, she made me promise to take care of you and the baby if something should ever happen to her. And I can't think of a better way to take care of your suicidal, manic ass, than to love you."

"Okay."

"Okay. I just tell you that I'm in love with you and I'm going to be with you and take care of you and the baby, and all you have to say is *okay.*"

"The baby?"

"Another thing I wasn't going to tell you. Well not until I found out if she was going to make it"

"She?"

"Yes, she. You have a daughter," I pulled out the picture I took before I left the hospital yesterday."

He stared.

"Well aren't you going to say anything?"

"I love you, Cheryl Cherry Sharell."

"Huh?"

"I said, I love you woman, and we will take care of each other, that is if I get out of this predicament."

"Not, if. When. And the when, will be soon," I put my palm against the wall of Plexiglas that separated us. "Trust me."

"I do."

"You do what?" I asked.

"Trust you. I trust you with my heart, my daughter, and my life. When you truly love someone, you give all of yourself and if you will have me you got me."

I opened my mouth, but nothing came out.

"Is that all you have to say?" he asked.

"Touche."

"I have a daughter."

"Yes, you do. Yes we do. She's still in critical care, but she's going to be alright. The doctors and nurses call her Miracle, because that is what she is, born three and a half months premature. The Umbilical chord was wrapped around her neck and it would have strangled her, but now her vitals have stabilized, her brain function seems to be fine, But she still needs to be in a sterile environment. It's her lungs. They're still developing."

"Miracle, huh?"

"Yep. Thats what they call her."

"Well then Miracle it is. Miracle Jones."

"Miracle Tameeka Jones," I said. "That's what I put on the birth certificate before I left the hospital yesterday."

"I have a daughter." He stood up. "I'm a father everybody. I have a daughter."

"Sit down and control yourself, Fifteen, before your visit is terminated," a faceless voice shouted from behind the Plexiglas on Trane's side.

"How are we going to deal with this?" I asked.

"Deal with what?"

"Us," I said. "The baby."

"One day at a time Queen. One day at a time."

Queen. The way he called me queen. a hard K a wind blowing W and a drawn out een.

"Oh God!" His eyes got big.

"What?"

"Karen. What if she..."

"Trane, she doesn't know that Miracle even exists."

He sighed. "You're right. If she knew, Miracle would probably be..."

"Don't say it Trane. Don't even put that kind of energy in the air."

Ten minutes later, our visit concluded. Thirty minutes later, I was in Miles's Cougar on my way to Rome. This time I wasn't wasting money or time renting a car trying to be discreet.

To help pass the time while I drove, I called Rev.

"What it do?"

"No you didn't answer the phone like that."

"It's like dis here shawty. I'm jus trynna relate to our shorty's, smell me."

"By speaking incorrect English."

"Sometimes you gotta be incorrect to show incorrectness. The same response I am getting from you, I hope to get from parents and our youth. Can you dig that?"

"Okay, Rev you went a little too far back with the 'can you dig that'."

"So, what's up Cheryl?"

"On my way to Rome, to check out this Roger character."

"Who?"

"The guy that Father Sheppard spoke of."

"Who's father Sheppard?"

"Rev, stop trippin'. You know good and well that he's the priest you introduced me to at your house."

"Cheryl, are you alright? Maybe we should have taken you to the Emergency room after you fell."

"Okay, now what are you talking about?"

"That nasty fall you took stepping down into the den, when you arrived at the house yesterday. You know you were out for a good ten minutes," he said. "Now, I feel bad."

"For what?"

"I should have insisted on taking you to the emergency room."

I remember falling when I walked in, but I don't remember hitting the ground or getting up. "Rev, me, you and Rhythm sat in your den. You introduced us to Father Shepherd. He told us all about the Parkers and Karen."

"No, Cheryl. It was just me, you, and Rhythm at the house."

"Okay, what about the person who you'd called me about. The one you wanted me to meet?"

"And you did. Winnie Mandela's book *'Part of my Soul Went With Him.'*

"The book you gave me before I left, that's...

"Exactly. I thought it would help you on your journey to self discovery and revolutionary thought. As I told you before you left the house yesterday, other than being Mandela's wife, Winnie will probably never be taught in schools or mentioned in history books, but she inspired a nation, like you have. I promise you Cheryl, you read her story and you won't feel so alone."

"How do you know how I feel?"

"All revolutionaries fighting for justice get lonely. They're always fighting against a genocidal system of traditions and principles that have been instilled into the socio-consciousness of the society they are fighting to uplift. The fight is always against a system controlled and manipulated by the megarich power mongers."

Back to the subject at hand, I asked, "So you're telling me that you don't know a Father Gene Shepherd?"

"Not personally, but I've read about him."

"Read about him."

"Yes, he lived during the 1800's, during the time of Charles Darwin and Francis Galton. Charles Darwin's theory of evolution and his cousin, Francis Galton's theory of racial superiority were then the new guiding forces in Europe that would eventually lead to Hitler's rise and the emergence of Social-Darwinism also known as Jim Crow in America.

Gene Sheppard was an Austrian priest that single handedly toppled a revolution that was on the rise in mother England, one that was going to reinstate slavery of African peoples. One that was led by Francis Galton himself. The potential revolution was fueled and inspired by the theories of Darwin and Gal..."

****

212

I looked at my cell phones screen. Dammit, I lost my signal as I drove through the small town of Rome. Even when I picked the signal back up I didn't call Rev back. I knew what I saw and who I spoke to. And I even had the address of Roger Naismith. Soon enough, I'd find out if Father Shepherd was real, although I knew he was. Just like I knew I wasn't crazy. I knew what crazy looked like, and it's spokesperson is the woman that I am going to destroy.

Chapter 32

Karen Parker Rose

"**I am going to destroy** you, if you don't run my piece." I crossed my legs while I sat in a chair outside on Neil Shorthouse's patio overlooking his olympic sized swimming pool.

"I can't. There is absolutely no way. My boss over at FOX killed the story. Cheryl Cherry Sharell has way too big of a following. At least that's what my boss thinks."

"So did Bill Clinton, but you guys broke the Monica Lewinsky scandal. So did Bishop TJ Money, but you broke that story," I said. "Come one Neil, what you're saying is complete and utter bullshit. The bigger the subject, the harder the fall."

The FOX news producer pulled out a stuffed envelope. "I am just telling you what I was told. I can only do what I can do." He slid the envelope across the marble topped stainless steel table.

"What is this?"

"The money you gave me. It's all there. You can count it."

"No need." I picked up the envelope and put it inside my Coach bag.

The forty something year old news producer seemed to relax a little. "I'm really sorry about this. I am sure the feed would've been a hit. You should think about streaming it on the web. I bet it would go viral in no time."

"No necd." I pressed a couple buttons before sliding my Iphone across the round table. "Take a look at this."

He picked up the phone. "What is this?"

"Come on Neil, you're a smart boy. You know exactly what this is."

"Are you trying to blackmail me?"

"No, not at all." I smiled.

"What do these pictures prove?"

"Again, you're a smart boy. Surely you see that the pics are time and date stamped."

"All you have is pictures of me getting into your Range Rover, and pictures of me taking money and a thumb drive."

"You left out the pictures of us watching the feed. I am not going to sit here and go back and forth with you Neil."

"You bitch," he stood up. "You fucking bitch."

"Thank you, Neil, but flattery will get you nowhere." I uncrossed my legs and slid my chair back from the table.

"You set me up."

"No. You set yourself up." I pulled my dark shades below my nose before batting my eyelashes. "A girl has to cover herself."

"A minute ago you said that you weren't trying to blackmail me."

I leaned in. "I'm not *trying* to do a got damn thing. I am blackmailing you."

"I'll lose my job."

The October suns intensity so late in the afternoon prompted me to place my shades back over my eyes. "You can find another job, but if these pics get into the hands of the proper people you will be charged. And granted, in the end you will probably get a slap on the wrist, but the only job you'll be able to get in the news industry is a... You know what, I can't think of a job you'll be able to get in the industry."

He picked up my phone and slammed it on the granite patio floor. "I'll kill you," he snarled.

"You could try."

Neil was around six foot, not a big man. Not a small man. An angry man, yes. I smiled as he took a couple steps and put his hand around my neck. "I will make your life a living hell if you do this." He lifted me from my chair.

I was like Edward Scissorhands, the way I used my nails on his face and arms.

"Shit!" he screamed, let me go and grabbed his face, specifically his right eye, the one I tried my damnest to gouge out. Now that I was free I kneed him in the groin. He bent over. I lifted my left leg and slammed a three inch heel into his knee. He was busy falling to the ground and screeching in agony when I reached into my bag and pulled out old faithful, my .380 Baretta. "I think you were supposed to kill me right? How did that work out for you?"

He was obviously in too much pain to answer. So I continued, "The feed will run today. Not tomorrow or the day after. Today. If it doesn't you are finished. Oh, and just so you know, I recorded you attacking me and me beating your ass. So, now you will not only be through in the news, but you will be laughed at and talked about years after I have killed you." I turned to leave. I was so proud of myself for staying so calm and in control.

"What about the money?" he asked, from his crawling position.

I had the .380 pointed at his ass when I decided not to shoot him. I wanted to, but what would it prove. I'd done enough to his body and his pride, so I put the gun back into my bag and pulled out the envelope. I knelt down beside him. "You mean this."

He nodded, but didn't reach for the money.

I stood up. "You forfeited this when you slammed my phone on the ground and put your hand around my neck." I smacked him on the ass before I put the twenty-grand back into my bag. "Don't get up. I can show myself out. Oh and you have a lovely home. I didn't know news producers lived so well. Sure would hate to see you lose all of this."

I had so much to do, and this idiot had thrown all of my plans off. I should have been in Rome helping Roger, but no, I get a call from numb-nut Neil telling me what he couldn't do. I put the gear shift in drive. St. Judes Children's Research Hospital was on the way. I turned my head. My wig and make up were in the backseat along with my other tools.

Chapter 33

Cherry

I turned my head. My wig and make up were in the backseat along with my other tools. Fortunately, I didn't need a disguise. Roger and Bumper were alike in that they both lived off the beaten path. Hillbilly's without the hill. Mile's would die if he knew I'd driven his baby through backwoods dirt roads, mud patches and over high grass and weeds. I reached in the backseat of the Cougar and unzipped the leather tool case. Six scalpels, a pair of scissors, a razor knife, and two poison darts. I got out of the car and strapped my tool case over my shoulder, before walking through the high grass and leaves.

A minute later I knocked on the black wood paint peeling door of the old Amityville horror looking two story house. There was no answer, so I walked over to the oversized garage and looked inside one of the windows. A red 2014 Chevy Silverado truck and a green expensive looking tractor thingy were parked inside. I retraced my steps through weeds, leaves and high grass. I stopped at a bay window. The white and black paint around it and on the entire front of the house was badly peeling. I cupped my hands on the huge window and peeked through the curtains. Damn. The inside of the house looked nothing like the outside.

"Click. Click." The sound of a pump action shotgun. I froze.

"Give me one reason why I shouldn't put a hot one in you," a scratchy voice rumbled behind me.

How the hell had he snuck up on me. All these damn leaves, and I hadn't heard a thing.

"Talk fast or die fast. Makes me no never mind."

My back to him, as calm as a carrot I said, "Roger Naismith, I presume."

"Who in hell wanna know?" He turned and spit.

"I work for Karen Parker-Rose." I said. "She sent me."

"Jesus Christ Mary mother of Jesus." The deathly slim white man said. "Sometimes I swear, if brains were cotton that gal wouldn't have enough to make a kotex for a flea."

I turned in time to see him slap himself upside the head. "Why in God's name didn't Karen send a hardleg? You be 'bout as useful as a back pocket on a shirt."

I tried my best to keep a straight face.

"Why in hell you grinnin' at me like a possum eatin' shit."

"I don't know. I'm sorry."

He finally uncocked the double barrel and let it rest at his side.

"You look greener than goose shit." He smiled, "But I swear fo' Jesus and all the apostles, you 'bout finer than a frog hair, split four ways and pertier than a glob of butter on a stack of flapjacks."

Please don't let this crypt keeper be flirtin' with me. He was tall, thin as paper and old as Moses. He put me in the mind of an emaciated Abraham Lincoln. Same funny looking beard and hairless upper lip. His skin looked like worn leather. It was really hard to believe that this man was capable of doing the things that Father Shepherd had said.

"Come on Suga' Dumplin'. You got me sweatin' like a two-dollar whore in church." He stopped, turned and waved the shotgun at me. "Come on now."

I did as told, and not because he had the gun. I could've unzipped my tool case, pulled out a dart, threw it, and before the thought of turning around could enter his mind, he'd be dead.

"We goin' inside. Don't worry Suga' Dumplin', I ain't gon' bite," he smiled, showing a mouthful of gums and chewing tobacco. "Couldn't bite if'n I wanted to. Lost my teeth in a poker game a coupla weeks back."

I didn't know what to say, my only thought was, who the hell would wear someone else's teeth.

"My cellular don't pick up to good out here," he said while unlocking the door. "Gotta use the house phone. Karen gon' have to 'splain to me how in hell I'm s'posed to dig up three stiff ones wit' you."

In one swift motion, I disarmed the old billy and pushed him to the floor.

He turned over on the hardwood floor only to find himself staring at the wrong end of his shotgun. "Karen ain't sent you, did she?"

"Nope."

"Well butter my butt and call me a biscuit." He pointed. "You that Scary woman, ain'tchu."

"Who?"

"That Wild Scary woman."

I laughed. "She's funny?"

"She who?" He asked, playing dumb.

"Your boss."

"Mike Malarchy. Been working for him for over fawty years at Myrtle Hill."

"Digging graves," I said.

"More than that, Suga' Dumplin'. I'm the grounds manager." He spoke with as much pride as someone like him could muster. "Mind if I stand, I'm stiffer than a three peckered billygoat on Viagara at a sheep breeding contest."

"Go ahead."

"Just prefer to die on my feet."

"If you tell me what I need to know and show me what I need to see then I won't need to kill you."

He grabbed the barrel of his gun and put it to his chest. "Suga' dumplin' you might as well send me to my maker, cause I ain't saying nothin' bout nothin'."

"Click! Click!" I pumped a shell into the double barrel. "You wanna rethink that."

The old fool laughed. "Suga' dumplin' If you haven't noticed, I'm not the healthiest sixty year old man you've ever seen. I'm on my way to greener pastures sooner or later. Might as well be sooner."

"Earlier, you mentioned God," I said, still holding the shotgun to his chest. "Are you a religious man, Roger Naismith?"

"What'n tarnation that got to do with you pullin' that dere trigger?"

"Nothing." I shrugged. "I just wanted to know how you could leave this world without repenting for all the bodies you've buried for Satan."

He reached into a blue jean overall pants pocket, pulled out a can of chewing tobacco, opened it, hawked and spit into it, before putting the lid back on and placing it back into his pocket. "I ain't done nary a nothin' for Satan. And furtha' mo', Suga' Dumplin', my relationship and my business with the Almighty is my own, whether I done repented or not ain't your business."

"Maybe not. But an innocent man... The man I love, Albert Coltrane Jones is in the Fulton County Jail facing Capital Murder, for what Karen Parker-Rose did."

"You talkin' bout that Jones boy," Naismith shook his head. "Damn shame."

"The damn shame is for a so called man of God to let evil get away with setting another man of God up for taking life, God's most precious gift."

"Whatever wrongs I may have done and whatever wrongs I may do, is me and the Almighty's business. I've made my peace."

"How can you say that? You think you can just go to confession, confess your sins, make penance and expect God to forgive you?"

He nodded. "Pretty Much."

"Repent means to turn from sin. Feel sorry for past conduct. How are you doing that by continuously repeating the same acts you're asking forgiveness for? You really think Father Shepherd..."

"Father Shepherd." His eyes got big. "You know Father Shepherd?"

"How do you think I know about the bodies you buried in unmarked graves at Myrtle Hill. The bodies you cut up and put down garbage disposals in the basement of the Parker Estate."

"He sent you."

"Yes."

"You really know Father Shepherd?" he asked as if he were in a drugged haze. "He really sent you here."

"Yes. He told me that you could help me."

"And he wants me to help you?"

"Yes."

The emaciated old man reached into another pocket and pulled out a different chewing tobacco container, opened it, stuck two fingers in the brown goo and put a gob in his mouth before closing the lid and putting the container back into his pocket. Next, he pushed the shotgun away from his chest and walked past me. "I swear, you and Karen is like two cheeks on an ass, only thing you got in common is a fart."

I tried my best not to laugh, but my voice broke a couple times while asking him where we were going.

"The kitchen. If Father Shepherd done sent you, than I must don't have long, which means we don't have long, and I got a heap of mess to pour on your brains."

Roger Naismith looked like trailer park trash, walked like trailer park trash, talked like trailer park trash, and even dressed like trailer park trash, but the inside of his home was antebellum Home and Garden. After walking into the kitchen I took a seat at the mahogany wood antique dining room table.

He closed a kitchen drawer, and turned. "This here," he held a stack of papers to his chest. "These here is me and Karen Parker's hist'ry."

****

I'd gotten to Naismith's house at around nine this morning and it was a quarter til nine in the evening when I opened the front door to leave. Naismith put his crusty, funky, skeletal fingers on my bare shoulder.

"Now, you just take heed to everything I done said. I done told you Karen done took leave of her senses. So, don't take her lightly. She nuttier than squirrel shit."

"Thank you Roger, for everything."

"No parting kiss." He puckered his dark curled in lips.

"I ain't Halle Berry and you sure ain't Billy Bob Thornton."

"Who?"

"The movie, Monster's Ball. The one that Halle got the Academy for."

He looked confused.

"Nevermind."

"Come on now, Suga' Dumplin' one eeny teensy little kiss for a dying man."

I looked into his jaundiced dark brown eyes. "Roger, there are just some things that a black woman will not do." I walked out into the quiet windless night, through the leafy jungle high grass. I opened the car door and pitched my tool case and the sheath of papers on the passengers seat.

Before getting in, I had a thought. One I hadn't thought of all day. I shouted. "Roger?"

"Yeah?"

"Where can I find Father Shepherd?"

"You said you knew him," he shouted back.

"I just met him yesterday. He came to me."

"Thats the way he works."

"What do you mean?"

"Father Sheppard," he said. "You don't find him. He finds you."

I was so anxious to get away from Amityville horror and it's crypt keeper. As soon as I stopped to thank Father Shepherd I was out of Rome, hopefully, prayerfully I would never have to return. I continued, "I understand all that, but where is his church, cathedral, whatever you Catholics call it."

Out the corner of my eye I could've sworn I saw a streaking shadow of a winged man. Best believe, I didn't turn to see if my eyes were playing tricks on me. I jumped in the car stuck the key in the ignition, turned my head, put the car in reverse and hit the gas. I'd just have to thank Father Shepherd some other time. As I'd told Roger, this ain't the movies. That's the only place you had people going into haunted houses and running after ghosts.

I was so busy trying to get the hell out of them woods, I wasn't paying attention to anything else.

Chapter 34

Karen Parker Rose

I wasn't paying attention to anything else. Day had turned to night and I hadn't even noticed. My mind was preoccupied with pleasant thoughts of the intense pain that Coltrane would suffer after he found out that his daughter had been murdered while in St. Judes critical care unit.

"Bammmmmmmm!"

My body jerked forward as the airbag engaged. What the fuck.

After being smothered under a big ass gray balloon for two whole minutes someone finally came to see if I was alive.

"Miss? Miss? Can you hear me ma'am." He touched my arm.

"Owwwww." I screamed. The airbag blocked me from looking anywhere but down. So I could only see the man's black shoes.

"I'm sorry. Didn't mean to scare you."

"You didn't scare me retard. You hit my fucking truck."

"Ma'am?"

Damn, his deep Vin Diesal voice was so damn sexy.

"You ran into my van," he said.

"Help me out of here, will you?"

After opening the door he put his arm under my airbag. I winced in pain.

"You wanna wait for a paramedic?"

Each vowel, each consonant he put together made me wet.

"No, please. I'm okay, just soar."

He reached across my chest and unbuckled my seatbelt. Next he pulled the airbag back toward the steering wheel.

"A little bit more," I said as I squeezed out of my seat. My face, knees and chest were on a crash course with some concrete until he grabbed and pulled me to my feet. "Thank you," and for one of the rarest moments in my life, I really meant it. I couldn't imagine ruining my fifty-two thousand dollar facial reconstruction. But that's what would've happened if my face crashed into the pavement.

"Are you okay?"

His deep voice made the wind in my ears rumble.

"I'll be fine." For the first time I was about to see who my savior was. I poked my twenty-five thousand dollar Beyonce ass out. I even made my butt clap a couple times while I smoothed out my dress.

I turned and looked at Mr. Sexy voice. "You have to be fucking kidding me. My eyes went from toe to head, and head to toe. A priest. An old ass white priest." I couldn't believe Father Time had turned me on. In sheer frustration, I threw my arms in the air. "Ow," I grabbed for my chest and ribs as I screeched in pain. If that airbag damaged my sternum or anything else, I was gon' sue. I turned, looked at my smashed in front end, and then at the other vehicle. I nodded, and blew out a long breath. "Yep, I fucked your van up pretty bad."

Serves him right, old ass white bible pimp with a Vin Diesal laced Teddy Pendergrass voice, causing me to now walk around in a sticky wet thong.

"The van is of no concern to me." The bible pimp looked deep into my eyes. "What concerns me is you."

I turned, looked at the van again, and then back at the priest. There was no way he came out of that without being at least a little fucked up.

"You are one lucky Father?"

"Blessed."

There is that blessed bullshit again. Blessed. Blessed. Blessed. How the fuck are you blessed when I just tore your van out the frame. You're old as Adam, about to die any damn minute and you're blessed. "You would think the cops would be here by now, an affluent white area." I took out my phone to call 911.

Five minutes later I was finally off the phone with the operator. Three of those minutes I was on hold. Hell, I could've died on hold.

I looked up. "Father?" I walked around to the back of my tore up SUV and to the rear of his smashed in van. "St. Judes Children's Research Hospital." The logo on the van read. I looked across the street. St. Judes Children's Research Hospital, right across the damn street. So close but yet so fucking far. I squeezed my hand into a fist. I could not believe my luck. So busy day dreaming about the pain I was about to cause Coltrane. The intense indescribable pain. I was less than a hundred yards away from strangling his precious parasite wittle baby. "Father," I called out. No answer again. We were in the middle of a usually busy street. A major thoroughfare. Granted, it was night. 10:07 PM to be exact.

I looked across the street in every direction. The man had just disappeared. And I would have, right into the critical care unit of St. Judes, but the Range Rover was registered in my name.

Sirens blared in the distance.

Chapter 35

Cherry

Sirens blared in the distance. I don't know and I can't explain it, but I couldn't stop thinking about Miracle. A little baby. A baby that I had fallen deeply in love with the day she was born. Her little bitty chest fighting to breath in that incubator. Her tiny pink hands balled into a fist. Miracle was a fighter. And there was nothing miraculous about her being alive. She was the daughter of two bonafide warriors. The miracle will be the mark that I and her father will help her make on this world.

I was tired. Bone tired. Been in Rome all day talking to Roger the cryptkeeper. It was late. A big day was in store for me tomorrow as I would deliver the evidence that would exonerate my man. But for now, I had to see Miracle. I had to let her know how I felt. For some reason I couldn't wait until tomorrow. It was as if something was tugging at my heart. Pulling me to the children's hospital.

A police car got behind me as I turned the corner. The hospital was just up ahead when the blue lights lit up and the siren blared.

"Pull over," A masculine voice blared from the cop cars loudspeaker.

I was sleepy but I know I wasn't weaving. But, in any case I pulled to the side of the road.

The cop walked up to my window.

After letting my window down, I asked, "What did I do?"

"License and insurance."

Another police car pulled in front of me. I reached in my purse and took out my license and insurance card. Call it intuition. I had a strong feeling that me pulling over was a mistake. Despite my reservations, I gave the cop my credentials anyway.

He opened my door. "Get out of the vehicle ma'am."

"Huh?"

He pulled his gun. "Get out of the vehicle. Now!"

"Okay, relax. It ain't that serious" I slowly stepped out with my hands in the air. "Okay, I'm out."

The other cop came up beside me, grabbed my arms, and pulled them behind my back. "Cheryl Sharell, you are under arrest. You have the right to...

"What am I being charged with?"

"If you can't afford an attorney...

He kept reading me my rights as if I hadn't said a thing.

After he finished, him and his partner roughly grabbed me and took me to the squad car that was parked behind me.

Before the cop pushed my head inside, I said, "You rednecks don't know who I am."

"Oh we know exactly who you are Wild Cherry."

"No, you really don't know, because if you did, you wouldn't have had your hand all over my ass and coochie. Don't worry I ain't gon' report you. I got better plans for you two junior rapists."

"Is that a threat?" One of the officers asked.

"No sir. Not at all." I decided that my best bet would be to stay quiet until these knuckleheads got me downtown. Whatever I was being charged with had to be a mistake.

The drive to the station was uneventful. I didn't say a word and the cop didn't either. It wasn't until we got to the station when the cop following us got out of his car and opened the back door and helped me out. I didn't give either arresting officer the satisfaction of a response during and after they copped a few more feels.

By the time I was processed and put into a holding cell, I was too tired to speak, almost too tired to keep my eyes open.

"Hey, I was going to use that," the half naked hooker that was sitting on the toilet said.

"I'm the wrong one and this is definitely the wrong time," I said. "There's two more rolls of toilet paper on the floor beside you," I went to a corner and slid down the wall to the dull gray concrete floor and used the roll of toilet paper as a pillow.

My eyes were closed when I heard the toilet flush. I was halfway to dreamland when I heard a voice say, "Bitch must think she the queen of fucking England. Just gon' come in here and take a roll of shit-paper for herself. It's seven of us in here, and three rolls, now two rolls of shit paper. All of us can't have a roll for our personal pillows."

With my eyes closed and my senses one hundred and ten percent alert, I said, "I don't think I'm the queen of England. Just the queen of *me* and my surroundings. The word queen and the word bitch don't go together. Now I know you think its cool to address your sisters as bitch's, but I don't play that. I am not covered in fur and I sure don't walk on all fours and I definitely don't copulate with dogs, so I'd appreciate it if you would address me as queen or Ms. Sharell.

"You got me fucked up. You got all of us fucked up, trick."

I didn't want my one phone call. I didn't want anything to drink or eat. I just wanted sleep. Sleep. That's all.

"Queen, my ass," the woman continued.

I still hadn't forced my eyes to open. "I'm extremely tired. But, I know I just explained to you who I was and who I was not. And yet you not only continue to disrespect me, but you are trying to draw others into your mess."

"Freak Nasty ain't drawn' nobody into nothin'," a phony deep voiced woman replied taking up for the hooker who was preventing me from sleep.

"Can you just leave me alone and let me sleep?"

"Bitch please," Freak Nasty replied.

"That's the second time you called me out of my name."

"Third," the deep voiced woman corrected me.

"Okay, third time." I still hadn't opened my eyes, but I had an idea that the deep voice belonged to the bald headed high yellow, sagging jeans, breast strapped, big bull that looked at me like I was a Longhorns steak dinner when the deputy pushed me inside the cell. "Don't make it a fourth. Tell you what. I'll put the toilet paper back if you'll leave me the hell alone."

"Bitch, you think someone wants to wipe they ass or dab they twat with shit paper you done had your nasty ass hair on," Freak Nasty said.

"Why me? Why now?" I said opening my eyes and standing.

"The queen bitch has risen. Let us all bow down to the queen," Freak Nasty said.

While the women in the holding cell snickered, I stretched, walked up to Freak Nasty, and slapped her so hard you could see my fingerprints on her face.

As she fell to the wall in seemingly slow motion I said, "You're a beautiful young queen. There are so many positive

232

things you could be doing with your life if you only knew you were a queen and not a whore, a bitch, or a prostitute."

Stunned was the best way to describe everyone in the cell besides me. It was so quiet, you could hear an ant piss. Freak Nasty looked up at me with her hand to her reddened cheek.

The big linebacker man/woman, grabbed me from behind. I banged my head into her nose.

She grabbed her face. "My nose, you broke my nose."

I kicked her in the knee and on her way to the ground I grabbed her arm twisted it around her back and guided her head into the metal toilet bowl.

"You wanna be a man, than respect me like a man should," I dunked her head in the toilet, let her arm go and flushed.

She struggled alright. Although she was twice my size, she had way too much fat on her to fade me.

I pulled her head up. "You wanna be a man, but you wear your jeans like a boy who wants to excite gay men."

"Fuck you," she said.

I dunked her head back into the toilet and flushed again. "That's your problem. You fucked with me. I warned you. Both of you. But no, you didn't listen. Now, listen to this." I pulled her head out of the toilet. She struggled to catch her breath, struggled to break free. "Read a book, free your mind. Read about Harriet Tubman, Winnie Mandela, Assata Shakur, Queen Bathsheba, Queen Catherine, understand the queendom within you, and learn why the powers that be want you to forget who you were, who you are. See why they want you to emulate late the ways of animals, being used primarily for breeding purposes. Selling your bodies for crumbs when you're worth more than all the gold that ever came out of the ground. Trying to be a man when God created you as a woman." I turned her bald head to me. "Queen, you are a black woman, strong, beautiful. God is beautiful and She created you in Her image.

Perfect. Love who you are, black Queen. Understand that you are a nurturer, the mother of creation. The glue that keeps the black family together.

The seven women in the small cell were quiet, attentive. I stood and pulled the woman up. The woman I had been dunking into the toilet. I turned her to me, wiped her face with some toilet paper before hugging her. "I was like you and I am like you."

"You don't even know me," she said.

"No, but I know the women who came before you. The queens that looked like you, who died because they refused to be slaves, refused to let men use them like toilets, refused to be beaten down by men and a system that perpetuates the ideology that women are only good for Child rearing and domestic duties." I let her go, put the roll of toilet paper back were I'd gotten it from and went back to my corner, where I slid back to the floor.

"Put this behind your head," Freak Nasty said, as she pitched the roll of toilet paper back at me.

Before I knew it I was knocked out. Several times I tried to force myself awake. I tried to will my eyes open but they wouldn't comply. I had to get up. I had to call Rhythm. I had to...

Chapter 36

Karen Parker Rose

"I had to. It wasn't like I had time to stop. He pulled right out in front of me." I explained my version of what had happened to this black dyke cop that stood in front of me.

"We know you didn't have time to stop. You were going fifty-eight in a forty-five when your SUV collided with the hospital van."

"There is no way I was speeding. If I don't do anything else, I abide by the laws of the land. Now, I am in a hurry."

"That's the problem."

I looked at her name tag. "Officer Branch is it?"

She nodded.

"Officer Branch, you obviously don't know who I am?"

She looked down at my license and then back up at me. It says here, that you are Karen Parker-Rose."

I smiled. "Judge Royce Roses wife."

"He's the judge that turned down the presidents offer at becoming the next Attorney General."

"That's my husband." Stupid fuck. How you gon' turn down an offer of becoming the top dog attorney in America. If anything, Royce becoming Attorney General would expedite his rise to the Supreme Court.

"He's seems to have the next Supreme court appointment sewn up," she said.

If he doesn't continue pissing me off. "He does have it sewn up doesn't he. And I assure you, he would not like his wife being detained."

"I'm sorry to hear that," she said.

"So can we wrap this up."

"Sure. As soon as I finish doing my job."

"I'm sure there is someone breaking into a house, selling drugs, robbing a liquor store, committing serious crimes, something more pressing than keeping me here in the wee hours of the morning."

"Lying to an investigating officer is a serious crime."

"I am not lying. I told you that I was not speeding."

"Satellite photos and computer analysis say different."

"Satellite photos and computer analysis?"

"Atlanta is one of three test cities using experimental satellite technology to record, analyze and process anything that happens in public areas of the city."

"Experimental. That means there are or could be flaws and bugs in this technology. Flaws that would have recorded me traveling at ridiculous speeds." If that satellite shit was true than I would've been on death row long ago. You can not bullshit a bullshitter. Now, I probably was speeding but there was no way for Dickless Van Dyke to know.

She looked at my license again and then back up at me. "You're saying that you weren't speeding?"

"That is exactly what I'm saying."

The paramedic that had attended to me walked up and asked, "Are you sure you don't want us to take you inside..."

"I am not going to be treated at a Children's hospital."

"They do treat adults in emergency situations."

"This is not an emergency situation, and I am fine."

The male officer shrugged. "Suit yourself." He turned to Officer Branch. "I think we're done here."

"Thank you," she said.

"When can I leave?"

"I don't know yet. We're trying to get to the bottom of a problem we're having?"

"What problem?"

"St. Judes has no record of this van being signed out." She looked up. "You say a priest was driving and he just disappeared after helping you from your vehicle."

"For the hundred million time, yes. Yes. Yes. An old white man in a priests get up was driving the van and yes, he disappeared when I was on hold with your 911 slow ass operators. Why don't you download satellite pics and see for yourself."

"I'll be right back." She walked back to her cruiser.

Two hours and thirty-seven minutes. Two hours and thirty-seven fucking minutes. This was ridiculous. I took out my phone and looked up Yellow Cab. A minute later I pressed end.

I had way too much to do, and a small window to do them in. I'd been in car accidents and car purposes and I had never had to go through half the drama this afro wearing dyke cop was taking me through. She needed to be getting a perm and taming that black sheep's wool on top of her head, instead of holding me.

Seven minutes passed before she stepped out of her cruiser and began walking my way.

"Look, I've been patient for close to three hours. It's one-thirteen in the damn morning. It ain't my fault that some fake ass geriatric priest that you can't find, stole a hospital van. You can write me a speeding ticket. Write me ten damn tickets.

237

Keep the damn Rover, tow it, I don't give a rat's ass." I pointed to the cab that had just pulled up. "I'm going...

"To jail," she slapped handcuffs on my wrists and made me drop my phone before I could react. "Karen Parker-Rose you are under arrest. You have the right to remain silent...

"You black dyke bitch."

She put her hand around my arm.

"So, you're just going to leave my phone in the street?"

"What phone?" she said, looking everywhere but the ground where my phone was.

"You must be planning on changing careers. Maybe moving to another country, cause when I'm finished with you, you want be able to get a job as a minimum wage dayworker."

"Your empty threats don't rattle me," she said ushering me to her cruiser.

"Future facts, not empty threats." I changed my harsh tone to one of seduction. "Don't be angry because you're ugly. So ugly that you don't even take the time to wear make up or do your hair. I know you wish you looked like me, had my body, my beauty, my long blonde hair. I bet deep down inside you wish you were white like me."

She waved at the tow truck driver, before pushing my head into the back of the police car.

Seconds later she was behind the wheel.

"Humor me, Boozilla, what am I being charged with?"

"I haven't cursed you one time. I hadn't become irate. I had not raised my voice. I hadn't called you out of your name. But, you've done all of the above to me. Yet, you want me to bend to your will."

"What do you expect? After the way I have been treated."

"I expect courtesy. Respect. Why do you think I've had you out here for three hours?"

"Because you are a racist, or maybe you're jealous of my looks, my money, my standing in the community."

"You don't even believe what you just said."

I shook my head. "Dyke."

"I wear my hair in it's natural state, and don't put wax, powder, or chemicals on my face. That doesn't make me gay, it makes me confident and assured of who I am. You see Mrs. Parker-Rose, I recognize Satan's manifestation in Eurocentric thought. The Social Darwinism in Eurocentricity that causes you and your ancestors to try and bury the beauty of Afrocentricity in your own ugliness."

"Huh?"

"You are the one that is jealous. So jealous that you paid for surgically enhanced lips. Lips that God naturally blessed me with. You wear make up to add color to your naturally ghostly pale skin. Make up that I don't need, because every morning I wake up, I'm already made up. And your shape. You paid to have your butt enhanced. Again, mine is all natural no additives no preservatives. Even the silicon in your hips, all natural on me, and I didn't pay a penny for them. Oh, and my hair. Your stringy dead looking hair can never look like mine in it's natural state. I said dead looking, because whenever a black woman ads chemicals like lye to her hair, she kills her hair. Like dead bodies, the hair lies down exactly like yours. You see Mrs. Parker-Rose if you do any kind of research you will find that my full of life kinky hair coils acts as receptors for the suns vibrant energy. Energy that feeds the mind and body with life sustaining essentials that help fight off disease and improves human thought process."

"That all sounds good, Boozilla but the fact remains that in this society I am the standard of beauty and the way you look is cause for a straight man to go gay."

"The society of the dead," she said. "A society that doesn't even realize that their standards of beauty are dictated by those that are so insecure that they turn truth around in their favor in order to make insecurity zombies of peoples of color all around the world."

"Miss me with that psychobabble. This is America. This is the way it is, and the way it's going to always be."

We turned into the precinct at one fifty-seven a.m. I was pissed. Pissed beyond pistivity. So pissed that I hadn't thought about calling Royce until now, and Dickless Van Dyke left my phone in the street. So pissed that I seriously contemplated coming back for the dyke after I cleared this mess up.

It was 3:01 AM when I finally got my one fucking phone call.

"Royce!"

"Karen, it's three in the morning where are you?"

"Where the fuck you think. Now, tell me, where do you think I am making a collect fucking phone call from at three in the damn morning?"

"Jail?"

"That's why I married you. The ability to outsmart a third grader."

"Why must you always be so negative? So condescending."

"You're right. I'm sorry Royce. I've just had the worst night of my life."

"What happened?"

"I don't know. I got pulled over by the most disrespectful, abusive black female cop."

"Are you okay? What did she do to you?"

He genuinely sounded concerned, but I knew better. "She hit me in the head repeatedly, and slammed my phone on the pavement."

"What is the officer's name?"

"Oh, I don't want to cause any trouble."

"Her name Karen. What is her name?"

"Branch. Innocence Branch."

"I'm on my way. What jail are you in?"

"Fulton County."

Chapter 37

Cherry

"Fulton County done seen the last of my black ass," Freak Nasty said. "Queen, you sleep?"

The cold hand on my shoulder awoke me. I jumped up.

"Chill queen. I just wanna tell you thanks. I ain't never thought I'd be thankin a bitch, I mean a queen after being slapped by one."

"I'm sorry for laying hands on you, and you too queen," I spoke to both women I'd dealt with earlier.

"I don't know about Khadijah but I deserved it. My momma used to threaten to slap some sense into me, and you did." She hugged me. "You was right. I'm to good to be a ho, givin' my money to a nigga who ain't gotta lay on his back and get bounced up in down on. He ain't gotta sit in a nasty, funky ass jail cell all night. I know I'm a long way from where I'm goin', but at least I know what I'm not going back to. You helped me see that."

"Kill that noise, and hurry your butt up Hollywood, you know you'll be right back on the strip before the streetlights come back on," the jailer outside the door said.

"Fuck you Preacher, you just mad, cause a bitch," she looked at me, "I mean a queen ain't never served your pencil dick bible totin' ass."

"Go on, get outta here queen. And do the right thing. Just remember, your mind is your power, your blackness is your strength and your womanhood is your glory."

"Ah, thats gangster." she walked to the steel door. "Didn't I tell you she was gon' kick some more gangster shit before I left. You bitches," she closed her eyes and shook her head, "I mean you queens stay up. This queen thing gon' take some getting used to. Ain't nobody ever called me a queen before."

I got up and went to the steel door behind her. "Can I please get my phone call?" I asked the jailer who escorted the queen out of the cell.

He pointed. "You're that Wild Cherry woman?"

Oh lord.

"You ain't had no phone call?"

"No sir."

"I ain't no sir. I'm Sergeant Buck Williams."

"Damn, Preacher," a girl behind me asked, "Can you please process me out this piece? I got hearts to break and money to make."

"Come on Hollywood," he said. He waved a small bible at me, "I'll be right back."

He wasn't lying. He was back before I finished stretching.

"Come on Ms. Wild Cherry."

I walked out of the cell and was blinded by the bright lights on the other side of the door.

"You damn sho' don't look like no killer."

Funny. No matter how many times I heard that, no one has ever been able to tell me how a killer looks. I picked up the pay phone and placed the call.

After accepting the charges Rhythm loudly exhaled. "Thank God. Thank God, you're alright. You are okay aren't you, Cheryl."

"A little tired, but physically, I'm fine."

"Okay, I'm on my way."

"You know where I am?"

"In jail. I just need to know where."

"The collect call gave me away."

"Uh, yeah."

"This may sound like a dumb question, but would you happen to have any idea why I've been in jail since eleven o'clock last night."

"You've been locked up since last night and you're just calling me."

"What time is it?"

"Twelve-thirty. I've been calling you, the hospitals, and the morgues all night. Cheryl, you scared me to death."

"And me too," I heard her husband Moses say in the background.

"You've been all over the news. I've been on the case since the story broke yesterday at six."

"What news?"

"FOX news, the company we are about to own. Them A-holes aired a video of you hitting Miles with a hammer."

"What?"

"Miles was shown in a wheelchair with gray duct tape all around him, and you were hitting him with a hammer."

"I didn't...

"I know. The video was doctored."

"I'm going to kill...."

"Cheryl, you're talking on a monitored jail phone."

I was so mad I could barely hold the phone. It's one thing to play with my life, but now she messing with my freedom.

"The tape also showed you strangling Ezekial Paulk."

"This is crazy."

"Where are you Cheryl?"

"Fulton County."

"The charges should be dropped by the time I get to you."

"Don't hang up. I know everything. Karen had Miles and Coltrane's places bugged. She had been in the condo and Trane's house at least ten times before she took..."

"You don't have to say it. I know how much you loved him. How much you miss him. Just like I know how much you love Coltrane."

"That's another story. But look, Rhythm, Karen watched Paradise and Trane for I don't know how long. She waited until Trane spilled his seed on the towel."

"Excuse me?"

"You know, the towel. The one used to protect the bed sheets after sex."

"Oh, that towel."

"Yes, she had a key to both homes and she had both alarm codes. She just waited for the right time, went in and got the soiled towel, took it back to the apartment, and smeared it inside and around Ezekial Paulks mouth. And how about she found a guy who resembled Trane and paid him to lease an apartment in Trane's name, using a fake Georgia's driver's license with Trane's picture on it."

"Okay, I'll be there in..."

"One more thing, Karen killed the man that leased the apartment, and Roger Naismith cut him up and flushed his body parts down a heavy duty super garbage disposal."

"Let me get off of this phone so I can come and get you."

"Okay, but there is so much more, and I have all the proof in Mile's Cougar, which is probably in the city impound yard."

Chapter 38

Karen Parker Rose

The city impound yard is the last place where I wanted to be. I needed my sunglasses. The sun was too damn bright and it was too damn hot for fall.

"Ma'am," the grease, grime and dirt covered attendant pointed, "Your Range Rover is right over there."

City impound my ass. This place was a junk yard, literally. I stepped over all types of shit I couldn't identify as I made my way over to the Rover. "Dammit!" I shouted after nearly twisting my ankle on a broken beer bottle hidden in the muddy-dirt.

I was already in a foul mood. I hadn't slept in forty-three hours. Tired was an understatement to describe the way I felt. But I wasn't about to sleep until I dealt with baby Parasite.

Miracle was a good name for the damn thing. It was a miracle that I hadn't gotten to her. A rocks throw away from St. Jude Children's hospital and a car jacking old ass priest drives a stolen hospital van in front of my Rover. And after he checked to see if I was alright, he just disappeared.

To make a bad night worst, a dyke with a nappy baby Erykah Badu afro arrested me for speeding, and driving without insurance. If she would have told me why I was being arrested I could've just called State Farm insurances 24 hour access emergency number and saved us all a lot of time. Instead, I go to jail and my wrecked Rover gets towed.

And now, nine hours later, tired had turned into exhaustion and exhaustion had transformed into sheer will power. I looked up to see how much further I had to walk. Why in the hell had they towed my Rover this far back into the bowels of Junk Yard hell, I wondered before thinking back to my crazy morning.

It had only taken Royce fifteen minutes to get to the station. I was just glad I hadn't been thrown in one of those horrible, unsanitary holding cells. I was way too gorgeous for jail and too tired to step off in a tramps ass for trying me. I could just picture a black bull bitch coming up to me and putting her meathooks under my dress. At the least, I'd catch an assault charge, but knowing my temper the assault would probably be upgraded to murder.

After two hours of Royce, schooling the night Lieutenant, he had apologized to me and Royce for the misunderstanding. Only reason I hadn't cursed the lieutenant's heart-attack-waiting-to-happen-fat-ass out was because I had to save what little strength I had left to tie up the rest of my loose ends.

At 6:00 A.M. I'd signed my release papers, the Lieutenants signature was all I needed so we could go, but no, Royce wanted the abusing officer's head on a platter. We were there another hour and three minutes while the Lieutenant scrambled to find out who had brought me in. All the papers were signed by an Innocence Branch, but there was no one on the force by that name, or so lieutenant Lard ass, had said.

It was 7:06 when we finally left the precinct. The lieutenant had promised to get to the bottom of the mysterious, missing, Officer Branch, before days end.

After we left, whatever bug Royce had up his ass, I hoped it stayed there. His silence was golden as he drove me to Enterprise car rental.

****

And now it was 8:53 AM. I was two car lengths away from... Right behind my Rover... It can't be. Were my eyes playing tricks on me?

A couple minutes later I was standing behind my Rover holding the tire iron I had just removed from my wrecked SUV. Now what in the world was Scary's precious mint condition 1969 convertible Ford Cougar doing at a junk yard. The car had to be worth at least a hundred thousand. Nothing worth that much should be in a junkyard. So much could happen in a junkyard.

Thanks to the Rover, no one back at the junkyard's office or garage could see me. Fifteen minutes later, I was exhausted. This had been more strenuous than my seven A.M. advanced Pilates class.

I was bent over sweating like a pig, when I remembered why I came to the junkyard in the first place. I opened my back hatch and threw my tire iron back inside, before walking to the passenger's door, opening it and taking my spare iphone and my Gaultier shades out of the glove box. After grabbing them and my car charger I walked back over to the Cougar to admire my handiwork.

Something on the Cougar's back seat caught my attention. I reached through the rear broken window and removed the paper clipped stack of papers.

I started reading the first page. I flipped to the second. The third. Forth. Fifth, "You fuck!"

248

I made a beeline toward my rental. "Mother fucker." My mind was on auto pilot.

"You have to come to the office and sign for those ma'am," I heard a junkyard attendant say in the distance.

I heard him, but my mind was telling my body to stay the course it was on.

"Ma'am, you can't take those without signing for them."

I put the gear shift of my rental into drive when the attendant caught up with me. He dove out of my way after I hit the gas.

I picked up my phone as I turned onto the expressway.

"Hi. I am probably home, I'm just avoiding someone I don't like. Leave me a message, and if I don't call back, it's you."

"Roger, call me back it's important and it involves a lot of money. More than you've ever made."

After pressing end, I looked at the time. Nine forty-eight. Roger was probably still sleep, or at the hospital.

Fifty-three minutes later I sped past a billboard advertising the Floyd County State Fair. Seven minutes later, I passed a big green and white sign welcoming me to Rome. Seventeen minutes later, at exactly eleven o'clock I pulled off the dirt road and into the paved driveway of Roger's paint peeling two story.

I stood outside banging on Roger's door.

"I'm coming. Im coming. Don't get your panties in a bunch."

If I stuck a finger in a bucket of ice water it would boil. The word hot was an understatement to describe my mood. My fists were in tight balls. My entire body was coiled and ready to strike.

He answered the door wearing a white robe and holding a shotgun. "Look, I'm too old to fight, too sick to argue, so if you still wanna squabble Karen, then why don't you crawl up my ass and fight for some air."

I pushed past him.

"Where'n hell you think you're going?"

I was in the kitchen drawer when he caught up.

He grabbed my arm.

I turned and brought the blade of his own butcher knife across his neck.

He dropped the gun, and reached for his neck as blood spurted everywhere, painting the kitchen walls, floor, cabinets, table and chairs.

He fell to one knee. I hawked and was about to spit in his face, when I thought about DNA evidence. I swallowed, walked out the door, got into the rental and backed out of the driveway. I looked at my phone. It was ten after eleven.

One hour and forty seven minutes later, I walked into my bedroom, which had been Royces and dropped the stack of papers in the fireplace before stripping naked, and dropping my blood splattered clothes on top of the papers. Next, I bent down and picked up a container of lighter fluid.

Sixteen minutes later, the clothes I had worn were ashes. Twenty-eight minutes later I was showered, changed and sitting behind the wheel of my rental guzzling a four pack of Red Bull. I closed my eyes and tried to think how I was going to get the four bodies out of the ground and to the basement where I would dismember the parts and run them down the disposal.

My buzzing phone brought me back to the task at hand.

"Hello?"

"Why haven't you..."

I pressed end. How the hell did TJ get the number to my private cell phone. Dumb question. Nicole Kyle, that Don't-worry-be-happy-attorney-bitch of his. Fuck her and fuck TJ.

I put the key in and pushed the ignition button. I'd figure out my next move after I left St. Jude. Wouldn't it be great if Scary was there. I decided to run back inside to get my gun.

Chapter 39

Cherry

I decided to run back inside my condo and get my gun just in case someone had stolen my tools out of the Cougar. As soon as the elevator opened, I said, "Rhythm, I'll be right back. I left something upstairs."

"Okay, I'll wait in the lobby library."

A few minutes later, I was tapping her on the shoulder. "You ready."

"I should be asking you the same. She looked at me before rising from the antique looking throne chair.

On the ride to the city impound, I explained everything that I had learned from Roger.

"You do know we will need Roger to co-oberate everything you've said."

"Well, we better hurry and get those papers from the...

She interrupted, "Without him, the papers are just hearsay."

"What about the bodies?"

"Without his cooperation, or Karen's, the state won't even entertain a motion to exhume Jonathon Parker's body, or any of the alleged bodies buried in unmarked graves at Myrtle Hill."

The sun was beaming. It was way too hot for early October. We pulled into the city impound.

"I'm going to stay here, if it's fine with you," Rhythm said, "I'll make some phone calls, see if I can hunt down Nathan Beckford."

"The DA?"

"Yes. Don't worry, Nathan is self-centered, but he's good people. We could really use him on our side, especially with all the incriminating evidence you have against Karen."

"Okay, you know the law and the people that work for it better than me. I'll be back in a few," I said, taking my license and auto-release papers from my purse. "Okay girl, I'll catch a bootleg cab," I said.

Rhythm rose up. "Girl, what was I thinking I forgot all about the Cougar."

"Sit right back down and handle your business girl, ain't no trip. I see a cab now." I said running out of the sliding glass door."

****

I walked up to an office door where a sign that read, CITY-WIDE TOWING greeted me before I turned he knob and entered. "Sir, I need to see about getting my..."

"Office down yonder," the tobacco chewing redneck junkyard mechanic said.

"Where is that? North, South, East, West."

He put a hand on his hips and pointed to a trailer like building, "I said, down yonder gal."

"I will fuck your redneck-hillbilly-gay-ass up white boy. I'm a black queen and you will speak to me with respect."

He kept walking, saying nothing while I walked out of the trailer in the opposite direction toward the office trailer.

I walked into the glass patio office door and handed my release papers to the lady behind the window. "These are my release papers ma'am. I'd like to pick up my baby."

"Elmer Leroy, get the keys and take this nice lady to the 69 Cougar."

"The white convertible?"

"How many 69 Cougars are on the lot."

"One. The white convertible."

The lady shook her head, "Dumb as a stump, bless his heart."

I pulled out my wallet.

"No, the city took care of it. You don't owe us anything, sweetie."

"Ms. Ma'am."

I turned. The young man was the longest man I'd ever seen. They should've named him lightpost. If he was my son, Trane and I would've started calling him NBA once he reached six-four. "How tall are you?"

He put his legs together and stood straight up, and put a hand right above his head. "This bout tall as I can get."

Dumb as a stump. And I thought she was exaggerating.

I followed Elmer Leroy out the side door.

A few minutes later I screamed.

Elmer hit the golf carts brakes.

I screamed again.

"Jesus H. Christ! What is wrong with you, lady?"

I pointed.

"Good God a'mighty." he picked up the CB. "Momma. Momma pick up."

"Hot Momma, dumb ass. My signal is hot momma. How many times I gotta tell you, when we on the job we ain't no kin."

"Momma, somebody done tored up that-there Cougar."

He pointed as if his mother could see my totaled car.

"Whachu mean tored up. Boy, ain't I done told you 'bout using ebonics."

I got out of the golf cart. The closer I came to Mile's most prized possession the tighter I got. My eyes began at the smashed rear light and worked their way up to the scratched and dented trunk and rear fender. The torn top. The smashed in windows. The scratched and dented hood. Suddenly, my whole body froze. I started trembling. I walked forward, teeth grinding together. I stopped when I was standing between Karen Parker Roses, mangled Range Rover and Miles's now deceased 1969 convertible Ford Cougar.

Ten years, it took Miles to restore the muscle car. No mechanics, just Miles, his tools, and his old car manuals. Ten years and over thirty thousand dollars. I turned to the back door of Karen's SUV. As soon as I opened it, my eyes shot to the only thing on the floor of the rear compartment. A lug wrench with white specks of paint on it. I turned and looked at the Cougar. My eyes particularly focused in on the scratched, and dents on the hood and the sides. Scratches and dents that were made by a black eighteen inch L shaped lug wrench.

"Shit!" I shouted before running to the car, opening the drivers door, and looking over the front seat and into the back.

The papers were gone, but my tool case and my tools were intact. She really shouldn't have left my tools.

"Ms. Ma'am, I'm sho' is sorry. I ain't never heard of anything like this here ever happening." I stayed quiet during the short drive back to the front office. I just needed two minutes with her, maybe not even that long. A public restroom, an elevator, anywhere that it was just me and her. After Elmer Leroy pulled up to the front office, I got out of the golf cart and said, "I'll be back."

"The Terminator," he said.

"Much more dangerous," I turned to him. "Wild Cherry," I said before turning and walking off. After calling

Rhythm and asking her to come get me, she didn't ask why or what happened, her exact words were, "on my way."

While waiting for my girl, I thought that I'll dig the bodies up my damn self. I don't care. I'll even pay for the medical examiner and the autopsy on her brother.

Before the sun rose again, four things were about to happen. First, I was going to St. Jude's to check in on Miracle. Second, I was going to find Karen and kill her, nothing fancy, no long drawn out torture, just cut a smile across her neck. Third I was going to march Roger down to the DA's office. And fourth, I was going to fulfill my promise to Paradise. Take care of Trane and Miracle until death do any of us part.

Before I was finished imagining all the ways that I wanted to kill Karen, Rhythm pulled up.

I opened the passenger's door.

"Wheres your car? Rhythm asked. "Don't tell me the state hasn't removed the computer hold on the Cougar?"

"How did you know?" I said, not having an earthly idea as to what she was referring to.

"Makes no difference if you have release papers that are stamped, whenever the city foots the bill on a tow, they have to remove a computer hold and that could take a couple hours," Rhythm explained. "If you want, we can got to Stonecrest, kill a couple hours in the mall."

"I really wanna go check in on Miracle."

"That's a great idea. It's about time I meet my grand Godbaby."

Thirty, forty minutes later, we were pulling into the parking deck at St. Judes when I panicked. I got out of the car slammed the door and grabbed my head. "Shit! Shit! Shit!"

"Cheryl, what's wrong?" Rhythm walked around the car over to where I was pacing. She stood in front of me, reached out and took me in her arms.

"Roger's dead."

"Who?"

"Roger Naismith. Karen's...

"That Roger Naismith." In a soothing, quiet tone she asked, "What makes you think that he's dead?"

I contemplated telling her the truth, that Karen had stolen all the evidence that Roger had given me, evidence that would take down Karen and free Trane, but if I did she would be an accessory to murder after I had killed Karen. Instead I just shrugged my shoulders and said, "I don't know just paranoid, let me call him."

With my phone to my ear, I said, "His answering machine picked up on the first ring. His phone is either off or dead."

"Do you still have his address?"

"2241 General Lee Trail, Rome Georgia 30161."

"Oh-kay now. You got that Rainman thing goin' on, huh Cheryl?"

"I sort of got a photographic memory. Places, dates, quotes, phone numbers, I hear them one time and they're etched into my brain."

"Look, you go spend some time with Miracle. I'll be up in a few. Gotta make a call. One of our church members is a state Trooper up in Floyd County. I can get him to go and check up on Mr. Naismith."

"Go ahead handle your business girl, I'll wait."

"No, go ahead," she shoo-shooed me. "I'll be up in a few."

Did she just shoo-shoo me? In any case I got out of the car. Minutes later, I was walking through the hospitals sliding doors. I made a couple turns before I stood at the correct elevator. With terrorism being on the rise and so much racial tension in the air, you would think there would be better security at a Children's hospital.

The elevator opened.

Chapter 40

Karen Parker Rose

The elevator opened. 2:15, the digital white lights read. After checking the time I got off the elevator and placed my phone back into my white St. Jude's lab coat, the one I took from the hospital laundry earlier, when I first arrived. The stairs, where were the stairs? I looked a little further down the hall. There they are. Just in case the elevator wasn't an option when I made my exit.

But by the looks of things, I didn't foresee me having any problems with my escape, especially with everyone being so busy. It was as if I were a ghost walking down the hall, the way everyone ignored me. Doctor's were doctoring, nurses were nursing, and families were familying. The door to the CCU flew open just as I was about to grab the handle. A couple of nobody's with scrubs on where wheeling a baby out of the CCU.

As I went from table to table looking for Miracles name on each clipboard, I couldn't help but shake my head. The little ugly sick pissers could haunt a house. This was the third time I looked. "I know this is the right unit," I said to myself as I walked out of the CCU and over to the nurses desk.

I smiled. "Uhm, I'm looking for Miracle Jones."

A coke bottle glasses wearing, shriveled up, liver spotted, pink prune looked up from a stack of papers. "You must be new."

"Yes, ma'am."

"Well what are you doing on the critical care floor?"

"I don't understand?"

"Who's your immediate?"

"My Immediate."

"Supervisor."

"Smith?" I said, pulling the most common name in the world out of my head.

"He knows better than to send a newbie up to CCU. I ain't got time to go back and forth with him today." She looked at her Ipad screen. "They just took the Miracle baby to 1442, prep," she pointed, "Down the hall first door on the right past the restroom."

I turned as the same elevator I got off of opened. She stepped out wearing all black. What a great outfit to die in. She looked right at me. Not a sign of recognition. My disguised look was perfect. I quickened my pace. I decided to step into the bathroom next door to 1442 prep. Wait for her to go in. Then I'd come out and kill everything breathing inside of 1442 prep.

After the heavy restroom door closed, I sat on the restrooms only toilet, opened my purse and pulled out my pink .32 and it's matching silencer. After screwing the silencer on, I stood up loaded a bullet into the chamber and pressed my ear against the door. I was listening for heels clacking on the hospital floor.

All of a sudden, the door blew open and I was thrown back into the bathrooms lone porcelain sink.

My gun slid across the small bathroom floor, as I fell between the sink and the toilet. The gun was right at her feet. But she didn't pay any attention to it. I don't think she saw it. She was busy locking the door from the inside.

I swung my fist and tried to move at the same time she dove onto me.

My badly aimed swing gave her the room and the time to wrap both hands around my neck.

"Say a prayer bitch."

I couldn't talk. Her grip was superhuman. My eyes bulged.

"Die!"

Somehow, I managed to spit in her eye, relinquishing her iron grip just enough for me to turn and buck my hips.

She grabbed for my hair. Instead of pulling it, she fell back into the wall with my brunette wig in her hands, giving me the opportunity to palm the back of her head and push it up against the porcelain commode.

"That the best you can do?" she asked, while I scrambled to get my leg untangled from hers.

Behind the door in the corner. My gun. So close.

"Nah bitch, how's this?" I sunk all thirty-two in her left breast. I couldn't tell if the blood in my mouth was hers or mine as bad as my teeth and jaws were hurting.

When I looked up to see the pain on Scary's face, I didn't get a chance to enjoy her anguish. I was busy trying to get my face out of the way of her flurrying fists. In the process my legs came free. Out of instinct, and not by choice, I grabbed my broken and bloodied nose and tried to cover up as a barrage of blows continued pummeling my face and head. Blood was everywhere. On me. Around me and even on my gun that was still, against the wall behind the door.

Suddenly the beating stopped. She lurched toward the gun.

"Shit!" she hollered while slipping on my blood and falling back into the commode.

When Scary looked up, I was standing over her, gun in hand. I smiled, aimed and...

Chapter 41

Cherry

The heavy oak, bathroom door swung open.

"Pff. Pff. Pff. Pff. Pff." Karen turned her aim to the door. The crackling sound of bullets penetrating wood as they went right through that detective that came to the condo.

I was scrambling to my feet when the detective motioned me to not move. "Stay, please."

Normally, I wouldn't have listened. But Detective Branch had opened a door that I'd bolted from the inside and I saw bullets go right through her. No blood, no holes, nothing. She was way more than a suit with a badge.

"We meet again." Detective Branch glared at a confused looking Karen.

She pointed the gun at the detective. "The dyke cop?"

I looked at Innocence and then at Karen.

"Quit shaking your head at me bitch," Karen said.

She was so focused on Detective Branch that she wasn't paying attention to me.

"Dyke bitch, didn't I tell you to quit shaking...

I had her. Had the chance to return the detective's favor. I lunged, slipped and fell again. My head crashed against the side of the toilet.

"This ain't your day Scary." Karen said, as she turned the gun on me. I watched her trigger finger as it moved in slow-motion. The sadistic smile on her face. I couldn't believe she'd beaten me.

"No, queen. She didn't win."

Now, this was crazy. I looked at Detective Branch. Was she reading my thoughts?

Detective Branch's right arm was extended. Her right hand balled into a fist aimed right at the gun Karen had pointed at me.

I turned to Karen. Her gun arm trembled. "What... What is happening?"

I turned back to the detective, wanting to know the answer to Karen's question.

The loud thud on the bathroom floor caused my head to turn back to Karen. The gun.

I scrambled for it.

"Leave it," Innocence said.

Karen began scratching at her chest.

Innocence squeezed her balled fist and slowly turned her arm.

"Can't breathe," Karen said.

"Then I am achieving my goal," Detective Branch replied.

"Please?" Karen begged.

"I will be, pleased that is, when all like you are burning in the lakes of hell. I will be pleased when my sisters realize their queenship and takes back their queendom. I will be pleased when God becomes more important to man than Gold. I will be pleased when more Wild Cherry's rise up against depression, repression, and oppression."

Detective Branch unballed her fist.

Karen inhaled.

Innocence Branch looked at me. "Vengeance was never yours Queen." She turned her attention back to Karen. "By the way Mrs. Parker, I am, I was, and I will always be, what you strive to be but could never be." she clapped her hands together.

Karen was dead before she hit the ground."

"Who? What are you?"

"I am who you once were. I am who you will one day become," she smiled. "I'm Innocence."

"You have to do a little better than that?" I said.

"You are who you were."

"Who am I?"

"Seek and ye shall find."

"Why can't you just...

Chapter 42

Cherry

"Why can't you just tell me the truth?" Rhythm asked.

"I don't know what else to say. And frankly, there is nothing else we can do for her."

"How much?"

"How much for what?"

"How much will it cost for you to put her back on life support?"

"It's not an issue of money Mrs. One-Free."

"Then what is it?"

"Ms. Sharell was brain dead when the paramedics pulled her out of that hospital bathroom two weeks ago. And since then she's been in a coma and her brain activity hasn't changed.

What. A coma. I wasn't dead.

"She's breathing, her bodily functions are normal, but because your machines say she's dead, that gives you the right to play God."

"Mrs. One-Free, I understand how you feel. Letting go of a loved one is extremely difficult. I've consoled many like you that felt the same way. But what I've found over my twenty years of treating coma patients is that after seventy-two hours of no brain activity, the patient has a zero chance of recovery."

"You didn't answer my question, Dr. Tanner?"

"What was your question?"

"I asked you if readings from machines gave you the right to play God?"

"The medical field is rooted in science. Theories and ideas that can be proven. I am not questioning your beliefs, but they are beliefs, not substantiated and not proven. If doctors left medicine and healing up to a an invisible God...

"God is not invisible." My voice was low, but the look on Rhythm's and the doctors face let me know that they had heard me

The doctor was the first to speak. "I-I don't know what to say."

Rhythm came to my side and took my hand. "I don't know how, but I knew you would come back to us."

"Doctor Tanner," I said. "God lives in everyone, even the worst of us. You just have to believe." I coughed.

A couple weeks ago, I would have said that I had no idea where all this was coming from. But, after what happened in that bathroom, I know exactly where the words were coming from. Just like I know exactly who I am.

"Amazing," the doctor said, his feet were still planted in the same spot they were when I first opened my mouth.

"Yes, He is," Rhythm remarked.

"Karen?" I questioned.

"Dead and cremated," Rhythm answered.

"Miracle."

"She's fine."

I took a deep breath.

"Roger."

"Dead."

"Karen."

She nodded in the affirmative.

"Damn."

"I'm sorry."

I closed my eyes, not knowing if I wanted to hear the answer to the question I was avoiding. Roger was dead. Karen was dead. That meant Coltrane was...

"Excuse me. I have to take this."

"Cell phones aren't permitted in here," Dr. Tanner said.

"I'll be right back," Rhythm stepped out of the room.

Before Rhythm had left my room at four, my eyes were closed.

****

When I opened them the clock on the wall in front of me read 6:15.

Dr. Tanner and two of his colleagues where in my hospital room, discussing something.

"Hello."

The medical staff turned to me. "Ms. Sharell. Just your being here defies all medical science. There is no logical explanation for your recovery."

I said, "Your misunderstanding of God's logic is why you are all so blind. When you find a cure to any ailment, any disease. Antibodies from the disease are used to cure the disease, am I correct."

"You are," one of Dr. Tanners colleagues remarked.

"So, wouldn't it be safe to say that man has everything within him or herself to cure themselves."

Outside of a slight nod, and a furrowing of the brow no one answered.

"God, has provided his seeds, us everything we need to sustain ourselves. We just have to find the God within us and

266

work toward the goal of unity and not money, to cure all of the worlds diseases, ailments, and problems. The key is coming together, a mass union of minds."

Rhythm, burst back into the room.

"He signed it!" She held her Ipad in the air.

"Signed what?"

She moved her hand across the twelve inch screen. A news podcast appeared.

A black queen with the grace of royalty began, "After being falsely accused and spending ten weeks in a six by ten dull gray basement prison cell for twenty-three hours a day, Albert Coltrane Jones has been exonerated on charges stemming from aggravated child molestation to first degree murder. This is the second time Mr. Jones, formally known as Mr. MVP has spent time in America's penal system falsely charged and accused of heinous crimes. And both times the perpetrator of the crimes turned out to be siblings. Jonathon Parker and Karen Parker Rose, both deceased, fooled the authorities, the courts, and the nation."

I shot up, knocking the Ipad to the floor. "Sorry, I'll buy you another one."

"What are you doing?" Dr. Tanner asked.

"Going to get my man." My muscles gave out as soon as I went to stand.

"Cheryl!" Rhythm shouted.

The doctors helped me back into bed.

"Your muscles have begun to atrophy because of the lack of blood circulation. We have you on blood thinners so your blood wouldn't clot while you were immobile. The good thing is that your muscles have memory and it shouldn't take more than a couple days before you are able to walk."

"Can you give us a minute, Doc?" Rhythm asked.

He nodded as he and his colleagues left the room.

"There's more to what Patricia Tucker was saying."

"Who?"

"The news analyst, you were listening to and watching on my ipad."

I waited.

"The day Karen died from a massive heart attack, the DA, Nathan Beckford went to see TJ on death row."

"Okay," I said wondering where this was going. The tone of her voice told me that it wasn't going to be good.

Before Nathan left, he'd struck a deal with TJ.

"What kind of deal?"

"TJ, told Nathan in detail about Karen's plot to kill everyone close to Coltrane, while Coltrane sat in jail for murders he didn't commit. He supplied dates, times and even led the DA's office to bodies buried in unmarked graves."

"Myrtle Hill Cemetery."

"Yes, and to the Parker Estate, where a typed written diary with Karen's name signed on the front page was retrieved from the attic, where Karen stabbed her brother to death."

"So they're going to dig Jonathon up?"

"They already did. A couple days ago. After reading the horrid details of the diary, they had no choice."

"I can't believe a woman so diabolically analytical would record anything that would put her away."

"So the courts communicated TJ's death sentence to a life sentence?" I asked.

"If everything he said checked out than the state would drop the murder charge and give him time served for the other charges."

"What? Are they insane? TJ's worse than Karen."

"You're preaching to the choir," Rhythm said.

"Help me up."

"What are you doing?" Rhythm asked. "You heard what the doctor said."

"I can't wait a couple of days."

"Are you going to help me or what?"

"I'll take the, or what. I am not going to help you hurt yourself."

"If you don't help me, than there is no telling how many people TJ Money will have hurt in a couple of days.

Epilogue

A couple days later, Miracle, was asleep in the room Trane and Paradise had made up for her before she was born.

We'd decided to turn off the outside and inside lights, hoping to sway any trick or treaters. The only light present was from the fire burning in the fireplace we laid in front of. My head lay on Trane's bare chest. My hand rested where his heart was.

He put his book on the hardwood floor beside the Polar bear rug we snuggled on. "Baby?"

"Yes King?"

"You know I love you, right."

"Yes."

"You also know that I trust and believe what you say."

I raised my head, and turned to him.

"I just finished reading the *'The Rise and Fall of Civilization.'*

"Was it good?"

"Depends on how you define good. Let's just say it was informative."

"So are you going to finally tell me about it?"

"Will you still love me if I do?"

"I will always love you regardless of what comes out of your mouth, Mr. Jones."

"The book chronicled the revolutionary life of a man who traveled throughout Europe. I won't go into too many details, but he was a parish priest from a small village in Austria. He preached against the evils of capitalism. It is said that Karl Marx quoted this priest, in The Capitalist Manifesto, when he said that *'Capitalists will eat themselves.'* And Marx being an atheist, of course he couldn't give credence to a man of God. Anyway Queen, This lilly white European priest spent his early years in the priesthood, studying and teaching Egyptian spirituality, and the mysticism associated with it."

"You're talking about Father Gene Sheppard."

"Yep."

"I know all about him," I said. "He also taught exorcism, demonology..."

He interrupted. "All Mysticism from ancient Kemet."

"Really?"

"Father Sheppard's secret organization, the Innocence Branch...

"Innocence Branch?"

"Yes, The Innocence Branch. Heres the kicker. The Innocence Branch were rumored to be Angels, soldiering, killing for God."

"What?"

"Not ordinary people. People that had been taken over by demons at birth. Demons that had grown too strong to be exorcised."

"At least, I know that there are black angels in heaven."

"Seek and ye shall find, Queen," Trane repeated, Seek and ye shall find."

"I thought that's what she meant."

"What who meant?" His eyebrows furrowed together.

"Innocence. When I asked her who I was, she said Seek and ye shall find."

"You just said, that you thought *that* was what she meant." What did you mean by *that*?

"*Queen*" I replied. "You said seek and ye shall find, *Queen*. My first thought, my first realization when I woke up was that I am a Queen. I had been searching for what I already knew. Or did I. I'd read about all the great African queens throughout antiquity. I've been told and had been showed that I was a queen. But I never truly visualized, believed that I was a queen until I spent those few moments in the bathroom with Innocence.

My cell phone vibrated off of the table and onto my man's chest.

I picked it up, looked at the caller ID.

"Important?" he asked.

"Don't know. Unknown caller."

"Answer it."

"You sure."

"Go ahead Queen."

"Hello. This is Cheryl."

"Cherry, Cherry, quite contrary, how does your...

"TJ, what do you want? And please lose my number."

"So much animosity in your tone. You should be kissing my....

"Terrell?"

"The diary. Wasn't it ingenious. Karen should have called me back the many times I tried to reach her. If she only knew what you knew, then she wouldn't have ignored my calls."

"I knew it. You planted the diary."

"Now, how could I do that from death row?"

"Your cult following. Folks like Bucky Barnes would do anything for their beloved false prophet."

"I'm crushed, that you would even think such a thing. I'm a man of God."

"Save it."

"The signature was good. Years behind bars studying her name and how she wrote it. What tangled webs we weave when we practice to deceive TJ Money. You helped put me on death row and you helped to get me out. I'd say we were almost even."

"Not by a long shot."

"70.3 meters to be exact."

"What?"

"70.3 meters is a long shot, but not too long. You see that's how far your head is away from the barrel of my Winchester snipers rifle. At least that's the reading I'm getting from the infrared night-scope I am looking at you and Mr. Jones through. Sweet dreams."

He pulled the trigger.